All About the Greater Good

Teri Ames

Copyright © 2016 by Teri Ames. All rights reserved. Printed in the United States of America by Catamount Publishing, Middlebury, Vermont.

Cover and book design by Kit Foster Design

Cover Photographs © Lucidwaters / DepositPhotos.com

Typeset in Garamond

First edition

Publisher's Cataloging-in-Publication data
Ames, Teri
All about the greater good / Teri Ames
p. cm.
ISBN: 978-0-9972484-0-1
1. Law—Fiction. 2. Vermont—Fiction. 3. Motherhood—Fiction.
I. Title.
Library of Congress Control Number: 2016903970

For Tom and our children,

who put up with a lot so I could write

CHAPTER 1

Sarah Bennett
Tuesday, September 4, 2012

Even though I am expecting them, I'm still not prepared when I open the door and find two uniformed police officers.

"Are you Sarah Bennett?" the male officer asks.

"I am." I nod.

"And you're in charge here?" he says.

"I am," I say, though right this minute I wish I wasn't.

"May we come in?"

"Of course." I move aside and gesture them toward the TV room. "Have a seat." I follow them in and sit on a couch. They stand inside the door, but make no move to sit.

Both officers seem vaguely familiar, but that's not unusual in a small town. The man, who's clearly in charge, is middle aged and barrel chested, not tall, but he looks like he could hold his own in a fist fight. The name tag on his chest reads, "Sgt. Patterson." The woman, whose name tag says, "Ptl. Driscoll," stands slightly behind him. The bulletproof vest she's wearing under her uniform makes her look like a child playing dress-up. She stands stiffly with her hands near her hips.

"What can I do for you, officers?" I say. I wish I was still standing. It feels awkward to have them staring down at me.

"We're here to search the premises," Patterson says.

"Do you have a warrant?" I hope they didn't pick up on the tremor in my voice.

"No, ma'am. We were told we wouldn't need one as long as someone in charge gives us permission to search."

"Well, I'm the director, so that would be me," I say.

"Then you'll need to sign this consent form," Patterson says. He takes a folded paper out of his breast pocket and produces a pen.

"Wait a minute." Involuntarily, I put up my hand. "Why should I give permission?"

"Because it's the right thing to do, ma'am. As you probably heard, someone pulled a knife on the clerk at the Quik Stop last night, took more than three hundred dollars."

I did hear. It was the first thing that Betsy, the assistant director of the shelter, told me when I walked in the door. The sergeant continues, "Scared the girl near to death."

"I'm sure it was horrible for her," I say.

The sergeant nods. "Anyway, the longer it takes us to find the knife and the money, the less likely we are to apprehend the perpetrator. We think it was one of your residents."

"Which one?"

"Bryce Anderson."

"I doubt Bryce would do something like that," I say. Bryce was pretty upset when he told me the police had questioned him this morning. Not that I blame him.

The sergeant stares at me silently for about five seconds before he speaks. "Then it might've been one of the other black fellas. We'd like to search all the rooms and the living areas." His eyes move around the room. "If you'll let us, that is."

"But, why do you think it was Bryce, or anyone at this shelter for that matter?"

"Well, the perp was a dark-skinned male wearing a bandana. And the Quik Stop is only a few blocks away. The guy obviously needed money real bad if he was willing to commit armed robbery for three hundred bucks. The people here are all a little...," he pauses as if searching for the right words, "more motivated than most folks."

The woman nods. Patterson goes on. "Bryce Anderson was in the Quik Stop an hour before the robbery. He admitted it."

"Anything else?" I say.

"Yes, but if I tell you, I might compromise the investigation. Besides, there's quite a few more black people around here than average," he says.

I count to three in my head. Even though I've been the director of the Murdoch Shelter for five years, the prejudice still gets to me.

"I understand the difficult position you're in," I say. "And I want you to catch whoever committed that robbery. But I'm also in a difficult position. When people are homeless, they have near nothing. We try to offer them something like a home. A bit of privacy and respect. If I let you come in here without a better reason, they'll view it as a betrayal. I'll lose their trust. That will make my job very difficult."

"So, you're going to let him get away with it," Patterson says.

"You're making some pretty big assumptions. You don't even know if anyone here was involved."

"We think there's a good chance."

"Well, if it's good enough for you to get a warrant, I'll cooperate completely."

"You realize you can be charged with aiding and abetting if you help someone get away with a crime." The sergeant gives me a steely look. The female officer appears to be smirking.

"Are you suggesting I would help someone hide stolen money?"

"Just reminding you of your responsibilities." He draws out the last word.

"I have no intention of committing any crimes. I'm only protecting the rights of our residents. If they want to let you search their rooms, that's their choice. But I'm not going to make that decision for them. And I'm not going to let you search the common areas without a warrant."

"Even though you have the authority to let us search the entire place?"

"That's right. Save us both the trouble and go get a warrant."

The sergeant turns to go and the officer follows his lead. They saunter, letting me know they are leaving on their own terms. Last in line, I notice the woman's strawberry blond hair curling up from under the back of her cap, a feminine contradiction to her demeanor.

When we reach the door, the sergeant turns to me. "We'll see you later, ma'am."

"Have a good day, officers." That probably sounded more snide than I intended.

After they're gone, I head back to my office and flop into my chair. I'm glad that's over, but I'm still tense from the confrontation. I dial my husband's direct line.

"Did the police show up yet?" James says.

"They just left."

"How'd it go?"

"I'm glad I talked to you before they got here. Otherwise, I wouldn't have had the guts to stand up to them. Thanks for the legal advice."

"One of the fringe benefits of being married to a lawyer. But don't forget that criminal law is not my thing, and I only did about five minutes of research. Did they give you any more information about the robbery?"

"Not really, but it's clear they're focused on Bryce."

"Any chance the guy did it?"

"I don't see it."

"Why not?"

"I've known Bryce for three years. He's a Gulf War vet, so he's got issues, but he strikes me as honest."

"But he could've done it."

"He'd have no reason to. He gets disability benefits because of his service. And he spends most of the year living in a tent in the National Forest, so he doesn't have a lot of expenses. The reason he's at the shelter right now is that he just had surgery."

"You're right, it doesn't sound likely. Any second thoughts about telling them no?"

"Not really. It was the right thing to do. I appreciate that the police have responded the few times we've needed them. But I don't want them showing up at the shelter every time a black guy commits a crime just because we have a few black guys. It reeks of racism."

"I agree."

Betsy is peeking around my office door. "Um, we have a situation on the third floor," she says.

"Sounds like you'd better go," James says.

"Yup. Anyway, thanks," I say to James. I hang up and turn to Betsy. "Please tell me you didn't just find a pile of money wrapped in a bandana."

"No, nothing like that. It's more of a plumbing problem."

"I'll be right up," I say. I'd rather deal with plumbing than police any day.

CHAPTER 2

Karen Driscoll
Tuesday, September 4, 2012

Patterson is driving and chewing spearmint gum. He must have put in a couple of fresh pieces before we got into the cruiser because the smell is driving me crazy. It's not that I dislike spearmint. I just don't like that I can practically taste his breath. Of course, if he'd offered me a piece, it wouldn't be so offensive. When Patterson asked me to go out to the shelter with him, I was surprised. He usually avoids me. Maybe I was the officer who looked least busy.

"What a bitch," Patterson says, shaking his head. "Sarah Bennett."

"Do you really think it was Bryce?" I say.

"I'm almost positive," he says.

"What do you know that you didn't tell that Bennett woman?"

"It's simple logic. How many black males do we have in this county?"

"Counting the migrant workers that live out on the farms?"

"No, they're all Jamaican or Mexican. And the perp didn't have an accent."

"What about college students?"

"Keep them out of it too. Someone who pays fifty thousand bucks a year for tuition isn't going to rob a convenience store."

"Okay. A dozen, maybe two?" I say.

"A dozen sounds about right," Patterson says. "Where are they?"

"All over."

"I'm not talking about professionals with families." He looks at me like I'm stupid. "I'm talking about the ones that might rob a convenience store."

"There's Cyrus Wilson and his buddies over on Depot Street." Cyrus showed up in town a few months ago. In a town as white as Middleton Falls, Vermont, he sticks out like a sore thumb. His companions seem to rotate weekly after visits from vehicles with Massachusetts plates. And since he has no visible means of support, it's assumed he's trying to establish himself as a drug dealer. I'm not sure that's fair, but I'm not sure it isn't either.

"That's right. So," Patterson says, "Cyrus and his crew live near the Quik Stop?"

"No. It's a couple a miles."

"Those guys have a car?"

"Not that I know of. Cyrus always walks around town or takes the shuttle unless he has friends from the city staying with him."

"Any out-of-state plates over there lately?"

"Haven't checked."

"I did and there weren't," he says with a nod.

"Okay."

"What time was the robbery?"

"Approximately 10:15 p.m."

"What time do the buses stop?"

"Around 8:00 p.m."

"You gonna rob a convenience store then walk home two miles?"

"Probably not."

"So, it's gotta be someone lives closer, right?"

"Probably. Or someone with access to a car," I say.

Patterson ignores my comment. He's on a roll. "What's closer?"

"The shelter."

"How many black guys they got there?"

"Maybe three or four."

"Like I said, simple logic. Where're we gonna find the perp?"

"It could've been someone from out of town," I say.

Patterson shakes his head. "That's what the state's attorney said. But if that's the case, we'll never catch him unless someone turns him in. Without another lead, we've got to assume it's someone local. So where should we look?"

"At the shelter," I say because it's the answer he wants to hear.

"Who was casing the Quik Stop an hour before the robbery?"

"Bryce Anderson."

"That's right. That's why he's our prime suspect."

I see his logic. While I'm not convinced it was Bryce, the odds are good that, if it was someone local, they live at the shelter.

"How come there's so many black guys at the shelter?" I say. "It seems weird."

"Mostly, they come up from the cities to go to the job training center. They decide they like it here, but they can't find jobs."

"Makes sense," I say. "So, what are we going to do?"

"We're going to get a warrant and go back and stick it in her face."

"Why didn't we just get one in the first place?"

"State's attorney didn't think there was enough there. He said we'd be better off trying to get consent."

"I guess he doesn't know the shelter director," I say.

"Sarah Bennett. She's probably one of those liberals moved here from somewhere else."

"I really don't get her," I say. "I heard what she said about trust, but I don't see how they would blame her. It's a homeless shelter, not the Ritz. It feels like she's just trying to keep us from doing our job."

"Like I said, must be a liberal. She sure talks like a liberal. Either that or she's a criminal. Maybe she got the job because she used to be one of them. You know, like AA counselors."

It doesn't seem likely, but I shrug. "Could be. Anyway, this is a serious crime. When was the last time we had an armed robbery in Middleton Falls?"

"A few years back. Some guy used a gun to get oxycontin at Kinney Drugs."

"Must've been before my time."

"He was stoned. We caught him before he made it out of the parking lot."

"Anyway, I really don't understand that woman. There's some whacko out there with a big knife who's not afraid to use it. I'd think everyone would want to help us out."

"Preaching to the choir, kid. We're just trying to keep this community safe. You want to be part of the search team after we get a warrant?"

"Absolutely." I hope I'm on duty when the judge signs off on the warrant. I know Patterson won't go out of his way to include me and I'd like to be there when they catch the guy.

CHAPTER 3

James Bennett
Friday, September 7, 2012

I can think of at least a hundred things I would rather be doing than sitting in this room right now. Let's see. Going to the dentist? Yes, unless of course it was for a root canal. Buying feminine hygiene products for Sarah? Definitely preferable. Cleaning hair out of the drains? That's probably my least favorite household chore, but it's still better than marriage counseling.

I'm only here because Sarah forced the issue after the "French Door Incident," which we have yet to talk about with the counselor. I'm not going to be the one to bring it up, that's for sure. At our first session a few weeks ago, Jasmine, the counselor, asked us why we thought we needed counseling. Sarah just said that we'd been arguing a lot lately, which I had to agree with. But I didn't say that the whole counseling thing was Sarah's idea, not mine.

Jasmine's actually quite sharp. I like debating with her. We've spent most of this session discussing parenting. That's just fine with me and there's no shortage of material.

"Nick had to stay after school for not doing his homework," Sarah says.

"Is that a problem?" Jasmine says.

"Well, my problem with Nick is that he lied when I asked him if he did his homework. Probably because he wanted to watch TV."

"That's certainly an issue," Jasmine says.

"I agree. But, my problem with James is that when the school called to tell us, James got him excused," Sarah says.

"I don't want my kid sitting in a room with a bunch of budding delinquents," I say.

"He needs to learn that there are consequences for not meeting his responsibilities," Sarah says. "It sends the wrong message when you get him excused."

"I can impose consequences," I say. "How about I spank him every time he lies about having done his homework?" Jasmine furrows her eyebrows. "Only kidding. I've never been allowed to spank the kids." Jasmine's face returns to her normal blank mask. It's clear this woman is in Sarah's camp on the corporal punishment issue.

"I think what Sarah is saying is that the school has consequences in place," Jasmine says. "Maybe you should let Nick experience those consequences. If he does, then he might learn that it's not worth it."

"It makes our family look bad, having a kid in detention," I say.

"It's not detention, it's homework club," Sarah says.

"Whatever you call it, it looks bad," I say.

"Well, sometimes that's a side effect," Jasmine says. "But it might only take a few times before he'd figure out he doesn't want to be there."

"Or he might make friends with the delinquents and decide to become one," I say.

"It's a risk," Jasmine says. It feels like I scored a point.

"It's also bad if he misses soccer practice," I say. "I'm the coach. My kid needs to be committed to the team."

"I understand that," Jasmine says. "I'm just suggesting that you should consider a 'natural consequences' approach to the problem."

"There's nothing natural about detention," I say.

"No, but it may be the closest thing in this case. Let me give you an example of what I mean. What's a required piece of gear for soccer?"

"Shin guards," I say.

"So let's say that Nick keeps forgetting to pack his shin guards for practice. He calls Sarah and she runs home to get them every time. He's going to keep forgetting because he has no incentive to remember."

"Okay," I say. It's hard to argue against that logic.

"But let's say she doesn't bail him out, and he has to sit on the bench during practice or a game. After a few times, he'll get more diligent when he packs up his gear. That's natural consequences."

There's an obvious counterargument. "I get that, but what if the team loses because one of the best players is on the bench? That's punishing the whole team. Seems a little harsh."

"Some of life's lessons are harsh," Jasmine says. "If the team gets mad at him, he'll be more likely to remember next time."

"As a coach, I need to put the team ahead of teaching my kid a lesson. And it doesn't really address the lying," I say.

"I agree that's also an issue," Jasmine says. I feel like I won that round, but Jasmine doesn't seem to care. She continues, "I'm not telling you what you should do here. I'm simply suggesting that there are multiple viewpoints. It's all about balance. As parents and partners you need to figure out how you're going to address the issue and present a united front. You can't undermine each other in front of the kids. And it's not fair for one of you to make an important decision without consulting the other."

That feels like a dig at me. I think we need to spread the blame around a bit. "I don't really care what the consequences are as long as they're meaningful," I say. "The time-outs that Sarah imposes are ridiculous. As soon as nobody's looking, the kids just play or read in their rooms until the time-out is over. How's that a punishment?"

"You've got a lot to talk about," Jasmine says. "Just try not to do it in front of the kids." She didn't take the bait.

Jasmine glances at the clock. It's 10:50. Time to end the session.

"I have a homework assignment for you guys," Jasmine says. "Before our next session, I want you to go on a date. It doesn't have to be dinner, but I want you guys to carve out time to do something together. No kids, get a babysitter."

"But Nick's too old for a babysitter," I say. "And he'd probably kill his sisters if we left him in charge."

"Figure something out," Jasmine says. It feels like she's being dismissive. "Send Nick to a friend's house for the night or an afternoon. Just set aside some couple time. You guys are good at giving each other personal time. Now you need to start thinking of your marriage as an entity with needs as well."

Sarah and I look at each other. We both smirk.

"I'm not talking about sex," Jasmine says. "I'm talking about connecting. Outside the realm of children. You guys have made the children a high priority, and that's positive. You're both good parents, even if you don't always see things the same way. Now you need to learn to be good partners at the same time. Again, it's hard to find the right balance."

We make another appointment for next week and head outside. That wasn't as bad as it could have been. I can have a date with my wife. We haven't gone out to dinner in a restaurant that wasn't "family friendly" in ages. This could be fun. I might even get lucky with my wife afterward. I smile and look over at Sarah. She looks exhausted.

"Have a good rest of the day, beautiful," I say, hoping to cheer her up.

"You too," she says.

I give her a quick kiss on the lips before I get into my Audi and head back to my office. Maybe marriage counseling isn't such a bad idea after all. Maybe Jasmine can get Sarah to appreciate me more.

CHAPTER 4

Sarah Bennett
Saturday, September 8, 2012

I wouldn't say I love to run. For me, running is sort of like vacuuming the dog hair. If I don't do it often enough, things get ugly. Plus, running makes me feel less guilty when I eat chocolate chip cookies with the kids.

It's Saturday morning. I'm walking in the front door from a four-mile run when Meredith and Camille run in front of me shrieking and chasing Nick. All three kids are shades of blond with my brown eyes and their father's trim physique. Nick is almost four years older than Meredith who is only seventeen months older than Camille. It would have been nice to have the kids more evenly spaced, but Mother Nature had a different idea.

"Mommy! Nick took my dolphin and won't give it back," Camille says.

"Nicholas, do you have the dolphin?" I say.

"Well, yeah, but she had my comic book," Nick says.

"Does she still have it?"

"Well, no."

"So, why do you have her dolphin?"

"I was just trying to make a point."

"And what point would that be?"

"That she shouldn't touch my stuff."

"He was showing me the picture of the bloody zombie," Camille says. "He gave me the comic book. It was really gross."

"Oh, Nick. I know you get bored, but it's no excuse for any of this."

"I wouldn't be so bored if I had a brother. Let's adopt a twelve-year-old boy."

"Zero chance. But nice try. Now give her the dolphin and don't touch it again. Ever."

He takes the dolphin out of his shirt and hands it to Camille. She hugs the stuffed animal while Meredith rubs her little sister's back.

"How about everybody picks up the living room and then you can have a little iPod time until it's time to get ready for ballet." Yes, it's bribery. But I want a chance to stretch before I have to start shuttling children for the day. All three children groan.

"Why do we have to clean up? Let us have our iPods now and we'll clean up later," Nick says.

"Not negotiable," I say.

The house is blissfully quiet while I do some gentle stretching. Sometimes the ends justify the means. At 9:15, I realize it's almost time for the girls' ballet lesson. I find James in the office writing an email.

"Are you taking the girls to ballet, or am I?" I say.

"Either one. I just need a few minutes to finish sending out this email to the soccer parents," he says.

"Well, if you wouldn't mind taking them, it would give me a chance to shower. I'm still pretty sweaty from my run. But if you take them, I'll pick them up. Deal?" I say.

"Okay, but can you make sure they're ready?"

"Sure thing." I head back to the living room where all three kids are still engrossed in their tiny screens. "Girls, you need to get ready for ballet. Nick, enough electronics. It's time to put the iPod away."

"Fine. I'm going to ride my bike to the library," Nick says. I know he plays games on the library computers while he's there, but at least there are time limits and he gets exercise riding his bike.

"Be home before lunch," I say.

"I don't want to go to ballet today," Meredith says.

"Yes, you do. You always say that and you always have a great time. Now go get ready."

"No. I don't want to go." Meredith is still staring at the iPod and moving her thumbs.

"You don't have a choice. Shut that thing down now."

Meredith shakes her head, but doesn't look up from the screen.

"Here's mine, Mommy." Camille hands over her iPod. "I'll get the ballet bag."

"Meredith, this is your last chance. If that iPod is not in my hands by the time I count to five, you will lose your screen privileges for the rest of the day. One… Two… Three…"

I'm holding out my hand, but Meredith puts the iPod on the table next to me. Scowling, she turns and follows Camille upstairs to their room.

I really want to get in the shower. My skin is clammy and I stink. It's a good thing James is taking the girls to class.

On my way to the bathroom, I peek into the girls' room. Camille is dressed in her black leotard and pink tights. She's struggling to put her hair into a bun.

Meredith is sitting cross-legged in the middle of the pink carpet. She's still dressed in skinny jeans and a T-shirt.

"Cammy, sweetie, do you want me to do your bun for you? You're doing a good job, but you know how Caroline is about stray pieces," I say.

"Yes, please, Mommy." Camille turns her back to me presenting her hair. It takes a few seconds to wrap her baby-fine hair into a bun and secure it with a clip. A couple of bobby pins ensure her hair is out of her eyes.

"Okay, all set. Now, go get a water bottle and get in the van. Meredith will be out in a few minutes."

When she is gone, I sit on the floor in front of Meredith. "You need to get ready for class or we're going to be late. You know how much Caroline hates when people are late."

"I'm not going."

"Yes, you are. Your father and I paid six hundred dollars for ballet lessons. You're going to go. Besides, you always seem so excited after class."

"Caroline's too strict."

"I've watched your class. I know you have fun."

"I don't want to go anymore."

"I wish I could do it, that's how fun it looks."

"You go then. I'd rather just stay here and play."

"Well, that's not an option. First you finish this session, and then we can talk about whether you take another one. Now get dressed."

"No."

"We don't have time for this. Get your ballet clothes on or you're going to be late."

Meredith shakes her head.

I don't have the energy for this right now. "I'm going to get Daddy," I say, knowing that I mean it as a threat and wishing that I didn't. James is still in front of the computer.

"Meredith won't get ready. She says she doesn't want to go to ballet."

"Why not? She loves ballet."

"I don't know. She said something about Caroline being too strict."

"It's ballet. It's supposed to be strict."

"She's just being stubborn. She probably thinks if she stays home, she'll get to play with her iPod all morning."

James raises an eyebrow which I pointedly ignore. He thinks the kids spend too much time with their iPods. "Look, I'm not getting through to her. Could you please go talk to her?"

James glances at the computer and frowns. "Yeah, okay," he says. He clicks the mouse a few times before he gets up.

I probably shouldn't get in the shower until I know the girls are on their way. I go to our bedroom and gather some clothes to put on after my shower. Then, I putter around picking up until I hear James and Meredith come out of the girls' room. I'm glad to see that Meredith is wearing her leotard and tights.

"Let's get your bun done quickly so you're not late," I say. "Get the brush and the clips and I'll meet you in the living room." After she's gone down the stairs, I turn to James. "What did you say to her?"

"You're right about her being stubborn. I finally told her if she didn't put her own leotard on, I was going to do it for her. I think she was afraid I would actually do it."

"Would you—forget it," I say. "Thanks for getting her dressed."

In the living room, Meredith has the hair notions lined up on the sofa. I quickly put up her hair and remind her to grab her water bottle and get in the van. She walks slowly, staring at the ground.

"James, they're ready and in the van," I say. He's back in the office in front of the computer. I can see him typing when I reach the doorway. "I thought you were going to take the girls to ballet so I could take a shower."

"I was. But I couldn't get this done because I had to spend my time getting Meredith dressed. I really want to get this finished before I lose my train of thought. You take them and I'll do pickup, okay?"

"I really need a shower." I'm trying to keep the frustration out of my voice. I decide to go for flattery. "Besides, it'll go more smoothly if you take them. Meredith really wasn't listening to me. You at least got her dressed. You should take them."

"Just make it clear to her that she's going to class. That's all I would do. C'mon, I've got to finish this." He gives me a crooked smile, the one that made me fall in love with him.

"Okay. But you owe me."

It's a beautiful morning when I go outside. The sun is shining, and the temperature has come up since my run. The girls are buckled into my blue minivan. I roll down the front windows to let in the fresh breeze.

The trip is less than a mile. The air smells of cut grass. The sawing hum of lawnmowers comes from all directions. We pass children playing hopscotch on the sidewalk and basketball in a driveway. In the rearview mirror, I see that the girls have their heads bent toward each other.

"What are you guys talking about?" I say.

"Girl stuff, Mommy," Camille says.

"Nothing to do with you," Meredith says.

The ballet studio is on the second floor of what used to be the American Legion a few decades ago. The neighborhood is on our side of town and is mostly residential, with stately Victorians mixed with duplexes. I'm not planning to be there long enough to park in the lot out back, so when we arrive, I do a three-point turn in a driveway and pull up in front of the building. There's another ballet parent dropping off. When they leave, I pull forward and cut the engine.

Camille unbuckles her seat belt, grabs the ballet bag, and opens the passenger side slider. She hops out of the van and turns to smile at me. "Bye, Mommy."

"Have a good class." I smile back at her. She skips away, leaving the van slider open. Meredith is still buckled in when I turn toward her.

"Meredith, you need to get moving. It's almost time." Meredith pushes her chin down against her chest and crosses her arms in front of her.

"I'm not going."

"Yes, you are. I already told you. We paid for the classes, so you need to finish this session. Besides, you know how much Camille loves ballet. Please don't ruin it for her."

"But I don't want to go anymore."

"I got that. But sometimes we all have to do things we don't want to do. Now, get yourself upstairs before you're late." Despite my strictest "strict mommy" tone, Meredith still doesn't budge.

What can I say to get her moving?

I take the keys out of the ignition and unbuckle my seat belt, turning my body to face Meredith. James would probably threaten to carry her up the stairs. I really don't know what else to say.

We're both just staring at each other when Camille comes back to the van. "Is Meredith coming to class? It's going to start in just a minute." Camille looks like she's about to cry.

"Of course she's coming. Go on up. She'll be right there."

Camille pokes her head in the open slider. "Hurry up, Em," she says. Then, she turns and runs back to the studio door.

"Come on, Meredith. Just do it for Camille's sake," I say.

Meredith unbuckles her seat belt and holds it while it retracts. She climbs out of her seat. She frowns at me as she steps out the van door and then pulls it shut behind her. I watch her as she walks toward the studio door. When she has almost reached it, she turns suddenly. I can tell by the change of pace that she has changed her mind about cooperating.

Instinctively, I find the switch on the driver's door and lock all the van doors. A second later, when Meredith pulls on the slider, it doesn't open.

"I want to go home!" Meredith says through the open window.

"That's not happening. Now get your butt upstairs to class."

Meredith moves forward and tries to open the front passenger door. She pulls on it a few times, but nothing happens. "I'm not going to ballet!"

"Okay, at this point that's your choice. But if you decide not to go to class, you're walking home. I'm not driving you. I think you should go to your class and be with your sister. I guarantee it'll be more fun than walking home by yourself." How's that for natural consequences? It's probably the kind of thing Jasmine had in mind.

I find my sunglasses and rebuckle my seat belt. With my foot on the brake, I start the engine and put the gear shift in Drive. A second later, I hear a clicking sound and remember the "unlocking" feature on the van. Then, the driver's side slider opens. I turn left and see Meredith standing on the pavement beside the open door.

"Don't you dare," I say. "If you get in this van, you'll lose your iPod for a week. Now get yourself upstairs right this second." So much for natural consequences.

Meredith and I stare at each other for what seems like a long time, but is likely only three seconds. I can tell she's considering whether it's worth it to lose her iPod.

I'm weighing my own options. If she gets back in the van, I may not be able to talk her out of it again. Also, if I take the time to shut the door, she may decide to get back in the van. There's nobody coming up the road, so I'm not going to give her any choice. I take my foot off the brake and slowly pull forward, away from her and out onto the road. The slider is still open, but who cares? I can shut it later.

I look in my rearview mirror expecting to see Meredith still standing in the parking spot. She's not there. I check the sideview mirror. I can see part of her face. She has to be running next to the van. Oh no.

"What are you doing? Get out of the road right now!"

Her face is still the same size in the mirror. I turn my head to the left and get a look at her whole body. She is holding onto the slider door handle and running on the yellow line.

Oh dear God, she's wearing Crocs. I have a split-second vision of my daughter stumbling in her slip-on Crocs and falling under the rear wheel of the van. My whole body starts shaking. If I touch my foot to the brake, I might hit it too hard and it might make her fall. I need to slow the van as gently as I can. I take my foot off the gas. My foot is convulsing in the space above the brake. *Please don't fall.*

"Meredith! Let go or you're going to get hurt. Let go right now, Meredith!" I don't recognize my own voice.

As soon as the words are out of my mouth, she lets go. I can see her in the mirror, continuing to trot after the van on the yellow line. For a second I can't breathe. Then the air fills my lungs. She's okay.

"Get out of the road, Meredith. You're not being safe."

The van is still creeping forward. I touch the brake and the car jerks but slows more. I watch as my daughter walks across the oncoming lane and stands in a driveway across the street from the dance studio. I don't know what to do. There's a stop sign, so I stop, my foot bouncing on the brake pedal, my hands gripping the steering wheel. I turn and watch my daughter. She's standing safely off the road staring at the van.

Thank God she's okay. There are a million ways that could have gone wrong. What could she possibly have been thinking?

Now, what am I supposed to do? If I go back and get her, then she did something terribly dangerous and got her way. That's not a behavior I want to reinforce.

I really didn't see that coming. I want to go back and ask her why she did it, but I probably shouldn't. I told her she was going to walk home, so she needs to walk home. There's no danger in that. Unless she runs into the road again. But if I leave, then she won't have any reason to run in the road. She'll use the sidewalk like she always does.

Or maybe she'll stay and go to her class. If I leave, that might happen. Worst case scenario, it takes her ten minutes to walk home. Best case, she goes to class.

On the other hand, if I show up at home with Meredith, James will label it as another example of my weak parenting.

Wait a minute. Why am I the one here dealing with this? James was supposed to be here, not me. This never would have happened if he'd brought the girls to ballet like he promised. Meredith would have done what he told her to do. She'd be at her class right now. But his email was more important to him.

Or maybe he was testing me. I can never tell these days.

I continue through the stop sign. As soon as I'm out of sight of Meredith, I stop to shut the van door.

Did I make the wrong choice? She knows better—and yet it happened. What if this whole thing is really about something else? Maybe I should go back. No, it would definitely send the wrong message. If I had thought she might run after the van, I would have handled it differently. But I really didn't. So there's no reason to waste the lesson.

She's probably on her way upstairs to her class. But if she's not, James needs to help with this.

James is still in the office at the computer when I walk in. I've been dealing with parenting hell, and he's happily typing away.

"James! Meredith ran after the van. In the road."

"Is she okay?"

"She didn't get hurt, if that's what you mean. She was out of the road when I left, but I don't know what's going on with her. It is definitely your turn to deal with this!"

"Okay." I'm surprised at how quickly he shuts down the computer. He must realize how frazzled I am. He grabs his wallet and keys from the table by the front door. A few seconds later, I hear his car start.

All I want to do is take a shower.

CHAPTER 5

Karen Driscoll
Saturday, September 8, 2012

Finally, I have a day off. I was looking forward to sleeping late and then sitting on my back deck, drinking coffee, reading the *Gazette*, and enjoying the mountain view. It's supposed to be a beautiful day—sunny, mid-seventies, probably one of the last real days of summer. The tops of the mountains are already turning yellow and orange.

My sleeping plans are foiled by Arlo, my ninety-pound German shepherd. He hears something in the backyard and starts barking at 5:20 a.m. Probably deer. Once he realizes I'm awake, there's no chance he's going to leave me alone until I let him out to investigate. I drag myself out of bed to open the door for him. It's tempting to just go back to bed, but I know from experience that, if he wants to come back in, he'll either bark forever or scratch at the screen door. Sometimes both. Unless I want to add repairing the screens to my "to do" list, I'm better off waiting.

It turns out to be a long wait. I can see Arlo's tracks crossing the dewy grass of my back lawn and disappearing into the cornfield next door. After ten minutes, I consider going back to bed because the longer I'm awake the less likely I'm going to get back to sleep. I've only had about four hours of sleep. I worked the three-to-eleven shift last night. I consider myself lucky I was able to sign out just before midnight. Friday nights in a college town can be a little crazy. As one of three officers on duty, I was kept pretty busy. I responded to one noise complaint and one domestic incident. Neither of those involved much paperwork because we didn't arrest anyone. I also processed one college student for DUI after happy hour at The Shack, the most popular bar for Friday happy hour, probably because of the free popcorn. Personally, I prefer Mr. K's Place because the crowd tends to run a little older and there's a pool table. Not that I go there often. The reality is that, in a town this small, you get to know most of the locals, which means that the guy you arrested last week could be the guy you end up sitting next to at the bar this week. It's easier to just stay home.

I'm standing at my kitchen window, waiting for the coffee to finish brewing, when I see Arlo come out from the cornfield. I go to the back door and open it. Fortunately, I smell Arlo before he manages to squeeze through the open door. Skunk—there's literally no other smell like it. I slam the door in his face. He whines. So much for a relaxing morning. I vaguely remember a handout from the veterinarian suggesting ways to get rid of the odor. It probably went in the trash. While Arlo scratches at the screen, I boot up my computer and Google "removing skunk smell from dogs."

The baking soda and hydrogen peroxide mix does pretty good on the skunk smell, but it isn't gone by any means. I'm going to need to make a trip into town for more supplies. Arlo is tied up in the shade to keep him from scratching at the screen. The first pot of coffee turned to sludge while I was giving him his anti-skunk treatment, so I'm forced to make a second pot. I don't really enjoy my first cup as much as I'd hoped because Arlo keeps staring at me like I'm betraying him while I sit and sip. I'm just pouring my second cup when the phone rings.

"I understand we're supposed to call you when there's a kid involved." It's Joe Langford. He's a part-timer. I swear he's been on the force since I was in elementary school.

"That's right."

"Better you than me."

"What you got?"

"Little girl got dragged behind a van. Witness said the mom didn't even stop. The dad's here with her, but he wasn't there for any of it."

"Wow. Okay, I'll be there in five."

I take two minutes to put on a uniform and holster my weapon. About fifteen minutes later, I walk into the Middleton Falls Police Department offices.

The MFPD building is a run-down brick building on the north end of town. It was supposed to be a temporary headquarters when it was built fifty years ago. Unfortunately, the taxpayers never seem to want to pay for a new building, so we have to make do. There are two interview rooms and a large common room with shared desks and lockers for all the officers. The chief has an office and the two sergeants share an "office" which might have been a janitor's closet at some point. The only part of the building that gets regular upgrades are the holding cells. Something to do with Federal regulations. We have two of them, though it's rare they're both used at the same time. The cells have cameras mounted high in the corners. They get painted once a year and cleaned thoroughly by the twice-weekly cleaners. Personally, I wish someone would put half as much effort into keeping up the rest of our space.

Joe Langford is in an interview room talking with a balding middle-aged male. I make eye contact with Joe through the glass window. He nods slightly. A minute later he comes out into the hall. Joe is tall and stooped, with sun-damaged skin.

"So, where's the kid?" I say.

"She's in Room 2 with the dad."

"What's the story?"

"Well, according to the witness, he saw the kid trying to get into a parked van in front of the ballet studio down on Sarandon Street."

"Yeah. I know where it is."

"The kid told him her mom was driving. The witness saw the mom turn the van around while the kid was in the road. Then the kid ran after the van and opened the door and the mom kept driving. The kid was holding onto the van and running for a while. We have another witness, lives up the street, saw the van moving with the door open. He didn't see anything to do with the kid, must have been after, but it corroborates the first witness."

"What about the dragging?"

"The dispatcher used the word 'dragged' when I got called out, but it's not what the guy told me."

"Was the kid hurt?"

"No, fortunately not. But still...."

"Yeah, I know. It's amazing what some people will do to their kids."

"It gets even better."

"How so?"

"The mom is that woman from the homeless shelter, Sarah Bennett, the one who gave you and Patterson a hard time last week."

"Really?" I can't help but smile.

"I guess you can knock her off her high horse this time." Langford smiles back at me and we both nod. "Do you want me to get a statement from the main witness?" he says.

"No, just write a summary of what he told you so far. If I'm going to be the primary on this, I'll need to talk to him anyway. Tell him I'll be in touch later today."

"Okay, will do."

"Thanks, Joe."

I enter Room 2 not knowing what to expect. There's a little blond girl sitting in the interview chair. Her legs don't reach the ground and she's swinging them, kicking straight up so her thighs come slightly off the chair each time. She's dressed in ballet clothes and green Crocs sandals. Her hair is wrapped tight in a bun at the back of her head. She's a cute kid who looks small in the adult-sized interview chair. Immediately, I feel sorry for her. She probably has real controlling parents. I didn't much like Sarah Bennett when I met her. Personally, I wouldn't be surprised if she's super strict. In my trainings I learned that you can never tell what an abusive parent looks like. Sure, abuse is more prominent with the poorer people, but child abuse is everywhere. Mommy Dearest and all that.

I recognize the dad, though I'm not sure from where. I've probably seen him walking around town. He's dressed casual, in shorts, a T-shirt, and flip-flops.

"Thank you for waiting," I say to him. "I have just a few questions."

"That's fine," he says, "as long as it doesn't take long. We've already been waiting in this room for thirty minutes, and I'd really like to take my daughter home. She wasn't hurt, and I want to find out from my wife what happened."

"You haven't talked to your wife?"

"No, she came home upset, said something about Meredith being in the road."

"Did she say anything else?"

"Yeah, but I wasn't really paying attention. I just know she wanted me to go check on Meredith, so I went. I got there the same time as Officer Langford. For some reason, he really wanted us to talk to you."

"Well, it's my job to talk to children, so I'd like to ask Meredith a few questions. Is that okay with you, Meredith?"

"Sure," Meredith says quietly.

I turn to the dad. "You can stay if you want, but usually it works better if the parents are not present when we talk with the child." I seriously hope he decides to leave. I don't like the vibes I'm getting from him, and I'm afraid he's going to take the kid and walk out. Most people don't realize it, but I can't make them stay for an interview.

"How long do you think this will take?" He looks at his watch.

"It's hard to say, five minutes maybe. It's just a few questions about what happened. We got called out, so we have to do some paperwork." I know I'm grossly underestimating the amount of time it takes for a forensic interview, but I also sense that if I'm honest with him, he'll probably take the kid and leave. "You can wait in the lobby if you want, Mr...?"

"Bennett. James Bennett. Will you be okay if I'm right outside, sweetie?" he says.

The child has stopped kicking and is holding very still. She's staring at her dad with big brown eyes.

"Meredith? It'll just be a few minutes, okay?"

I can barely hear her answer. "Okay."

The dad pulls his phone out of his pocket and nods once at his daughter. He looks relieved. "Okay, kiddo, see you in a few minutes." He opens the door about a foot, slips through the opening, and quietly shuts the door.

"Hello. Meredith, right?"

The kid nods very slightly. I can't tell if she is scared or if she's just a shy kid. I should probably try to follow the forensic interview format I learned in training.

"How old are you, Meredith?"

"Eight."

"When's your birthday?"

"August twenty-fifth."

"So you had a birthday last month?"

She nods.

"What grade does that make you?"

"Third."

"That's great. Where do you go to school?"

"Tully."

"Do you like school?"

Meredith shrugs.

"Do you have any brothers or sisters?"

She nods her head.

"Which?"

"Both."

I'm supposed to get a bunch of background information from her, but I'm literally afraid that the dad is going to barge in and take her away. I need to step things up if I'm going to get anything useful from the kid. On the other hand, if I don't follow the interview guidelines, I could get in trouble with the lawyers. What's most important? Probably the truth and lie thing.

"So, if I were to say that apples are blue, would that be the truth?" I say.

The kid tilts her head and frowns, but gives the correct response. "No," she says.

Good enough. That pretty much proves she can tell the truth. I don't want to waste any more time on preliminaries.

"So, let's talk about what happened today. It looks like you were going to ballet, is that right?" I say.

"Yeah."

"And your mommy took you?"

"Yeah."

"What happened?"

The kid looks at me with those big eyes, not even blinking. I try again. "Meredith, can you tell me what happened?"

She shakes her head.

"Did something happen with your mom's van?"

"Yes."

"Did your mom do something?"

"Yes."

"Did your mom do something to you?"

"Yes."

"What did your mom do to you?"

"She locked the doors."

"Why did she lock the doors?"

"So I couldn't get in."

"Okay, then what happened?"

"She left."

"Why did she leave?"

"I don't know. She was going home."

"Did she say anything to you?"

"Not really."

"Did you go to your class?"

"No."

"Why not?"

"I didn't want to go."

"Why not?"

The kid stares at me again, but doesn't answer.

"Do you like ballet?"

Still no answer.

"What happened when your mom left?"

"She drove away."

"Okay. What happened when you got to ballet this morning?"

"I got out."

"Then what?"

"I ran after the van."

"Were you holding onto the van?"

"Yeah."

"Were you running or were you dragged?"

"I was running."

"Are you sure?"

The kid stares at me and then shrugs.

"Were you dragged by the van?"

"I don't know."

"Did it hurt?"

"Not really."

This interview is not going the way I want it to. The kid is definitely holding out on me. Something happened between she and her mom that she's not telling me. On top of that, the dad is probably going to walk in any minute.

"Let's start from the beginning. I think it might help if we made a drawing." In training they taught us that sometimes kids will draw what they won't say. I get a piece of paper and pencil from the desk drawer. "Can you draw it for me?"

"I'm not a good artist," Meredith says.

"Okay. How about if I get it started." I take the pencil and draw a rough map of the area near the ballet studio, explaining to the kid what each part of the drawing represents. It's not to scale, but it hardly matters because I'm just trying to get the kid to open up to me. "So, can you show me where your mom parked when you arrived?"

"In front."

"So she parked here." I point to the front of the building. "Okay, and did you come from home?"

"Yeah."

"Where do you live?"

"Forty-seven Park Street, Middleton Falls, Vermont," she says.

"Very good. You practice that?" She nods. It takes me a couple of seconds to remember where Park Street is.

"So, your mom would have been coming from the east, like this." I demonstrate with my pencil. "And she pulled in here in front of the studio, right?" I draw a picture of a car parked in front of the ballet building.

"Sure."

"When she left, she would have turned the van around, right?" I draw an arrow showing the way the van would have turned around.

"I guess so."

"Which door did you get out of? Can you show me on the drawing?"

The kid shakes her head.

"Why not?"

"I don't know. It's not there." I have to admit that confuses me some.

"You want to draw it?"

"No."

I get a separate piece of paper and this time draw a picture of a van. "Can you show me which door you got out now?"

The kid points to the passenger slider.

"Did you go into the ballet building?"

"No."

"But you couldn't get back into the van, right?"

"Yeah."

"Because your mom locked the doors, right?"

"Yeah."

"And she turned the van around?"

"Yeah."

"And she drove away?"

"Yeah."

"But you got one of the doors open?"

"Yeah."

"Which door did you get open?"

The kid points to the driver's side slider on my drawing.

"So, how did you get from this side to the other?" I point to the doors on the van.

"I walked. Well, kind of a walk, kind of a run."

"Did you go in front of the van?"

"I guess so."

"And you ran after the van?"

"Yeah." The kid looks down at her shoes.

"And you opened the door?"

"Yeah." She's still looking down.

"And your mom didn't stop when the door was opened?"

"Yeah."

"And you were running, but you were dragged a little?"

"Yeah."

"And how long were you like that with the van?"

"I don't know." She finally looks up, but does not make eye contact. She's fidgeting, putting her hands under her legs and then pulling them out.

"Did your mom know you were there?"

"Yeah."

"How do you know she knew?"

"She told me to let go."

Incredible. Sarah Bennett literally locked her kid out of the van, turned around while the kid ran in front of a moving vehicle, and then kept going even after the kid managed to get the door open. And when the kid is being dragged, she just tells her to let go and keeps on going. I feel really badly for this kid. I have to admit I'm a little surprised. I wouldn't have expected that from someone who runs a homeless shelter. Of course, you never can tell about people.

Just then, James Bennett opens the interview room door. Meredith looks relieved to see her father. I look at my watch, surprised to see that thirty minutes have gone by. At least I got what I needed from Meredith before her dad came back. By the expression on his face I can tell the interview is over.

I'm writing a summary of my interview with Meredith when Joe Langford walks up to my desk. He drops a copy of his report on the corner, and waits for me to look up.

"How'd it go with the kid?"

"I think I got enough to nail that Sarah Bennett."

"That's great. What did the kid say?"

"I'm writing it up as we speak." I tell him what's going in my report.

"Wow. That's pretty bad."

"She says she wasn't hurt, but the dad pulled her out of the interview before I had a chance to make sure. Personally, I'd be surprised if she wasn't at least a little hurt after all that."

"The poor kid. I'd like to say I'm surprised, but I've been doing this job so long that nothing really surprises me. What are you thinking for charges?" Joe says.

"I need to talk to your witness first. What's his name?"

Joe glances at the report. "Dave Belkin."

"I won't know for sure until I talk to Belkin. But, based on what I have so far, it looks like reckless endangerment, gross negligent operation and maybe aggravated domestic assault and child abandonment. I should probably run this by the state's attorney when I'm done."

"Well, good work so far. Score one for the good guys this time. Serves her right for protecting the criminals she works with."

"Thanks, Joe, and thanks for the help." I can't believe he actually complimented me. That's got to be a first.

When I'm done writing up my interview with Meredith, I read Joe's report on his interview with Dave Belkin. It was really only an intake. The report is pretty short, but what little is there seems to confirm what I got from Meredith. I call the cell number listed for Belkin, but it goes to voicemail. I leave a message.

I check my police email account while I'm waiting. It's just after three o'clock when Belkin calls back. I know that I should probably talk to the guy today while his memory is still fresh, but I'm tired. He says that he's going down to Bennington for a wedding tomorrow, and that he has to work from seven to three on Monday, but he can come to the PD afterward. We agree to meet at three thirty on Monday afternoon. I tap out a few short email responses and make a call to the Department of Children and Families to make the mandatory report of suspected child abuse. I tell DCF we have an investigation ongoing. After that, I can't think of anything that can't wait until tomorrow, so I head out to my Trooper. Fortunately, I remember to get peroxide and baking soda before I head out of town.

When I get home, Arlo still stinks. I can smell him before I see him. As soon as he sees me, he starts whining. His strategy works and I feel guilty enough to let him off the rope. But I know that, if I let him in the house, I probably won't get the smell out of the furniture. Despite some early efforts to train him, Arlo spends a big portion of his day camped out on my couch. I could have trained him. It's not like I didn't know how. I worked at a kennel for two years while I was in college.

I sit on the back steps and scratch his ears. After a few minutes the smell doesn't bother me so much, but I still don't want it in the house. I change clothes and give Arlo another treatment. Afterward, I let him into the basement. It's got an old couch. I figure Arlo can sleep down there until the smell gets better. I can wash the slip cover in a few days.

As soon as I set Arlo up in the basement with food and water, I wash my hands thoroughly, grab a beer, and sink into the living room couch. I surf through the channels on the TV until I find a show on the Discovery

Channel about Brazilian tree frogs. About halfway through the beer, I fall asleep. I wake up a little after six o'clock feeling groggy, but less tired. I realize that it's Saturday night and, as usual, I have no plans.

I could drive up to Burlington and go listen to some music. Or I could watch a movie on Netflix with Arlo. Shit. Arlo's been banished. I take Arlo for an evening walk and watch a movie by myself.

CHAPTER 6

Nicholas Bennett
Saturday, September 8, 2012

Right after I get back from the library my dad walks in with Meredith. My mom is in the kitchen with Camille.

"Where were you guys?" I say.

"Where's Mom?" my dad says.

I point to the kitchen. Meredith walks by me going to her room. My dad goes to the kitchen. Something's going on and I'm going to find out what. I follow my dad into the kitchen just as Camille comes out.

"What's for lunch?" I say.

"Not now, Nick," my dad says.

"Give us a few minutes, okay?" my mom says.

I leave the room but don't go far. They can't see me, but I can hear them.

My dad tells my mom how he and Meredith had to go to the police station. It sounds like my sister ran after the van and someone called the police. Wow. That's bad. Worse than anything I've ever done. Or at least been caught doing. Timmy and I climbed the fence up at the power dam once. There were these big signs saying, "Danger" and "No Unauthorized Entry." It was cool in there, but I was afraid the police were going to come the whole time. I'm glad they didn't because my parents would have killed me.

Then, Mom and Dad talk about what Meredith's punishment should be. I'm sure it's going to be a big one, but they decide that having to go to the police station is part of the punishment.

I can't believe it. My sister got in trouble with the police and all my parents are going to do is take away her iPod for a week. If it was me, they would take away my iPod for the rest of my life.

I want to get the rest of the story, so I go up to my sisters' room. They're sitting on Meredith's bed. They don't even scream when I come in. They just stop talking. What's up with that?

"You're in such big trouble," I say. "You might lose your iPod for a year."

They both look at me. Still no screams. After about a minute of silence, I leave. It's only fun if I can get them worked up.

Meredith doesn't come down for lunch. She spends the whole afternoon in her room. Camille hangs out with her for a while, but then she gets bored and asks me if I want to play Wii Mario Kart. I even get her to play FIFA soccer for a while, but she sucks. She's better at Mario Kart.

When Meredith doesn't come down for dinner, my mom goes up to take her temperature.

"No fever, but she says she's not feeling well," my mom says.

"There's a stomach thing going around," my dad says. "If her stomach's upset, it's better not to make her eat."

After dinner, I ask Camille what's up with Meredith. She says Meredith was freaked out about what happened at the police station. Meredith told Camille that everyone there was wearing guns and uniforms. She thought they were going to put her in jail, but instead they asked her a bunch of questions before Dad finally brought her home.

I wish I could have been there to see it.

CHAPTER 7

James Bennett
Saturday, September 8, 2012

I probably shouldn't have let that police officer interview Meredith. Something about the situation felt wrong at the time, but I couldn't come up with a concrete reason to walk out. It's not like Sarah would do anything wrong, and Meredith is just a kid. Kids do stupid things all the time. You can't prosecute an eight-year-old for bad judgment.

When I got to the ballet studio, Meredith was standing on the side of the road near some bald guy I didn't recognize. While I was parking, Officer Langford arrived. I always see him around. He seems friendly enough. He spoke briefly with the bald guy. I only waited so I could thank him for his concern. I wanted to be polite. Then, he asked us to come to the police station to do some paperwork. I know I could have said no, thanks, I'm taking my daughter home now, but it's a small town. I didn't want to come across like a jerk. Lawyers get such a bad rap as it is.

"What happened when Mommy brought you to ballet?" I said while Meredith and I were in the car driving to the police station.

"I ran after the van." Meredith said.

"Why?"

"I wanted to go home."

"That's dangerous. You know better than that."

"I know. I'm sorry, Daddy."

"You okay?"

"Yeah."

"You know, Meredith, this has gone too far. We both told you that you had to go to class. There's going to be some punishment for this. Obviously Mommy and I need to talk first." Maybe I did learn something in marriage counseling.

"She said no iPod for a week." Really? I thought we weren't supposed to make unilateral decisions about the children.

"I'm not sure that's enough," I said. "We'll see. Now, let's go in there and get this over with so we can go home."

"Yes, Daddy."

It kills me. You spend so much time trying to teach your kids to be safe. Then, they go and do something stupid like that. It's a good thing Meredith didn't get hurt.

When I left Meredith with that police officer, I was planning to call Sarah and find out more about what happened. I didn't feel comfortable calling her from that room because I could see the cameras and I figured they were recording. I was planning to give them five minutes to fill out their paperwork and then take Meredith home. But, as the saying goes, life is what happens when you plan something else. As I was leaving the interview room my cell phone rang. It was a client who is trying to put in a twenty-home development on the west end of town. We're going before the planning commission next week to try to get a zoning variance for some of the common areas. I like real estate work because there are rarely real estate emergencies and after-hours calls. This client has my cell number because he's given me a fair amount of business over the past few years. I figured if he was calling me on a Saturday morning, he probably had a good reason. I didn't expect to be on the phone with him for half an hour. I didn't even have a chance to talk to Sarah until we got home. When I realized how long Meredith had been in that room, I went and got her.

Okay, it was stupid of me to leave. Not that I like to admit it.

I didn't tell Sarah that I left Meredith alone and I convinced her to give Meredith a little time to process before talking to her. I didn't want Sarah to find out what I did. She'd just criticize me like she always does. Then, she'd want to talk about it in marriage counseling. The last thing I need is Sarah and Jasmine ganging up on me. Even *I* know I made a mistake.

CHAPTER 8

Karen Driscoll
Sunday, September 9, 2012

I'm working noon to 9:00 p.m. for the next few days. I give Arlo another skunk treatment and then leave him tied to a tree again when I head out to work.

Things are pretty quiet at the PD. We get called out on a domestic disturbance. Two of our frequent flyers are going at each other again. Pattie and Travis. We literally get called to their place at least once a month. Apparently, the neighbors don't like their screaming matches. Or maybe the neighbors don't like their lifestyle. There's a few families in the building, mostly people who can't afford to live anywhere else, and Pattie and Travis are known drug users. They're both in their mid-twenties, but look like they're pushing forty. We usually get them to settle down and convince Travis to go somewhere else for a while, mostly because the apartment is in Pattie's name. Personally, I've gone out there at least three times before. Some people just shouldn't be together.

Pete Greene arrives in his cruiser at the same time I do. Pattie and Travis are in the front yard screaming in each other's faces. We agree I'll talk to Pattie while Pete deals with Travis. Pete is dark haired with a mustache. He looks like he spends a couple of hours a day in the gym. He's relatively new, having graduated from the police academy a year ago.

I can tell that Pattie has been drinking and possibly using. Her eyes are partially closed and her speech is thick. She keeps shifting her weight. Her breath smells like beer. Her flowered halter top looks like she bought it when she was a size larger and seems an inappropriate choice for today's sixty-degree weather.

"What happened here, Pattie?" I say, not expecting an honest answer.

"The bastard shoved me." That gets my attention. According to Vermont law, if you do something physical to someone else and it causes pain, even just a little bit, that's an assault. If you assault someone you live with or have a relationship with it becomes a domestic assault. Domestic assault has long-term consequences, including a prohibition on the possession of firearms. Vermonters love their guns, so it's definitely a big deal. My next question is critical.

"Did it hurt?" I'm hoping she says yes because it will mean a prosecutable case.

"Damn straight it did. I hit the corner of the coffee table. Look, I'm gonna have a bruise." She lifts up the bottom of her shorts and shows me a dime-sized red mark on her leg. She's right. It's going be a bruise in a few days. Bingo.

"It's okay, I got even," Pattie says. That doesn't sound good.

"What do you mean?"

"I'm not saying, but he'll think twice before he shoves me again."

Whatever she did, it doesn't change the fact that I need to get a statement. I'm afraid Pattie's going to have second thoughts about cooperating with me. I'm pretty sure that, if I ask her to come down to the station, she'll refuse. Without a statement the state's attorney will decline the case. Maybe I can get what I need here.

I have her sit on the steps while I get a statement pad from the cruiser. I quickly handwrite out a few sentences saying that Pattie and Travis live together, that Travis shoved Pattie, that Pattie has a mark, and it hurt. I ask her to read it and sign it if it sounds right. She doesn't ask what it's for, just reads and signs. When she's done, I get Pete's attention and show him Pattie's statement.

"What do you want me to do?" Pete says.

"See if you can get Travis to admit he did it. If you can get an admission, the whole thing is sewed up tight."

"How do I do that?"

"Sweet talk him. Tell him that everyone makes mistakes and that we just need to get to the bottom of it for our report. You can even tell him that he won't necessarily get in trouble if it was a mistake."

"Isn't that lying?"

"No. As long as you say it in a way that doesn't make any promises."

He comes back a few minutes later shaking his head.

"According to Travis, he didn't push her." He looks down at his notepad. "He says he lost his balance and fell down. She fell with him." He looks up at me. "He's under the influence of something, so it's quite possible."

"Yeah, she is too. What else?"

"He says she got up first and kicked him in the balls. He was down for a few minutes. Then he wanted to get away, so he came outside, but she followed him out here and kept screaming at him."

"If it were up to me, I would charge them both with domestic assault," I say, "but I already know the state's attorneys won't do it."

"Why not? Sounds like maybe they assaulted each other," Pete says.

"Man, do you have a lot to learn. We better call Tamara at the S.A.'s office and ask what she wants us to do," I say.

"If you say so. You want me to make the call?"

"Yeah. I'll keep an eye on Pattie and Travis."

Pete gets out his cell phone and goes over by his cruiser to talk. A couple of minutes later, he hangs up and shakes his head.

"We're supposed to arrest Travis. It figures."

"Yep, saw that coming. She never charges the women. You got Travis?"

"Yeah. I'm not expecting trouble from him, but hang out nearby just in case."

Pete has no trouble putting the cuffs on Travis. He's walking Travis over to the cruiser when Pattie jumps off the steps and comes charging over.

"What the hell do you think you're doing?" she says.

Pete has the cruiser door open and Travis is getting in.

"We're arresting Travis for domestic assault," I say.

"But I'm not pressing charges."

"It's not up to you," I say. "The state's attorney already made the call. We're just following orders."

She clenches her fists and, for a second, I think she's going to assault me. Instead she lets loose a string of swear words that I personally take offense to, and I'm used to hearing trashy language. There are half a dozen neighbors, including two teenagers, milling around, watching the drama. I'm tempted to arrest Pattie for disturbing the peace. It looks bad when we let people treat us that way, but I know the state's attorneys are pretty strict about their "one arrest" rule. I learned that one the hard way. I had a father and two sons get into it. We couldn't decide who to arrest. They were all so out of control and equally beat up. So, we arrested them all. The state's attorneys threw the case out, said they couldn't prosecute a case if there were only defendants and no witnesses. Then, we had this training where they basically told us that, if we arrested a guy for domestic assault, we couldn't arrest his girlfriend for possession, even if she was literally smoking a joint in front of us. It sounds like crap to me.

But I figure it's a safe assumption that arresting Pattie on a minor charge won't go over well if there's a domestic assault in the mix.

I turn and go back to my cruiser, pretending not to notice the bystanders. I'm supposed to counsel Pattie that she can get a restraining order and give her a referral to Safe Haven, but it seems kind of pointless. When I do the paperwork, I'll check the box that says I advised her. Nobody's going to know any different and I won't risk a scuffle with Pattie.

Pete is processing Travis when I get back. We agree that he'll write the affidavit of probable cause, so I only have to write a report about my interview with Pattie and fill out the domestic violence victim checklist.

Afterward, I respond to a noise complaint, but things have quieted down by the time we get there, so it's not much paperwork.

Before the end of my shift, I take a little time to clean up my report on the interview with Meredith Bennett. Poor kid. My parents may not have been perfect, but at least nobody abused me. No child should have to live in fear. Besides dragging her behind the van, I wonder what else passes for acceptable punishment in Meredith's house. Or maybe Sarah Bennett just lost it. It's possible she snapped. Either way, it's my job to make sure this kid is protected. Hopefully, I can get to the bottom of it tomorrow.

Time to go home to my stinky dog.

CHAPTER 9

Sarah Bennett
Monday, September 10, 2012

I need a vacation. Not a camping trip with the family like we did back in the summer, but a real vacation. On a beach. With waiters that bring an endless supply of piña coladas. I picture my handsome husband with his still trim physique relaxing beside me on a lounge chair in front of an aquamarine ocean while our kids splash happily in the surf. Of course, in my fantasy, I've finally lost the extra ten pounds I've been carrying around since my third pregnancy and I look great in the bikini I haven't worn in years. The reality is that we can't afford a vacation like that, and the kids would just bicker the whole time anyway, but it's nice to dream. Besides, we promised the kids a trip to Disney. That's going to eat up the vacation budget for a while.

James and I haven't even had our "homework date" yet. There just wasn't time last weekend. We were so busy with the kids' activities. And the thing with Meredith on Saturday morning really threw us for a loop. I wish I knew why she's been acting out lately. She's been going through a rebellious phase. Nick went through one too. Hopefully, Meredith's won't last long.

When I got to the shelter this morning, I found out that the microwave oven died over the weekend. From the look of it, someone tried to heat something in aluminum foil. I would have thought everybody knows you're not supposed to do that. I'd better post some signs.

I'm just getting back from an emergency microwave shopping trip. As I walk up the steps, the noise gets louder. A high-pitched shriek is coming from the west-end common room. I leave the microwave in the hallway and head toward the noise.

Three-year-old Cameron is standing in the middle of the room. His cheeks are tearstained. He keeps repeating something that sounds like, "A wa ba." Melanie, his nineteen-year-old mother, is slouched on the couch, staring at the television mounted high in the corner of the room. She's wearing sweat shorts and a T-shirt that look like she slept in them. She smells of stale cigarette smoke. There's no way she can hear Dr. Phil over the noise.

I wonder how long Cameron has been screaming. Several of the residents have mental health issues, which is why they have trouble holding down jobs and maintaining permanent residences. Any sort of violence is grounds for expulsion from the shelter. The residents know this, so everyone is on their best behavior, but it's better not to tempt fate. I grab Mr. Wiggle from the toy box in the corner.

"Cameron, I need your help with Mr. Wiggle. He's out of control," I say in a mock shriek of my own. I pretend to struggle with the toy and flick the "on" switch on the bottom. The toy begins to vibrate and make soft noises. I burrow it into the three-year-old's armpit.

"Oh my goodness, he's trying to get you." The child stops crying and looks at me suspiciously for a second. Then, he grins. I continue to pretend to be struggling with the out-of-control toy and Cameron starts to laugh. I stay and play with him for a few minutes. I show him how the toy works, leave it with him, and focus on talking with his mother.

"How are you doing today, Melanie?" I try to keep my tone neutral.

"Fine."

"What's going on with Cameron this morning? He seemed kind of worked up when I came in."

"He wanted to watch Bob the Builder, but I said no."

"How come he isn't at Head Start?"

"They made him leave because he had a fever." She sounds put out.

"Poor little guy. Did you give him some Tylenol?" I say.

"No. I didn't have any and you weren't here."

"What about Betsy?"

"I couldn't find her."

"Well, I'd be happy to give him some Tylenol or Motrin —which would you prefer?"

She shrugs. She has yet to look away from the television and make eye contact with me.

"By the way, why did you say no to Bob the Builder?"

"I can't stand that show. And besides, I been wanting to see this Dr. Phil."

I go to my office and get a dose of Motrin and some puzzles for Cameron. I'd like to give Melanie an earful, but it's not worth it. I can't help her if she thinks of me as the enemy. The problem with teenage parents is they're teenagers. They end up at the shelter either because they have no family to help them out, or because their families have given up on them after a long history of self-destructive behavior. The teens are afraid that their parents will try to take their children away, so they intentionally disappear and end up in shelters many miles from their estranged families. I think Melanie is from southern Vermont. Because she's a teenager with a child, there are other agencies working with her. Our goal is to keep Melanie and Cameron safe and off the streets until a long-term solution can be found.

I need to remember to check on Cameron later in the day.

I'm about to unpack the microwave when Betsy appears. "You're going to want to see this," she says.

"Give me a hint," I say.

"It looks like rodent damage to me."

Maybe if James and I start saving now, we can afford a beach vacation in a few years. Who am I kidding? We've got three kids to put through college.

CHAPTER 10

Karen Driscoll
Monday, September 10, 2012

When I wake up on Monday morning, I decide Arlo only needs one more treatment. It's supposed to rain tonight, so I leave him in the house when I go to work just before noon.

There's not much going on at the station. Most of the other officers on duty are out on routine patrol. I serve a couple of subpoenas for the state's attorneys and catch up on emails. It will be good to wrap up the case against Sarah Bennett.

Dave Belkin arrives just before our appointment time. I lead him to an interview room. He's average height, a little overweight and seriously balding, with near black hair and brown eyes. I estimate his age at thirty-five and then glance at Joe's report and see that he's only twenty-nine.

I ask him some background questions to put him at ease. I learn that he's a plumber and a volunteer firefighter in nearby Bridgeton. Then, I start what we call the "hard interview." The idea is to get the witness to give you as much detail as possible, to really nail down the specifics of what they saw. I personally find if you encourage them, most people can give you more information than they provided in their original report. That is, as long as they're the type of person that wants to help the police. Some people don't trust the police and don't want to help us. You can't do much with them, except take a statement and write up a report.

"So, you were on Sarandon Street Saturday morning?" I'm writing fast but neat. Personally, I like to take detailed notes during interviews. If I write down everything the witness says that helps my case, it only takes a few minutes to type up a statement at the end.

"Yeah, I was driving by, going west. I saw this little girl that looked like she was trying to get into this parked van."

"Okay."

"So, I went by, but I continued to look in my sideview mirror. The van changed direction. In the mirror, I saw the little girl running after the van and holding onto the door handle. She was running as fast as she could. And I was thinking, 'please don't fall, please don't fall,' because I also have some EMT training, and I know what could've happened if she fell." He's shaking his head.

I nod. "Yeah, I know. It's pretty scary the things some people do to their children."

"Do I take it you've had other incidents with this family?"

"Well, I'm not really allowed to say." I nod slightly, hoping to encourage him.

"Wow. Well, I really couldn't believe what I saw. So after the kid let go, and I saw the mom leave, I turned my van around to go back. The kid was holding her face in her hands, like maybe she'd been crying or she was going to cry. And when I got there I asked, 'who was that that drove off.' When she said her mom, that was when I decided to call the police."

"Okay, and the other day you talked to Officer Langford, right?"

"Yeah. So why am I talking to you today?"

"Well, I did the interview of the child, so I'm taking over the case."

"Right. I see. What did the kid tell you?"

"I'm not allowed to tell you what the other witnesses say. I'm sorry."

"That's okay, I understand. Well, what else do you want to know?"

"Well, I want you to think back to Saturday, and try and remember how you were feeling about what you saw. See if you can recall any more of the details. Okay?"

"Yeah, sure. I was mostly afraid for that kid, thinking about how she could've been hurt."

"Okay, good. Just try and remember and I'm going to ask you some questions. The idea is to try to recall as much detail as possible."

"Okay. Like I said, almost everything I saw was in my mirror, but I think I got a pretty good look."

"So the little girl was trying to get into the van, right?"

"Yes."

"And the van was parked facing west, right?"

"Yes."

"And the mom left and turned the van around?"

"Yep. She must have. Because I remember it being one way. Then, when I looked again it was the other."

"Okay, good. Now, which door was the little girl holding onto?"

"It would've been the driver's side slider. It was a minivan."

"Okay." I'm scribbling like crazy. "When the girl ran around, did she run in front of the van."

Belkin is sitting with his eyes closed. "Yep. I'm pretty sure."

"So, the mom would've seen her, right?"

"Absolutely. How could you not see your kid run in front of your van?"

"Now, how fast was the van moving when the door opened?"

"I'm not sure. It was probably ten miles per hour." He looks at me for confirmation. I nod and write it down. "I mean a kid can't run much faster than that," he says.

"And again, you think the mother knew she was there?"

"She had to have known. How could you not notice the door coming open?"

"Okay. Could you hear the child yelling or crying?"

"No, but I was pretty far away. I mean, I'd already gone by when all this happened."

"Okay, I understand. Now, did it look like the child was dragged at any point?"

He doesn't answer. I look up from my notes and he's studying me.

I try again. "Did it look like the child lost her footing, and maybe she was dragged a little bit?"

Now Belkin looks like he's concentrating. "You know, I think she did."

I nod. "Okay, good."

Belkin nods his head. "Yep, I'm pretty sure she did."

"Alright. Now, based on Officer Langford's report, it sounds like the girl was running and being dragged for about two hundred feet. Does that sound right to you?"

"Yeah. It was probably two hundred feet."

"Is there anything else you remember about the incident based on our conversation here today?"

"No, I don't think so. I was just so worried for the kid."

"Did you talk to her?"

"Not really, just for her to tell me it was her mom. Then I told her I was going to call the police and that she needed to stay right where she was. By the time I got off the phone with dispatch, the dad was pulling up."

I ask a couple of questions about his vehicle and then excuse myself to prepare a statement for him to sign. When I'm finished the statement, I print it and return to the interview room. Belkin is playing a game on his phone, but he quickly puts it away when I come back.

I read him what I wrote. "If this sounds right to you, I just need you to sign at the bottom of the page." He nods and quickly signs the statement.

Then, I ask him to accompany me back to the scene so we can get some more accurate measurements. We take my cruiser. Fortunately, it's only a few minutes to the ballet studio.

"Do you do a lot of kid cases?" Belkin says.

"I'm the official child interviewer for the department."

"You have kids?" he says.

"No."

"Me neither," he says. "But I like them. Hopefully some day I'll find the right woman and have a couple. So, how did you learn to interview kids?"

"I went to some trainings."

"How long you been doing this? The cop thing, that is."

"Five years."

"You look young. To have such an important job. When we're through, you want to go have coffee?"

I need to be careful here. I have no interest in this guy other than as a witness, but I need to keep him on my side. "Thanks, but I'm not allowed to fraternize with the witnesses. I could get in trouble."

"Oh. I understand," he says. "Maybe some other time." I give him a quick smile.

I stop in front of the ballet studio on Sarandon Street. We get out of the cruiser. I ask Belkin to put one traffic cone where he first saw the child grab onto the van and another where he saw her let go. He puts out two cones that are 193 feet apart. This is good. It's pretty close to the estimate that's in his written statement.

When we're done measuring, he says, "How'd I do?"

I smile at him and nod. "Great. Hey, thank you so much for all your time today. You've been a big help."

"I don't mind," he says. "I mean, whatever I can do to help that kid."

We go back to the office and Belkin leaves. I write up a quick report about the measurements he did at the scene. The case is coming together.

It's time to call Sarah Bennett. It's just after 6:00 p.m. She's probably at home. I look up her home number in the law enforcement data base. The husband answers and I ask to speak with Sarah. He asks who's calling and I tell him. I can hear muffled voices on the other end for about a minute before she picks up.

"This is Sarah Bennett."

"Ms. Bennett, this is Officer Driscoll from MFPD. I need to speak with you about the incident with your daughter on Saturday."

"Why would you need to do that? You already spoke with her and you know she wasn't hurt. Quite frankly, I can't believe you put her through that."

"Well, in matters like this we like to hear everyone's side of the story."

"What difference does it make?"

"Well, the prosecutors require us to get statements from everyone. So, I need you come down to the station."

"Prosecutors? Are you planning to charge someone? Oh my God, are you planning to charge me?"

"Ma'am, my job is just to get statements from everyone involved. That's why I need you to come in."

"I really don't know. I need to talk to my husband. He's a lawyer and I want to ask him what I should do."

"Okay. I'll be here until nine o'clock tonight. Then again from noon to nine tomorrow. I'd like to wrap this case up, but I can't do that without your statement."

She promises to call back and we hang up. I'm personally a little surprised to learn that the husband is a lawyer. He didn't act like any of the criminal defense attorneys I've dealt with. They never let anyone talk to us. He's probably not a criminal lawyer.

I'm hoping I get a chance to interrogate Sarah Bennett. I enjoy interviewing suspects much more than children. They almost always deny the accusations, but it's easy to tell they're lying. It's fun to watch them squirm. Of course, some people will tell you everything, after you convince them that confession is good for the soul. I wonder how Sarah Bennett will react to being questioned. She'll probably retain a lawyer. That's another thing guilty people do.

CHAPTER 11

James Bennett
Monday, September 10, 2012

How could I have been so stupid? It sounds like the police are trying to make a case out of this thing with Meredith.

Sarah is practically hysterical when she hangs up the phone. "She wants me to go in for an interview and give a statement. She wants to charge me with a crime. What crime could I have possibly committed? Is it illegal to drive with a van slider open? Because I did that. I just didn't think it was illegal."

"Calm down. I don't think it's illegal to drive with a slider open. I've seen other people do it. Tell me again exactly what happened."

"Okay," she says and takes a few deep breaths. "Meredith changed her mind about going to ballet and came back to the van. I locked the doors and told her to go upstairs. When I started the van, the doors unlocked," she says. "It's some weird safety feature."

I nod. "What next?"

"She opened the slider, so I told her she would lose her iPod if she got in."

"Okay."

"After a few seconds, I drove off. When I left she was standing in the parking area in front of the studio. I never thought she'd run after the van!"

"I know, I know. How many times have we told them to stay out of the road, right? What was she thinking? You couldn't have known."

"At first I thought she was just running in the road. Then I realized she had her hand on the door handle. James, I was scared out of my mind. I was so careful when I slowed the car down. Then she let go and got out of the road."

"How far did she run?"

"I don't know. Not far. The whole thing was over in under five seconds. How far can an eight-year-old run in five seconds?"

"Not far," I agree. "Plus, she was basically across from the studio when I got there. It doesn't make sense to me that the police are treating this like a criminal investigation. There's got to be something we're missing. Did anything else happen before you left?"

"Not that I know of."

"What happened when you left?"

"Nothing. I just left. I could see she was safe. She was standing across the street from the studio. I didn't know what to do."

"I can imagine."

"Part of me wanted to go back and get her, but it seemed like that would send the wrong message."

"I know what you mean," I say. "Like, okay kid, do something really stupid and dangerous and you'll get your way, right?"

"I was hoping she'd go up to the class, so I came home. Then, it just felt all wrong, so I asked you to go down there."

"I get that. It's always easier after the fact to analyze what you should've done differently. If it's any consolation, I probably would've handled it worse."

"Thanks."

"Have you heard anything more from the police since you refused to let them search the shelter?" My mind is churning. Sarah's clearly in over her head. It feels good to know that my skills may be useful in working through this.

"No. Do you think this has something to do with that?"

"I don't know, honey. I'd hate to think it does. But it's probably a good idea for us to talk to a criminal lawyer before we talk to the police any more."

Sarah's face turns white. "I need a lawyer?"

"I'm going to call Phil and see what he thinks. Don't worry. It doesn't sound like you did anything wrong. And the police can't charge people with crimes unless they have evidence. It will all work out. We just have to play hard ball with them. You'll see. They'll back down. I bet they're trying to make you squirm because of that stuff last week."

Her shoulders relax a bit and her face softens. I go over to her and put my arms around her. The irony of the situation is not lost on me. Sarah would never do anything to harm any of our children.

I call my law partner, Phil, and give him an overview of the situation with the police.

"I wouldn't talk to the police any more," Phil says.

"That was my gut reaction, but criminal law is not my thing. I've been racking my brain, trying to figure out who to call."

"I'd call Barry Densmore. From what I hear, he's a bulldog when he needs to be."

"You're right. I should've thought of Barry."

"Maybe he can head them off."

"Yeah. If anyone can get the police to back down, he can." I feel less anxious, more in control, when I hang up.

CHAPTER 12

Sarah Bennett
Tuesday, September 11, 2012

I feel like a little kid who poked a stick into a hole in the ground not knowing what was in there. I had no idea there would be consequences for tangling with the police, and I'm not sure I'm prepared to deal with them. I usually leave for work when the kids get on the bus for school. James frequently leaves earlier. This morning we hang out in the kitchen drinking coffee after the kids are gone. We're both already dressed for work.

"Did you sleep at all last night?" James says.

"A little."

"I heard you get up around one o'clock and then you were already up when I woke up at about five thirty."

"Sorry. I'm just scared."

"I don't blame you."

"What can you tell me about the lawyer?" I need to do something. I get up and start drying and putting away the breakfast dishes in the drying rack.

"I've met him a few times at bar meetings and CLE trainings. He seems pretty sharp."

"So why him?"

"He specializes in criminal defense work and he gets results."

"You mean 'not guilty' verdicts?"

"I've heard of quite a few which is unusual, but he's also pulled off some impressive plea deals."

"What do you mean by impressive?"

"Well, like a woman who embezzled half a million bucks and walked away with probation."

"Oh, that was in the *Gazette*. It bothered me at the time."

"Anyway, that's Barry."

At eight o'clock, James calls Barry Densmore. We put him on speaker phone. James does most of the talking. I just listen.

"Are you there, Mrs. Bennett?" Barry says when James has finished.

"Yes."

"I'm willing to represent you. Obviously, we don't know what the police have against you. But, whatever it is, let's not give them more. From here on, don't talk to them."

"But Officer Driscoll's expecting a call."

"I'll call her for you."

"Thank you."

"My billing rate is two hundred fifty dollars per hour, billed to the quarter hour. I won't ask for a retainer unless charges are filed. If this thing fizzles, I'll just send you a bill for my time."

"Thanks, Barry," James says and hangs up.

"I'm so glad I don't have to go talk to that woman. Do you really think they're doing this because of what happened at the shelter?" I say.

"I don't know. None of this makes any sense."

"Well, what exactly did Meredith tell them?"

"I'm not sure."

"What do you mean you're not sure? You were there, weren't you?"

"Not exactly. I left the room and then I got a call and lost track of time."

"You mean you left your daughter alone to be interrogated by the police? No wonder she was so upset when she got home. I just assumed you were there with her. Oh, James. Why didn't you tell me that? It was bad enough that they interviewed her."

"That's right. I screwed up again."

"Well, think about it. She disobeyed me and did something she knew was dangerous. Then, she got interrogated by a police officer. Oh my God! No wonder she's been so upset the past few days. She probably thought she was being investigated for her behavior. How could you let them do that to her?"

"You weren't there. At the time it seemed so innocent. You know, just filling in paperwork. How was I supposed to know they would come after you?"

"I'm not even talking about me. I'm talking about Meredith."

"Well, if you'd cared so much about Meredith, you shouldn't have left her at the ballet studio. You know what? Fuck you! I'm going to work. At least the people there respect me." He slams the door on the way out.

I shouldn't have been so hard on him. We're both out of our element here. The police are investigating me and I don't know why. I went over and over it in my mind last night, but I can't figure out how they could blame me for what happened with Meredith.

The only thing I know is that I need to talk to Meredith tonight. Now that I know more of the story, I have to find out what happened to her at the police station. I need to make sure she's okay.

CHAPTER 13

James Bennett
Tuesday, September 11, 2012

I'm in my office after lunch when Sarah calls me. She's hysterical and I have a hard time making out her words at first. I'm able to figure out that the police came to the shelter and arrested her. Goddammit! I promise her I'll call Barry. I have to look up the number because Barry isn't in my contacts. My hands are shaking so much that I drop the phone book before I find the number. While the line is ringing, I realize that Barry probably has a website.

"I need to talk to Barry right now. It's James Bennett."

"I'm sorry, Mr. Bennett, but he's in court," his secretary says.

"This is an emergency. My wife's been arrested."

"Well, in that case, I'll send him an Instant Message. I'm sure he'll get in touch with you as soon as he's done."

"I'm not sure you understand. My wife is at the police station. They arrested her at her work."

"Mr. Bennett, I know this is upsetting, but nothing will happen without Mr. Densmore. It's during normal court hours, so they probably won't let her go without an arraignment. Mr. Densmore is in a hearing with Judge Jenkins right now. I don't expect it will be long. I promise he'll get in touch with you as soon as he's free."

I thank her and hang up. Then I slam both palms hard against my desk. It hurts and feels good at the same time. I wish I could talk to Phil, but he's out of the office in depositions.

I need to talk to Sarah. I tell our secretary to cancel my afternoon meeting and I go to the police station. There's a female officer behind the window in the lobby. She smiles at me.

"How can I help you, sir?" she says.

"My wife called to tell me she was arrested. I need to see her."

The corners of her smile droop. "Your name, sir?"

"James Bennett."

"Just a minute."

She's on the phone for a few minutes. While I'm waiting, two uniformed officers come through the lobby. The desk officer glances at them and hits a buzzer so they can enter.

"I'm sorry. Only attorneys are allowed in the holding cells."

"I'm an attorney."

"Are you representing your wife in this matter?"

"No."

"Then you can't go back there."

"When can I see her?"

The phone on her desk is ringing. "Just a second," she says and picks it up. A few minutes later, she hangs up and looks back at me. "Okay, what did you want to know?"

"When can I see my wife?"

"Let me see if I can find out." She makes another call. "As far as we know, she's going to be arraigned at three o'clock. You could go to the courthouse."

"Do you know what the charges are?"

"I'm sorry, I don't."

"Could you find out?" Just then her phone rings again and she picks it up. "Forget it," I say, refraining from launching into a rant that might get me arrested too.

It's two thirty, so I decide to go up the street to the courthouse to wait.

The county courthouse is a stately brick building with the requisite white columns, located near the center of town. I have to go through a metal detector to go into the building. The probate court is in this same building, so I've done it many times before, and yet it bothers me today. The uniformed sheriff's deputy at the entrance tells me that all criminal matters are in Courtroom 1.

I'm sitting outside the courtroom when Barry comes out, looking impeccable in a tailored dark gray suit. He's clean shaven and his shoulder-length white hair is neatly pulled back in a pony tail. I'm not normally a fan of long hair on men, but it works on Barry. He is carrying a leather briefcase and is followed by a scruffy-looking guy in his mid-twenties. The guy is so thin that his chest looks concave. His keeps pushing his stringy black hair out of his eyes by swinging his head. They have a whispered conversation and then shake hands. As the guy walks by me, I get a whiff of him. He reeks of tobacco smoke and body oil with a slight undertone of patchouli. Barry gestures me into a nearby meeting room.

"I got a text from Marcy. Do you know what time the arraignment is?" he says.

"They told me three o'clock."

"Okay, you wait here. I'll go to the clerk's office and see if the paperwork is ready yet." Barry leaves his briefcase on the table and leaves the door open when he goes out. I want to follow him to the clerk's office, but I don't feel like I should leave his briefcase. I can hear him greeting people in the hallway before he disappears into the clerk's office.

After a few minutes, I consider packing up his briefcase and taking it to see what's going on. Instead, I go out into the hallway and pace in front of the meeting room.

Barry is back ten minutes later with a stack of papers.

"They have her downstairs in a holding cell. I need to meet with her to go over the paperwork. As soon as I'm done, they'll bring her upstairs for arraignment. After that, the three of us can meet to talk about the next steps."

"Can you at least tell me what the charges are?"

"Looks like attempted aggravated domestic assault, reckless endangerment and gross negligent operation of a motor vehicle. So, one felony and two serious misdemeanors."

"Are you serious? Meredith runs after the van and my wife gets charged with a felony? How can this happen?"

"Look. I only had a chance to skim this stuff. I need to go over it with Sarah. After the arraignment, we'll go over it more thoroughly."

"What's going to happen at arraignment?"

"They may or may not ask for bail. She'll be released with some conditions. Then, we'll figure out what's next."

"Okay," I say. It's really not okay.

Barry leaves, taking his briefcase and the stack of paperwork. I notice it's almost three o'clock, so I head into the courtroom. Bob Kessler is at a counsel table packing up his briefcase.

"Hey, James. You dabbling in criminal defense these days?" he says.

"Not exactly. I'm just here to assist."

"I thought I had the last hearing of the day."

"It's an add-on."

"Oh. How's your practice going?" Bob says.

"Fine, I guess."

"You see the inside of a courtroom much these days?"

"Just the occasional civil hearing. Phil does more of it than I do. And the civil cases always settle. Our firm hasn't done a trial in a few years."

"That stuff isn't juicy enough for me," Bob says. "Besides, I like being in court."

"What do you think of the judge?"

"Jenkins? He's only been here a couple of weeks, so it's hard to say. Ask me again when I get his decision on the motion I just argued."

"How long's he going to be here?"

"Rumor is a year. Judge Carney was here for two, but mostly they only stay a year. Good luck with your hearing."

When he leaves, I'm alone in this large, eerily silent official space. I've never been in here before when there wasn't something going on. I take a seat on one of the cushioned benches in the gallery and study the room. It looks just like the courtrooms in the movies: an ornate high ceiling, a row of tall windows along the west wall, a set of chairs for jurors, and an elevated bench and witness stand at the front of the room.

I'm starting to wonder if I'm in the wrong place when, at 3:15, everything changes. First, a young woman in a suit comes in the main door. She looks to be about twenty years old, with long brunette hair held back by a barrette. She's carrying a manilla folder and a legal pad. She passes through the gateway into the front of the room and takes a seat at the left-hand counsel table, and I realize that this near child is a prosecutor. Then, an old clerk and a younger dark-haired, heavyset woman in a sheriff's uniform come bustling into the courtroom. Almost simultaneously, a side door opens and Sarah is ushered into the room by two large male sheriff's deputies. They remove her handcuffs and direct her toward the counsel table where I've sat before. At this moment I'm grateful the courtroom is empty of spectators.

"Are you okay?" I say. The deputies are standing nearby, but don't seem concerned when I approach.

Sarah nods her head. I can tell she's fighting back tears. I don't even know what to say at this point. Just then Barry comes into the room through the main door and makes his way to the counsel table.

As soon as he has opened his briefcase, the heavyset female deputy bellows, "All rise. The Honorable Patrick Jenkins presiding."

The judge enters. He hasn't yet reached his chair when he says, "Please be seated." I sit directly behind Sarah in the first row.

"This is the case of State versus Sarah Bennett, docket number 12-9-837," the deputy says.

Barry stands. "Good afternoon again, Your Honor. I'm representing Ms. Bennett."

"Ah, Mr. Densmore, again." The judge smiles.

"I'd like to start by issuing a challenge to probable cause," Barry says.

"I did just review the charging documents and I have found probable cause. What is the basis for your challenge, Mr. Densmore?"

"Well, Your Honor, first with regard to the felony attempted assault. The charge requires a showing of intent to cause serious bodily injury. There was in fact no injury at all to the child. Nor is there any evidence that my client had any intent to harm the child, much less cause serious bodily injury."

"Does the state have any response?" the judge says.

The child prosecutor stands. "Yes, Your Honor. There is circumstantial evidence of intent. There is evidence that the child ran in front of the van while the defendant turned it around, and that the child opened the door while the van was moving approximately ten miles per hour. The child was dragged for a significant distance, as much as two hundred feet. And, during all this, the defendant did not stop her vehicle. Instead, she told the child to let go. So I'd say there's evidence of intent because there's evidence that the defendant knew of the possibility that her child could have been seriously injured, but she continued to operate her motor vehicle."

"Anything else, Mr. Densmore?" the judge says.

"Actually, yes, Your Honor. With regard to all the charges, there's simply no evidence that my client had knowledge of what her child was doing. All the charges require knowledge and there's no evidence of it."

"Ms. Goodwin?"

"Well, Your Honor, again, the evidence is circumstantial. Given everything that happened, she had to have known. Plus, if she didn't know, why did the defendant tell her daughter to let go?"

The room is quiet for a few seconds before the judge speaks. "As I have said, I carefully reviewed the charging documents. I'm going to stand by my finding of probable cause. As you both know, the threshold for a finding of probable cause is low. I think Mr. Densmore's arguments would be better made during a Rule 12(d) motion to dismiss."

"Thank you, Your Honor," both attorneys say simultaneously. Jinx. It has always struck me as funny how the attorney that loses always thanks the judge. God. I really can't take this in. How could they be saying that about Sarah? It doesn't make any sense based on what both Sarah and Meredith told me.

"Let's proceed with arraignment," the judge says.

"Yes, Your Honor," Barry says. "Waive the reading and Rule 5 rights, waive the twenty-four-hour rule, enter a plea of not guilty to all charges."

"What is the state requesting for conditions?" the judge says.

"Actually, Your Honor. In light of the seriousness of the felony charge, the state is requesting ten thousand dollars bail."

"Your Honor!" Barry bounces out of his seat. "My client is a fifteen-year resident of Middleton Falls with three children in school. Her husband is here in the courtroom. She has no criminal record whatsoever. She's a respected member of her community with a full-time position as the director of the Murdoch Shelter. She is no flight risk at all."

"Okay, I agree with Mr. Densmore. Bail request denied. What conditions are you requesting, Ms. Goodwin?"

"Conditions one, two and three, plus special conditions of no driving and no contact with the minor child, MB."

Again Barry is on his feet in half a second. "The child is eight years old! She lives with her mother. Where's she supposed to go? A no-contact condition is overkill."

"Ms. Goodwin, under the circumstances is the no-contact condition really necessary?" the judge says. "We could just issue a no-abuse or harassment condition."

"Your Honor, the state feels that a no-contact condition is necessary to protect the child as well as the integrity of the evidence. The defendant engaged in extremely risky behavior. In addition, the child is an important witness. If the defendant is allowed contact with her, the child's testimony may become tainted. And while we have a witness to what happened with the vehicle, only the child can testify about what her mother said and did. That evidence is critical to our case."

The judge nods. "Can the father take care of the child while this matter is pending?" He is looking at me.

Barry is shaking his head. "But then where's my client supposed to go? There are three school-aged children in the house. They need their mother to take care of them."

"Surely Ms. Bennett can find somewhere else to stay until this matter is resolved. I'm sure Mr. Bennett can manage the children by himself." The judge is looking right at me. I feel like a total idiot. No, I can't manage the children by myself. Every time Sarah is sick the house is in a state of utter chaos. Barry turns to look at me too. What am I supposed to say? No, I suck as a parent. I need my wife to take care of them. I shrug and nod weakly. "Of course, there would be nothing preventing Ms. Bennett from spending time with the other children," the judge says.

Barry is looking down at the desk, fiddling with his pen. "For the record, we think that a no-contact condition is not in the best interests of the child," he says.

"I'm ordering no contact," the judge says.

Barry looks up. "And a no driving condition is unwarranted. My client has a perfect driving record. There was no alcohol involved. There's no evidence that my client was speeding or disobeying any traffic law. We all know how necessary a car is to function in this state."

"I agree the driving condition is unnecessary. But I've already ordered no contact with the minor MB. Just so it's clear, Ms. Bennett, you are not to have any contact with MB by any means, including by phone or computer or through a third party." The judge glares at me before he continues. "I want initial discovery complete and everyone back here in four weeks. Anything else before we adjourn?"

"No, Your Honor," says the prosecutor. She sounds like a baby bird chirping. Barry just shakes his head.

The judge stands. "All rise!" the deputy bellows.

As we stand, I watch Sarah. I can see her chest and shoulders move with each breath. Her eyes are wide and her nostrils flared. As she turns toward me, her eyes open even wider. I look back to see what got her attention and notice Manny Rodriguez from the *Adams Gazette* closing his notepad. We both know him from an article he did when Sarah took over as the director of the Murdoch Shelter. I wonder when he came in and how he knew to be here.

Sarah is rubbing her wrists. Manny leaves and Barry ushers us into another one of the mini conference rooms in the hallway.

"Okay, so first off," Barry says. "Now that we know what we're dealing with, I'll need a ten thousand dollar retainer to start. If it looks like this is going to drag out or if it's going to trial, I'll ask for more." Barry looks at Sarah and then me, as if he is trying to read us.

I don't blame Barry for getting right to the money issue. I would have done the same thing. "I'll get a check to your secretary in the morning," I say. At least I can help with this. I'll have to transfer some money from savings to cover it, but I can swing that amount right now. We have some money left over from a life insurance payout I got when my mom died last year. It was supposed to be for a family vacation, but this is definitely more important.

Sarah is just staring into the middle distance.

"Okay, now we need to talk about our strategy," Barry continues.

Sarah comes back from wherever she was. "I need to talk to Meredith," she says.

"Well, you can't do that right now. Any contact with her and you could be arrested again."

"But she's my daughter. And she's only eight. I don't understand how she could have said I did those things. What did they do to her to make her say that? I have to talk to her."

Barry furrows his brow and faces Sarah. "Forgive me for this, but I have to be clear with you. There's a court order prohibiting you from contacting Meredith. If you violate that order, you could go to jail. I'll do my best to resolve this in a manner that works for you. But, if you violate that court order, you will only make my job harder. Do you understand?"

I have never seen Sarah look so defeated. "But none of that happened. All I did was drive away. I didn't even know she was there."

"Well, there is a witness who gave statements supporting the state's version of events."

"So you don't believe me."

"It doesn't matter if I believe you. My job is to represent you whether I believe you or not. If it helps, I'm sure that the witness statements exaggerate things. They always do. Most of the time, the affidavit of probable cause is the worst possible version of what happened. That's how the police write them. That's why I'm going to talk to any witnesses and try to poke some holes in the state's case. Then, I'll see if I can negotiate this down to something you can live with."

"How long is this going to take?"

"Well, as your husband will tell you, nothing happens quickly in our court system. We'll have a better idea when we come back in four weeks."

"You mean I'm not going to see my daughter for four weeks?"

"Not unless we make a plea deal."

"What would I have to do to see Meredith?"

"Well, the state's arraignment offer was one to three years suspended except thirty days. I never advise my clients to take an arraignment offer because I can almost always do better."

"But, what does that mean?"

"It means that, if you pled guilty to all the charges today, they would agree to a sentence of thirty days to serve with a substantial term of probation including counseling."

"They want me to serve time in jail?" Sarah's voice is reaching a strange, high pitch, almost like a child's.

"Look, that's why we didn't even discuss pleading at arraignment. I'm sure I can do better. Besides, we don't even know enough about their case to make a decision on this. There's a felony charge. That means I can depose the police officers and other witnesses. If we poke enough holes in their case, they'll probably back down some."

"But I didn't do anything. Can't you make this go away?" Tears are welling in her eyes now. I reach out to take her hand, but she snaps her arm back reflexively.

"It's possible. Like the judge said, I can file a motion to dismiss. But first I'll want to take some depositions. And I should probably talk to Meredith."

"No," Sarah says. "I don't want Meredith involved in this."

"Sarah, Meredith's already involved," I say. "There's nothing you can do. Besides, I have to tell her why she can't see you. You're going to have to stay some place else. It's not like we can keep it from her."

Sarah breaks down and sobs. "But she's going to think this is all her fault. She knows she disobeyed. She knows what she did was bad. Oh my God, poor Meredith." She looks at me appealingly, as though we're still parents, working together on a problem that has a solution. "We need to get her counseling."

"That's not a good idea right now," Barry says. "We don't know why she said what she said to the police. We don't know what else they may have suggested to her. Counselors are mandatory reporters of child abuse, so if she were to make further disclosures to a counselor, the state might be able to use that as evidence against you. Plus, there have been cases where well-intentioned counselors convinced children they'd been abused, even though they weren't. It's just too risky."

"Can I talk to Meredith about what happened?" I say. "I can probably get this straightened out if I talk to her."

"I would be careful. There are two problems. First, it might seem as if you're communicating for Sarah, which is a violation of her conditions. If the court interprets what you say that way, she could end up in jail. Second, if you try to get Meredith to change her story, you could end up facing an obstruction of justice charge. That one's a five-year felony. And you could lose your law license. Obviously, given what's going on, it's going to be hard to not talk about what happened. But I would avoid anything that looks improper. I'll talk to Meredith after we get the discovery. Which reminds me, James, you need to call the school first thing in the morning."

"Meredith's school?"

"Yes. Tell them that if the Department of Children and Families wants to interview Meredith, they cannot, under any circumstances, do that without you present. It may get the school to think twice."

"But why would DCF be involved?" Sarah asks.

"This is essentially an allegation of child abuse. DCF is overloaded, so they may not look any further than the police report. But sometimes they try to get around parents by talking to kids at school. If they try to talk to Meredith, we need to know about it." Barry turns toward me. "Obviously, Sarah is being investigated, so she can't make the call. If the school calls you, call me."

"Okay," I say. I'm glad he trusts me to handle this.

"Also, remember that right now the smartest thing your family can do is not talk to anyone about this. If anyone contacts you, refer them to me. Just in case this thing goes to trial, the only version of events we want the jury to hear is the one we present. And, whatever you do, no more conversations with the police, either of you."

"What do you mean? I didn't have any conversations with them," Sarah says.

"Well, looking at the affidavit of probable cause, we already have a few problems. The police report quotes James as saying that when you came home you were upset. You told him you knew Meredith had been in the road and asked him to check on her."

"But there was more to it and I told the police I wasn't sure exactly what Sarah said," I say.

"They left some things out," Barry says.

"And I never signed anything."

Barry shrugs. "It's still out there."

"And there's marital privilege. They can't make me testify against my wife," I say.

"We may need your testimony. Anyway, there's also Sarah's statement to the arresting officer." Barry glances at the paper in front of him. "Officer Driscoll."

"I didn't say anything to her," Sarah says.

"Well, according to her affidavit, when you answered the door at the shelter, before she arrested you, you said, 'Please, go easy on me.' The obvious implication is that you knew that you committed a crime, and that you were requesting leniency."

Sarah gasps. "I never said that."

"Did you say anything?"

"Let me think." Sarah is rubbing her wrists again. "Yeah. After she had gotten out her handcuffs, I said, 'I know you don't like me, but I would appreciate if you would not treat me like a criminal.' I was referring to the handcuffs."

"And you're sure you never said, 'Go easy on me'?"

"Absolutely."

"Okay. Well, the problem is that juries like to believe cops. We can present our version, but again, the other one is out there. I'll see if it was recorded, but if it wasn't, it's your word against hers. Now, both of you, no more statements to anyone. Police, press, friends, I don't care who."

How could I have been so naive? I decide to bring up the question of retaliation. I tell Barry about the recent issues at the shelter and Sarah's decision not to let them search.

"It feels like they're just trying to get even with me," Sarah says.

"Well, we can talk more about that later, but it's probably not going to do us any good with the prosecutors. In my experience, once they take a case, they hate to let it go. And prosecutors bend over backwards to support the police even when they do really questionable things. If we bring that up, we may just make them angry, and make them dig their heels in. Now, it'll be a different matter if we go to trial. Let me see what I can do with the witness statements first. I'll get back to you as soon as I get copies of all the documents."

Barry stands and I follow suit. When Barry is gone, Sarah slowly rises and leans toward me. I hold her for a few minutes. She feels limp in my arms.

It's four thirty and soccer practice should be ending. I completely forgot about it. I'm sure the assistant coach took over for me, but he's probably ticked I didn't call him.

I drop Sarah back at the shelter. She's planning to stay with Betsy for now.

On my way to pick up the girls from the after-school art program they're doing this fall, I think about how my marriage hasn't been perfect for a while. Everything changed after we had kids, but at least it was normal. Now I'm facing the reality of my wife's banishment and the impact it will have on me and my children. In all honesty, the family would be better off if I were the one expelled.

What am I going to tell the kids?

CHAPTER 14

Sarah Bennett
Tuesday, September 11, 2012

After James drives away, I stand in the driveway at the shelter. I'm relieved to see Betsy's car is still here. I know I need to go inside and find her, but it feels like a big step: walking through the door, facing the new reality. The last time I passed through the door I was wearing handcuffs.

I wasn't expecting the police this morning. Was it only this morning? I had gone through the scene with Meredith so many times in my mind and I was sure it wasn't my fault. I knew they would have to reach the same conclusion. But, they didn't. And now everything is different.

So, I just stand here. I don't know for how long. Eventually, Betsy comes out.

"James called to say he'd be back around six o'clock with your bag," she says. I nod.

"I didn't realize you were here," she says. I nod again.

"Let's go inside," she says. When I don't move, she takes my arm and gently tugs me toward the door.

"I felt like a caged animal," I say.

"I'm sorry," she says, still pulling me carefully.

It feels like the dam is breaking and the words are forcing their way out. "They kept me in handcuffs until I was locked in this room. They fingerprinted me. Look, I still have ink on my fingers."

"Let's get that washed off and you can tell me about the rest of it." She leads me to the closest bathroom and starts scrubbing my fingers.

"They took a mug shot. Then they put me in a cell at the police station."

"Really? A cell? This whole thing is over the top."

"I was there for a while. I don't know how long because they took my watch."

"You're kidding."

"Then, they put me back in handcuffs and put me in a police car. They took the cuffs off while I was in a cell at the courthouse. But they put them back on when they brought me up to the courtroom."

"Why?"

"I don't know. Barry said it was the normal procedure. All I know is that it was the most humiliating experience of my life. I thought I was going to be sick."

"The cops really don't like to take no for an answer, do they?"

"The judge said I can't see Meredith until this is resolved. I can't go home."

"I know. You'll stay with me."

"I was hoping you'd say that." I feel a rush of gratitude because the truth is that I don't have a backup plan.

Betsy settles me into her guest room then stays up with me until nearly midnight. I don't want to be alone, but I know she needs to sleep, so I tell her I'm fine. I'm not. I need to talk to somebody. It occurs to me that it's three hours earlier in California. I call my sister, Amelia. She's six years younger and perpetually single so we have little in common. But she's family. And she's probably awake.

"Saaaraaah!" she answers and giggles. "Long time no talk."

"I know, I'm sorry."

"That's okaaay," she says. There are voices in the background. Lots of them.

"Amelia, where are you?"

"At a bar."

"Oh. This is probably a bad time."

"Hold on a sec." I can hear muffled laughter for about thirty seconds before Amelia comes back on the line. "Okay, what's up?"

"I just wanted to talk."

"So, talk."

"You know what? I think it's a bad time."

"Well, maybe. Why don't you call me tomorrow?"

"Okay."

"Just don't make it too early. I met a guy."

I hang up feeling even emptier than before, if that's even possible. I don't know what I was thinking, calling Amelia. She probably won't even remember talking to me. Now that I think about it, that's a good thing. If she were to tell my parents about my arrest, they'd worry. And I don't want that. They've got enough on their plates right now. My dad's Parkinson's disease has gotten so much worse that they should probably be in assisted living. And they definitely should have stayed in Illinois. The move to Florida was so they could walk outside year round, but my dad hardly walks anymore. He needed a wheelchair to make his connecting flight the last time they came to visit. He was so mortified that I doubt he'll visit again. I'm not going to tell them about my arrest until after Barry takes care of this mess. That way, they won't worry about it.

I can't sleep. I keep reliving the nightmare of the worst day of my life. And I cry.

When the morning light starts to creep into the room, I hear Betsy moving around. I know I should get up, but I can't. Betsy taps on the door. "Are you coming to work today?"

I don't want to leave this room, but I can't afford to lose my job, so I say, "Yeah, I'll see you there."

I stay in the shower until there's no more hot water because the pounding water gives me something to focus on other than my pain.

When I get to the shelter, everything is the same. It feels like it should be different, but it's not. My head is splitting and I feel dizzy, probably because I haven't eaten anything since breakfast yesterday. I can't. I pour myself a cup of coffee out of habit and close my office door. Every time I sip the coffee, my stomach churns. I try to do some paperwork, but I can't focus on the page. After a while, I give up on the coffee and the papers. The phone on my desk rings, but it goes to voicemail before I'm ready to answer. I feel like I'm watching myself, unable to will myself into action.

Betsy comes in to check on me. "You don't have to be here, you know," she says.

"Yes, I do."

"I can cover for you. You're not actually doing anything anyway."

"I know. But I have to keep trying."

She brings me a styrofoam cup of chicken soup for lunch. The broth tastes acrid, but I manage to eat the two cellophane-wrapped saltines that came with the soup.

At Betsy's again for the second night, I cry until I'm so exhausted that I finally sleep. But only for a few hours. At two o'clock in the morning, the memory of being led around in handcuffs is suddenly in my head and

I am wide awake. I wonder how James has explained my absence to the kids and how they are dealing with it. I hope Meredith's not blaming herself. And poor little Camille. This is the longest we've ever been away from each other. I watch the clock roll by three o'clock and four o'clock. I finally get up at four thirty and take another long shower.

I am standing at my office window staring into the parking lot when Betsy comes in with the local paper.

"Is it in there?" I say.

"I think you'd better sit down."

"Why? What does it say?"

"It's not the what, so much as the where. Although the what is pretty bad."

"It's on page one?"

"With a continuation on page three."

"This is terrible."

"You should have talked to Manny Rodriguez when he called."

"I wanted to, but Barry told me not to."

"Then Barry should have talked to him. Or James. It looks worse because your side of the story isn't in here."

"Barry said that he tries to avoid talking to the press because they always change what he says to make it more dramatic."

"Well, Manny got nice quotes from the state's attorney and our dear friend, Janice Higgins."

"Of course, he has to find the one board member who I always butt heads with."

"According to the article, she's concerned about your fitness to run the shelter."

"What an imbecile."

"No argument there."

"Does she really think I'm a child abuser?"

"Who cares? She's a stupid old biddy who probably used to beat her own kids with a paddle."

"But she's a stupid old biddy who might be able to get me fired."

"Anybody who knows you is not going to believe this shit."

"I hope you're right. Wow. This is unbelievable."

"I can take care of things here if you want to cut out a little early."

"What I really want most is to go home and curl up in my bed."

"So do it."

"I can't risk being there when the kids get home."

"Then curl up at my house."

"It's not the same."

"I know." The concern in Betsy's eyes is palpable.

"And I don't want to give Janice any more reasons to get rid of me. What are the residents saying about this?"

"The ones who've said anything think you got arrested because you stuck up for Bryce."

"Who told them that?"

"Nobody. It's just the logical conclusion. They see you sending the police away. A week later, you get arrested. What else are they going to think?"

"It makes sense."

"Plus, Bryce is telling everyone how you believed him and didn't let the police bully you. I think you moved up a notch with the residents."

"But now there's this article."

"Don't worry. Most of them don't read the paper, even if they know how to read. Besides, they've got their own problems to deal with."

As soon as I get to Betsy's that night, I curl up. And cry again. James calls my cell. I can hear the kids in the background and it makes me miss them even more.

"I take it you saw the article?" I say.

"Yeah. The paper was in today's mail. Hard to miss the story, huh? Anyway, how're you holding up?"

"I'm not. How about you?"

"I've been better. And that article is definitely not going to be good for business."

"I couldn't read the whole article. It made me too sick. Did they mention you?"

"Yep. And my firm."

"Why would they do that?"

"It's a small town," James says. "The more gossip they put in the paper, the more papers they sell. What's worse is they mentioned Meredith's name."

I feel like my heart stops beating for a few seconds. "Oh my God! They're not supposed to do that. She's a minor!"

"I know. But they did it. Which means it's on the internet."

"And there's no way to get it back. How did they get her name? It's supposed to be confidential," I say

"It was in the police report, remember?" James says.

"This is definitely a vendetta."

"Yeah, it sure feels like it. I think you should go see Jasmine by yourself tomorrow. You've had the week from hell and you could probably use someone to talk to. Jasmine is safe for you. She's bound by confidentiality."

"But I don't want this to be the end of our marriage counseling. It's too important."

"I'm not suggesting we give up on our counseling forever. I just think you're going to need someone safe to talk to."

"You're probably right."

"Why don't you stop by my office after the session?"

"Okay. That would be good. I miss you."

"Try to get some rest tonight. This is not your fault. We will get through this."

"Bye," I say.

"Bye."

"I love you," I say, but James has already hung up.

I hear a noise, like a cat yowling before a fight, and I realize that I am moaning. I pull a pillow over my head and bring my knees to my chest. I can't stop the moaning, but it eventually uses itself up.

I'm not aware of sleeping for more than a few minutes at a time. When it's time to get up, I make sure that Betsy is first in the shower—I don't trust myself to leave her hot water.

Most people get their papers in the mail on Thursday afternoon, so I expect I'll get calls from everyone I know on Thursday night and Friday. I keep checking my cell phone to make sure it's charged and has a signal. The only thing wrong with my phone is it isn't ringing.

Janice Higgins from the board calls me Friday afternoon at the shelter.

"I just want you to be aware that we'll be discussing the future of your employment at the next board meeting."

"Are you calling because you want me to add it to the agenda?"

"No, I've already taken care of that. I just wanted you to be aware."

"In case I didn't read what you said in the paper? Did it occur to you that I might be innocent?"

"Well, now, Sarah, there seems to be a lot of evidence against you. And you have to admit, it's not the type of publicity the shelter needs." Mealymouthed as usual.

"Don't believe everything you read, Janice."

"I'm sure we'll talk about it at the meeting. Bye."

After my session with Jasmine, I stop by James' office.

"How're the kids doing?" I say.

"They're fine. They're taking it in stride. Their days are mostly the same as before. School, art class, and soccer. The biggest difference is you're not home at night or for breakfast."

"I miss them. And it's only been three days. How are we going to get through this?"

"I was thinking about that. There's nothing prohibiting you from going to the house as long as Meredith isn't there, right?"

"That's my understanding," I say.

"Do you think you could do the grocery shopping during the day and drop off groceries?"

"I suppose I could do it during my lunch break."

"That would be a big help. We're getting low on things and I'm just not used to shopping. I have my hands full doing all the shuttling and making dinner. I haven't quite gotten into the swing of that."

"Okay. I'll try to make sure you have what you need to feed the kids until this is over."

"Great. Do you think you could also do laundry?" James says.

James is capable of running the washer and dryer, but I want to take care of my children. So, I say, "Sure. I'll stop by the house as much as I can to make sure that things aren't getting out of control. The big question is how am I going to spend time with Nick and Camille?"

"I don't know. It's awkward. Meredith and I could go to the movies."

"Then, Nick and Camille will want to go with you. It'll be like spending time with me is punishment."

"The best thing would be if you have one-on-one time with them somewhere other than home."

"I'll have to figure something out. I hate to keep imposing on Betsy."

"And what are we going to do about ballet? I can't make sure the girls get there if there's a conflict with soccer. We have a lot of Saturday morning games coming up."

"I know. And I can't drive Meredith because of the court order. They could walk from the soccer field."

"Yeah, that's true. It's not all that far, and I can make sure they leave on time. But what if Meredith doesn't want to go anymore?"

"Under the circumstances, we can't force the issue."

"That's for sure. I'll talk to Meredith. If she decides to quit and Camille wants to continue, you can take Camille every week."

"Okay. By the way, have you gotten calls from any of our friends? You know, about the article."

"No. A few of my colleagues commented on how ridiculous it was that you'd been charged."

"Of course it's ridiculous. So why aren't people calling?"

"Most people believe what they read."

"Even if it's ridiculous?"

"Yeah, pretty much. The internet is proof of that."

"I wish we could've told Manny Rodriguez the truth about what happened. Let people know that this whole thing is just a police vendetta," I say.

"I do too," James says. "I look bad right now. I mean we all do. But I trust that Barry knows what he's doing. He doesn't give press conferences like the showy defense attorneys in Burlington, but he gets results. And, what we need most is results."

"In the meantime, it's hard to face people."

"How'd it go with Jasmine?"

"It helped to have someone to tell the whole story to. She's a good listener. But what I need is for someone to make sense of this, and that's impossible."

"It's good you went alone."

"Jasmine said you should come back next week because all the issues in our marriage will be amplified by the stress."

"Okay, if that's what's best."

The only call to my cell that night is from James. He says that his partner, Phil, called to tell him that Channel 14 had picked up the story of my arrest.

It's too much.

I ask Betsy to watch the eleven o'clock news. I stay in her guest bed in a fetal position, crying. At 11:25, she knocks softly.

"Was it on again?" I say.

"Yes."

"What do I need to know?"

"It sounds like they took the entire story from Manny's article, but because it was TV, they made it shorter. And picked the worst parts. They made it sound like a bunch of people saw you dragging Meredith behind your van and that you knew she was there."

"Did they mention Meredith's name?"

"No."

"That's good."

"It was a short segment. They showed your mug shot. The news guy said a few sentences. They didn't interview anyone. That's it."

"I guess it could've been worse."

"I'm surprised they didn't call to get your side of the story."

"I'm surprised they thought it was newsworthy enough to broadcast statewide."

"You could take it as a compliment. You're prominent enough that your misfortune is big news." Betsy attempts a smile.

"Funny how I didn't know I was prominent until I was misfortunate."

"It only makes a good story because nobody would ever expect someone like you to do something like that."

"And yet it doesn't occur to anybody that I didn't do it?"

"Then it wouldn't be news. People around here have to realize this whole thing is ridiculous."

"Then why aren't they calling?"

"Maybe they haven't read their papers yet. They'll call. You'll see."

CHAPTER 15

Nicholas Bennett
Saturday, October 6, 2012

I t sucks to be me right now. My family is so screwed up. My mom isn't even allowed to live with us. It's all my stupid sister's fault. What was Meredith thinking, running after the van? I understand not wanting to go to ballet. Ballet looks stupid to me. But Meredith knows she's not supposed to be in the road. And now, all because of Meredith, my mom can't live here. And it sucks around here.

My mom has picked me up after dinner a few times so we can talk. Mostly, we go down to the river and walk. I wish we could do it every night because I miss my mom. But I'm in middle school and I have homework. Seventh grade is much harder than sixth grade was. I also have soccer practice after school every day.

I try to spend time with my mom on weekends, but it's hard because she can't come home if Meredith is here. Last weekend my mom and I drove up to the mountains and went for a hike. She wanted to see the foliage, but most of the leaves were already off the trees up there. She seemed disappointed. I didn't care. It was just nice to have a few hours with my mom. Our dog, Samson, didn't care either. He's always glad to get out of the yard.

My mom keeps telling me not to worry, that the police made a mistake, and it will all get sorted out soon. But I don't buy it. She looks terrible. She's just not the same as she used to be. She doesn't smile anymore.

Not that I blame her for worrying. I read the article in the paper. I didn't tell anyone. I heard my dad talking about it on the phone and then he left the paper on his desk when he went out for milk. I was curious, so I took that section and put it back later.

The paper had this picture of my mom taken at the police station. The article said my mom could go to jail for fifteen years. It said there were witnesses who saw her drag my sister behind the van. One of the guys was quoted saying that my mom had to have known that my sister was there. That's stupid. My mom wouldn't do that. She's crazy about safety. She won't even start the van until everyone has their seat belts on. The paper said that Meredith agreed with the witness.

I asked Meredith if she was dragged. She said she didn't know. How can you not be sure if you were dragged behind a van? So I said, "Do you even know what the word 'drag' means?"

"Not really."

"Were you running the whole time?"

"Yeah."

"Could you let go?"

"Sure."

"Then you weren't dragged."

"Oh."

Adults are so stupid. If she was dragged, she would've been hurt. I mean, think about it. I saw her when she came home from the police station. She was fine, not a mark on her. She seemed upset about what happened with the police, but she definitely wasn't hurt.

Then, my mom got arrested and, from what my dad said, she has to stay away from Meredith until the court thing gets wrapped up.

It just sucks having my mom not here. I especially miss her cooking. My mom still does the shopping, so at least there's food in the house. Not that my dad cooks it. The first three nights in a row we had Annie's Mac and Cheese. When I complained, he made frozen pizza the next night. My mom buys all these fresh vegetables, but most of them are just getting slimy in the fridge. One night my dad was so busy on the computer that he forgot about dinner. I went in to remind him, but he yelled at me before I could talk, so I made eggs for me and my sisters. I like making eggs. I put a little milk and some shredded cheese in them.

My dad gets really angry sometimes. He spanked me once that I remember. My mom yelled at him. He hasn't done it since. But with my mom not here, I don't trust him. I've seen the way he acts when he's mad. Like with the glass door last summer. I saw my dad smash the chair into it from the top of the stairs. I came out of my room when things started getting loud. They were both yelling. But only my dad was swearing. I just sat at the top of the stairs wishing things would quiet down so I could get back to sleep. Then, he smashed the door. I thought he was going to swing the chair at her next, but he didn't. I was glad when he left because I knew it was over and I could go back to bed.

The next day, I saw the broken door out behind the garage. I didn't say anything about it. A week later it was back in place, like nothing ever happened.

Don't get me wrong. My dad is not a bad guy. He's a good soccer coach. It's just that he can be a jerk when he's mad. I've never really seen him get mad at anyone except my mom and us kids. Mostly my mom.

My parents used to argue, especially last summer. My mom said that sometimes couples argue, but it doesn't mean they don't love each other. I hope she's right.

Two of my best friends had their parents get divorced. Timmy's parents split when we were in fifth grade. Evan's parents split last year. It really sucked for the kids. Timmy's dad got this crappy apartment. Timmy had to spend the weekends there. He didn't even have a TV for a long time. And Timmy had to share a room with his sister. It was worse for Evan. His dad moved in with this woman in Boston. Now, he almost never sees his dad. But at least they both got to stay with their moms. I don't understand why my mom had to leave. She's the one who takes care of us.

Because of the newspaper article, a bunch of kids from school know about what's happening with my family. I had an argument with Kenny Tyminski in gym class. We had free time at the end. I wanted to play dodgeball. He wanted to play basketball. We decided to vote and the other kids voted with me. Kenny got mad and said something about my mother being a child abuser who's going to jail. I wanted to deny it, but anyone who saw the paper knows he was telling the truth. My friend Timmy stuck up for me and said Kenny didn't know what he was talking about. Then, we played dodgeball, but it wasn't much fun.

We studied the Constitution in school, so I know that my mom is innocent until she's proven guilty. But the paper sure made it sound like she's guilty, so it's probably not as simple as the way it seems in the Constitution. I don't know what I'll do if my mom goes to jail.

Meredith and Camille aren't doing very well either. At least Camille gets to see my mom sometimes. Meredith is just sad all the time. She doesn't do anything anymore. And she looks kind of like she's sick. I should probably mention it to my mom, but I don't want to worry her any more than she already is.

My dad has been spending more and more time on the computer in the office. He used to go back to work after soccer practice in the afternoons and then we would all eat together at around seven o'clock. Now, with my mom gone, he works at home in the evenings. We pretty much have to take care of ourselves. We do okay. I try to remind my sisters to brush their teeth, but sometimes I forget to brush my own, so I'm not the best person for the job.

My mom used to read to my sisters every night. They were reading the second Percy Jackson book when my mom got arrested. I loved those books. I read them all when I was in sixth grade. Sometimes I used to sit outside my sister's room and listen, just because they were such great books, and I like the sound of my mom's voice. The book is still sitting on Meredith's nightstand. I asked my mom if she wanted me to finish reading it to my sisters, but she said that she'd be home before I knew it, and that she was looking forward to finishing reading the book out loud.

The only good thing to come out of this is that we've been getting tons of iPod time. My mom used to be really strict about how long we could use our iPods. We figured out that, if we stay in our rooms and don't make much noise, my dad has no idea what we're doing. Besides, we can hear him coming up the stairs, so we just pretend to be reading if he comes in the room. Which he almost never does. Sometimes, I get carried away and forget to do my homework first. My mom always used to ask me if I did my homework. I lied a couple of times and got in trouble. Since my mom got arrested, nobody asks me anymore.

It's a Saturday, so I have a soccer game this morning. My sisters will be there because my dad is the coach. That means that my mom can't come and see me play. This totally sucks.

CHAPTER 16

Tamara Goodwin
Tuesday, October 9, 2012

I decided to become a lawyer when I was in high school. My father used to call me his "little contrarian" because I was always challenging his reasoning. I won lots of those arguments, so I knew I could be good at it. Besides, I realized that medical school was not an option after we dissected frogs in ninth grade biology. I didn't want to opt out of the dissection because I thought it might impact my grade. Let's just say I would have been better off opting out.

"We just got funding for a new position in the PD's Office. Any chance you're interested?" Will says. We went to law school together. Now, he works in the Public Defender's Office and I work for the State's Attorney's Office. We are sitting in our conference room, each with a chest-high pile of manilla folders in front of us.

"It's about time. You and Benny have been handling all the cases since I started here."

"Yeah, it'll be nice to get some help."

"Do you guys ever win trials?" I say.

"Every once in a while. We're more about fighting for the underdog. Defending the rights of the downtrodden. That kind of thing."

"I'm eight and three right now. Two of the losses are thanks to Barry. I don't think the PD's Office has ever beaten me."

"I stopped keeping track after my first year. Too many of my clients are guilty—"

"You mean they're all guilty." I know that not everybody who gets cited or arrested is guilty, but we thoroughly screen the cases that the police bring to us, and the questionable cases are declined. If our office files a case, it's because we're confident we can get a conviction.

Will rolls his eyes. "—And they only go to trial because they can't seem to wrap their heads around the consequences. Of course, if they had to pay for my services, I'd do even fewer trials."

"Isn't it depressing?"

"The money helps me forget."

"They pay you guys more than us?"

"No. We're on the same pay scale."

"So, I work for you guys, I still only make forty-one thousand dollars a year, and I get to lose all my cases?"

"That pretty much sums it up."

"I think I'll pass."

"I figured you would."

"Let's see if we can resolve some of these cases. What've you got?"

"Josh Leonard," he says and opens the top file. "No record. Shoved his girlfriend during an argument. Pretty minor stuff. He's got no problem with probation, but he can't do the counseling because of his work schedule. He drives a truck, has a weekly delivery on Monday nights."

"You know I won't budge on the counseling."

"Even if his girlfriend recants?"

"They all recant. That's why we have a 'no drop' policy on domestic violence."

"They have a kid. If he loses his job, the family will be in trouble."

"He'll have to figure out a way to do the counseling. There's a class on Wednesdays up in Burlington if he can't do Mondays." Counseling is not negotiable, even in first-time domestics. That's something they stressed at training. Apparently, the men who do counseling are much less likely to reoffend.

"Okay. I'll tell him to work on it."

"Who's next?"

"Tom Bisson. Second offense, so you charged a felony."

I find the file and open it. "His wife wrote a letter last week. I sent that to you, right?"

"Yup. She wants him to come home."

"Of course she does. That's why I love no-contact conditions. The family puts pressure on the offender to make a deal."

Will laughs. "Are you suggesting that my client is violating his conditions of release and having contact with his wife?"

"We both know they are. But at least he's on his best behavior because, if he gets caught, it's straight to jail."

"It was a minor incident, and it's been ten years since his last offense. How about a misdemeanor and probation? With counseling, of course."

"You want me to give up my felony?"

"You don't care about the felony. Most of the time you just charge those so my people will plead to misdemeanors."

"Are you accusing me of overcharging?"

"If the shoe fits. C'mon this guy doesn't need a felony."

"Fine."

An hour later, we've resolved eight cases. The remaining six will get revisited in a few weeks.

"How's it working out for you, having all the domestics?" Will asks. He's organizing his folders in a cardboard box.

"It has its ups and downs. The cases are more challenging than what I was doing for the first couple of years. The biggest downside is that I'm the one called in the middle of the night when the police can't decide who to arrest."

"I guess it's karma. We get called in the middle of the night by all the drunk drivers."

"It's more like an occupational hazard," I say.

Will shrugs and picks up his box.

"Anyway, there're probably more drunk driver calls," I say. "You're definitely not going to sell me on going over to the dark side."

"I wasn't really trying."

I eat lunch in the office kitchen, which is really only a microwave, a toaster oven, a mini refrigerator, and a round formica table. Lunch is leftover spaghetti in a Tupperware that I heated in the microwave. Just after I sit down, Sanjiv comes in with his sandwich and joins me.

"How's your afternoon looking?" he says.

"I'm going to be in court all afternoon," I say.

"You mind covering a four o'clock status conference for me? My kid has a tee-ball game at four and I'd like to go. I miss so many of the games, but most of my stuff should be wrapped up by three thirty today."

"Sure. What do I need to know?"

"It's a felony sex assault. We'll be taking depositions for a few more months. Just tell Judge Jenkins that we want to come back in six weeks for another status."

"Sounds easy enough."

"I'll drop the file on your desk after I eat. Thanks."

"No problem."

"So, what do you think of Judge Jenkins so far?" he asks.

"So far, I like him. He seems to lean toward the prosecution."

"As he should. We're the good guys."

"Yeah. But he surprised me last week."

"What'd he do?"

"I had a motion to suppress. A young couple was parked at the entrance to the Black Mountain hiking trail."

"Nothing illegal about that, probably just making out."

"One of MFPD's finest pulled in behind them and blocked the exit. Then he approached and tapped on the window. The officer testified that he smelled marijuana, so he had the kids exit the vehicle." I lean back in my chair as the scenario flicks through my mind.

Sanjiv holds up a finger and finishes a bite of his sandwich before he speaks. "Who was the officer?"

"Tim Bartlett."

"I'm not sure about him."

"Me neither. Anyway, he said the kids gave permission to search. They said they didn't. He didn't find marijuana, but he did find a small baggie with two ecstasy pills under the front seat."

"Let me guess. The defense attorney argued it was a seizure." Sanjiv gently slams his fist on the table.

"Of course. If the cop had found marijuana, it would have been a tighter case, but he didn't. The defense attorney argued that because the cop blocked them in, the kids didn't feel they could leave, and that the officer's story wasn't believable because there was absolutely no sign of marijuana in the vehicle."

"Judge Jenkins denied the motion?"

"Yup. I got the decision this morning. I thought I was going to lose, but Jenkins said that the fact that the officer was mistaken about the source of the marijuana odor didn't diminish his reasonable suspicion to stop the kids. He also believed the officer's testimony that they gave permission for the search."

"So, where did the marijuana smell come from?" Sanjiv says.

"I suppose it's possible that there was someone else in the woods smoking marijuana or that the kids had been smoking and had already disposed of all the roaches and paraphernalia when Bartlett got there."

"Anything's *possible*," Sanjiv says.

"Exactly. Except he didn't even find a lighter. And if Bartlett lied about the marijuana smell, he might have also lied about whether they gave permission for the search. I really didn't think he was believable."

"No point in second guessing the judge."

"I know. And, now that I can use the pills at trial, I'll probably get a guilty plea."

"Don't beat yourself up. If they weren't guilty, they wouldn't have had ecstasy in the car."

"Good point," I say as we clear the table. The spaghetti wasn't great, but I always enjoy talking with Sanjiv. He's got a lot of experience and seems to have a good attitude about the job.

I arrive at court well ahead of one o'clock. I have a number of discovery deadlines today, and I want to hand out all the envelopes before court starts.

Discovery is when the state turns over all the evidence to the defense. Usually that means copies of all the reports, affidavits, interview recordings, and 911 calls. I had to work over the weekend to get it done, but I have a stack of large yellow envelopes for the defense attorneys in my cases. With my caseload, I don't have time to watch all the interviews and listen to all the recordings. Mostly, I just go through the police files and make sure that everything we have gets turned over. Some judges will dismiss cases if we don't get everything to the defense in a timely fashion.

Inside the courtroom, the judge is not yet on the bench. A couple of dozen people are milling around. Most are defendants and family members. Barry Densmore approaches the prosecution table, so I paw through my envelopes to find the ones for him.

"You got a minute?" he says.

"Sure," I say and hand him two envelopes.

"I want to talk about Sarah Bennett. I'd like you to consider lifting the no-contact condition. Apparently, the kid is not doing well without her mother. I'm planning to ask the judge, but I thought I'd try to convince you first."

I shake my head. "No can do, Barry. If you want to talk about a plea bargain, we can do that, but as long as this thing might go to trial, I need that condition."

"But what about what's best for the kid?"

"What's best for the kid is seeing her abusive parent get counseling and monitoring."

"My client is adamant the cops got it all wrong."

"They all say that, Barry."

"Maybe sometimes they get it wrong."

I shrug.

"Okay, I'm still going to ask the judge," Barry says. "I need to take at look at this discovery, but I want to get depositions scheduled as soon as possible. I'll call you tomorrow."

When the Bennett case gets called, Barry makes his way to the counsel table with his client. I glance at her and notice that she looks thinner than I remember her from four weeks ago. In general, I try not to look at the defendants when we're in the courtroom. It's easier if their faces don't pop into my head every time I pick up their files.

"Where are we at?" the judge says.

"I just received the discovery here in court," Barry says. "I'm assuming it's all there."

"How long do we need for depositions?" the judge says.

"I'm planning to take three," Barry says. "I can do those next week and file motions within four weeks."

Four weeks? Did he mean four months? And why is he only taking three depositions?

"Ms. Goodwin, can you be available next week for depositions? If the defense wants to expedite this, I'd like to accommodate them." Not me. The longer this drags on, the more likely I am to get a plea deal.

"Actually, Your Honor, my schedule is full. I'm scheduling depositions at least four to six weeks out," I say.

"Okay then, I'm going to order depositions be completed by the next status. I want everyone back here at the beginning of December. Anything further?"

"Yes, Your Honor, we'd like to request the removal of the no-contact order," Barry says.

"File a written motion and we'll set it for a hearing in a few weeks," the judge says.

"This is something of an emergency, Your Honor. My client has not seen her eight-year-old daughter in four weeks. This has been very difficult for both of them, especially the child. The father is here and can testify about the impact this has had on her."

"Mr. Densmore, I don't have time for a motion hearing this afternoon. As you can see, we have a full docket. Why don't you proffer what Mr.—" The judge looks down at the bench for a second. "—Mr. Bennett would say if he were to testify? Or you can file a formal motion and we'll deal with it as soon as we can fit it in."

"Well, Your Honor, we'd rather not wait. This is a critical issue for the family. If Mr. Bennett were to testify he would say that, since being questioned by the police, the child, MB, has not been herself. She hasn't been eating or sleeping normally. She's been crying at school and at home. She's told her father repeatedly that she needs her mother."

The judge scowls. "Ms. Goodwin?"

"Your Honor, the concerns we raised at arraignment are still the same. The child is a critical witness in the state's case. We don't want that testimony tainted. For the record, the behavioral changes are likely the result of the assault by the mother. I respectfully request that the condition stay in place."

"I'm thinking this would be a good case for supervised visitation," the judge says. "Of course, the defendant would need to understand that under no circumstances can she discuss this case with the child. Any objection, Ms. Goodwin?"

I don't like it, mostly because I don't trust the women from Safe Haven who run the supervised visitation program to report back to the court if Bennett tries to talk to her daughter about the case. But it would be politically dangerous to make that argument. I have no choice. "No objection, Your Honor."

"Okay, I'm modifying the condition to allow weekly supervised visitation. Let's get that set up through Safe Haven."

Oh well. I doubt the supervised visitation will affect my chances of getting a plea. If the mom wants to get her daughter back, she'll have to plead out.

The afternoon goes quickly. I have about a dozen status conferences, including the one for Sanjiv, but there's time in between to talk to the defense attorneys about pending cases and do a little negotiating.

Court wraps up at quarter to five and I head back upstairs to my office. After I organize my files, I call my best friend, Sherry.

"Are you going to spinning class tonight?" I say.

"I don't know, I'm kind of tired," Sherry says.

"Come on. Exercise is good for the body and soul. Besides, it's Tuesday."

"So?"

"Last Tuesday those smokin' hot guys were in class. Remember?"

"They were both super cute."

"It's worth it to rally just for the chance to see them in gym shorts." I can say things like that to Sherry. She's the bluntest person I know. Besides, maybe I can get her out of her funk.

"Probably. But I haven't seen them around before, so maybe they were just visiting."

"You won't find out if you go home and watch TV."

"Okay. I'll see you at six."

Just in case, I touch up my makeup before I head to the gym. It is definitely hard being single in a town this size.

True to his word, Barry calls me late Wednesday morning about the Bennett case. He wants to depose two officers, Karen Driscoll and Joe Langford and one civilian witness, Dave Belkin. We schedule them for early November. I tell him I'll get back to him when I decide whether I want to take depositions. I don't like to waste my time taking depositions unless it looks like a case is going to trial. In most of my cases, after the defense attorney takes depositions of the state's main witnesses, they realize that the state has a strong case, and we negotiate a plea.

Before we hang up Barry says, "Look, I realize you haven't had a lot of time to look at the details of this case, but this one never should've been filed."

"You telling me how to do my job, Barry?"

"No, not at all. It's just that my client is adamant she had no idea the kid was in the road. I believe her. Kids do the damnedest things. You have any kids?"

"No. And I don't see what that has to do with anything."

"Look. Sarah Bennett's a good mom. She's a good person. She's known and respected in the community. Before this thing takes on a life of its own, I'd like you to consider dropping it. This family has been through hell over the past few weeks. If this drags on, it will only get worse. The kid is not at risk."

"If memory serves me, the mom almost ran the kid over and then dragged her behind the van. How can you possibly say I should drop this?"

"According to my client, none of that happened. She just drove away. I don't know why the police report describes it that way because you gave me the discovery yesterday. But, my client is afraid she's going to lose her job over this. Once we start heading down the trial track, it's hard to come back. I'd just like you to consider doing what's best for this family now—before it's too late."

"Barry, my job is to prosecute crimes. Sarah Bennett should've thought about her job before she committed a crime. After she's convicted, the shrinks can figure out what's best for the family."

"And what if you're wrong? What if she didn't commit a crime?"

"Then the jury will acquit her and she can go back to her life."

"If only it were that simple. I'm just saying I think your ethical obligations require you take a second look at this."

"Now you're *definitely* telling me how to do my job. Thanks, Barry, but I passed the bar exam, so give me a break. I'll see you at depositions."

"Hold on, Tamara. I didn't mean to offend you. I just want you to consider that maybe you made a mistake in taking this case. We all make mistakes. Just consider whether there might be another side to the story."

"Okay, Barry. Anything else?"

"No."

"Then have a nice day." I hang up. Just because he's beaten me in two trials, doesn't mean that he has the right to treat me like I'm a law student and he's the professor. It sounds like this case is going to trial unless I can put enough pressure on to get a plea. Hopefully, this will be the first time I beat Barry. Of course, this will probably be a high-profile trial, which puts the pressure on both of us.

When I took the Bennett case, I didn't realize who Sarah Bennett was. Karen Driscoll had stopped by my office with the paperwork.

"I have a case for you," Karen said.

"We've had a lot of cases together lately. Are you doing anything other than child abuse these days?" I said.

"Not much. The kid cases are taking most of my time."

"What've you got?"

She handed me a stack of papers and dropped into one of my guest chairs while I read it. "You're recommending a felony domestic? Why the felony?"

"I want to arrest her. Handcuffs and cruiser ride."

"You don't need a felony to do that. The reckless endangerment is enough, but I would still just cite her."

"But what if the kid's at risk?"

"Then flash cite her. Get her in court tomorrow."

"You're the one that always tells us to arrest in domestics."

"That's usually my policy. It sends a strong message. Nothing like a night in jail to remind a guy that it's a bad idea to beat his wife."

"So we need to send a strong message to men who assault their wives, but not women who assault their children? Personally, it sounds hypocritical to me. At the very least sexist. You know if this were a male defendant, you'd be jumping up and down to charge a felony and arrest," Karen said.

"I'm not sure the felony will even hold up."

"I think the evidence is there and it's a stronger message. Besides, you can let her plead to a misdemeanor like you always do."

"I don't always reduce to misdemeanors."

"Maybe it's just my cases."

"Fine. Go ahead and arrest her," I said. "I'll charge the felony too, but only because there's a kid involved." I knew she was manipulating me, but she had a point. Besides, we have a symbiotic relationship with the police. I figure we'll get along better if she feels like I respect her judgment.

I realized who Bennett was at her arraignment. I had asked for bail, fully expecting that I would be turned down, just so the judge would be more likely to give me the no-contact condition. That was when Barry mentioned she was the director of the Murdoch Shelter. Not to say that I would have done anything differently if I had known. I like to think I'm an equal opportunity prosecutor. Apparently, the Bennetts are a prominent couple in town. I also didn't realize that the husband was an attorney until I read the article in the paper.

After the arraignment, Manny Rodriguez from the *Gazette* asked me to comment on the charges. My boss has an office policy that the deputies are not allowed to talk to the press. I had no choice but to say, "No comment." Apparently, Manny went to my boss afterward because Fred came into my office late that afternoon and asked me about the case and how tight it was. I told him that the evidence looked strong and gave him a quick summary. He used my exact words when he spoke to Manny. It's not fair that Fred gets to be in the paper even though it's my case. The only reason Fred has that policy is that, once every four years, he has to run for office. He likes to make sure the voters know he's doing his job, and one way to ensure that is to get himself in the news on a regular basis.

Most of my cases don't get any attention from the newspaper. Our office handles over a thousand cases per year, yet only a handful get mentioned outside the court log, where the print is tiny. I doubt anybody reads the court log.

Sarah Bennett's arrest warranted an entire half page on page 3 of the paper. It was obvious that Manny had copies of the court file because he quoted Karen Driscoll's report extensively. I was a little surprised that neither Barry nor the Bennetts made any comments to Manny. I have to give it to Manny. Driscoll's report made Bennett look bad, but Manny's article made her look worse. Nobody's going to give her the Mother of the Year Award. I can see why her job is in jeopardy. We probably shouldn't have someone like her running a shelter that has children as residents. It sounds like she's unstable.

Barry is crazy if he thinks I'm going to dismiss the charges against Bennett. What would Fred say when Manny calls again? Oops, we made a mistake? I don't think so. If this case needs to go to trial, then so be it. Bring it on, Barry.

CHAPTER 17

Sarah Bennett
Thursday, November 1, 2012

There are very few defining moments in a lifetime. Life is an evolution that, for the most part, we don't see happening. We have vague memories of times and places, but few experiences change us enough to stand out. Certainly, getting married to James was important, but I'm not sure I remember it so much as I have daily reminders from the wedding photos that are scattered around my life. The birth of Nicholas I clearly remember. Your life changes when you become a mother.

Beyond that, I now see my life in two distinct parts—before the arrest and after. Even if the case against me were dismissed tomorrow, I can't imagine that I would ever view the world the same way. I'm a different person. I'd like to think I'm less judgmental, but I know it's much more than that. I'm also more cynical.

I've lived in Middleton Falls for fifteen years. I thought I had friends. Yet, none of them have called. Not one. Not that first weekend. Not in the weeks that followed.

At least nobody I know posted opinions on the news websites. It was a few weeks before I was ready to read the articles about me. When I finally got up the courage, I was shocked that a couple dozen people who don't know me felt it was their due to express opinions about my moral character. I know that the news services allow postings to drum up interest in their stories and increase ratings, but it's hardly fair. They publish a completely skewed story and then invite people to comment. I wanted to post something myself and tell the people who posted what sheep they are to believe what they read. Tell the truth about what happened. But I'm paying Barry a lot for his advice, so I probably should follow it.

The interesting thing is that the few people who questioned whether there might be more to the story or suggested that it was unfair to judge without more information were all male. Or at least had male-sounding names. Are women naturally more judgmental? Or are they on the verge of losing control so often that they can imagine assaulting one of their kids? Did they judge me as a way of congratulating themselves?

Despite my resolve not to worry my parents, I couldn't resist calling my mother the weekend after my arrest. She's been great. She calls me every day to check on me. She must sense how much I need her right now. I guess that's part of being a mother—knowing when you're needed. She insists that she and my dad are coming for Christmas this year. I think she needs to see for herself that I'm okay. I know the travel will be hard on my father, but I'm glad they're coming. Maybe this nightmare will be over by then and we'll have even more to celebrate. I'm also glad my mom promised not to tell my sister about my legal mess. If Amelia knew, she would probably start calling too. Her intentions are always good, but she's got so many issues of her own, and I don't have the energy to deal with her drama right now.

I'm waiting for Meredith in the supervised visitation room at the courthouse. As usual, I'm early. It's our third visit in as many weeks. It's an unsatisfying substitute for parenting, but it's not like I have another option. I've spent more time with Barry Densmore in the past month than I have with my own daughter.

I met with Barry yesterday afternoon at his office, a converted single-family home on Main Street. The space is simple, but tasteful, with hardwood floors and high ceilings.

"I don't know how much more of this I can take," I said. "I feel like I'm trapped on an airplane that's been circling the airport for hours. And the fasten seat belt sign is on so I can't go to the bathroom."

"I'm sure this is frustrating, but you need to be prepared for the worst," Barry said.

"What's the worst?"

"A trial. We'd be lucky to get dates six months from now."

"Six months!"

"If we're lucky."

"Would I need to be away from home for six more months?"

"Quite possibly."

"Why can't we explain to the judge that they made a mistake and get this to end?"

"We're going to try. We'll file a motion to dismiss. But it's not as simple as it sounds."

"Why not? They got it all wrong!"

"First of all, judges don't like to step on prosecutor's toes. In many ways, we're better off trying to convince Tamara to drop this."

"So, why don't we do that now?"

"I tried. But she's not ready to see it yet."

"What do you mean?"

"She took the case, so she's responsible," Barry said.

"Exactly."

"We need to be able to prove to her that the police made an innocent mistake and gave her misinformation."

"I don't think it was innocent."

"Probably not. But we need to present it that way. We don't want her feeling defensive. Even then, she may not be able to see how badly they acted."

"Why not?"

"It's called cognitive dissonance," Barry said.

"Oh my God. She can't see her mistake because then she would be on the wrong side."

"That's right." He pointed a finger at me. "I think you're the first client of mine who actually knew what that meant."

"But the judge should be able to see it. He's not emotionally vested in the outcome."

"Except that he doesn't want to step on her toes."

"I thought that was the whole point of checks and balances."

"It is. In theory. But in practice, the whole system is skewed against the accused."

"So how do we convince her?"

"I've already watched the videos of the interviews."

"Did you figure out why Meredith said those things?"

"Mostly. The officer asked a lot of leading questions, essentially telling her their theory of what happened. Meredith just didn't correct her. It's not unusual for kids."

"Are they allowed to do that?"

"They're not supposed to, but they get away with it so much that they keep doing it."

"So, explain it to Tamara."

"She's not going to take it from me. She has to see it for herself."

"So, get her to watch the videos."

"That might help, but she's probably not going to do that either. The quality of the recordings is not great, and it takes too long. She won't want to see it and she won't necessarily know what to look for."

"What do we do?"

"First, we get an expert. I know an expert forensic psychologist who can testify about suggestive interviewing techniques. I've used him before in child sex abuse cases. He's excellent."

"What will that cost?"

"I don't know. A lot. At least ten thousand dollars. I'll call him and get back to you."

"What else?"

"We take depositions and see how much damage we can do to Tamara's case. Even if she can't see her mistake, she may be able recognize a loser of a case."

"I want to see Meredith's interview."

"That's not a good idea."

"I need to understand this," I said.

Barry just looked at me.

"I've spent the past six weeks wondering why my daughter would say things that made it look like I committed a crime. I need to know what happened."

"Okay. Marcy can burn you a copy of the DVD before you leave."

I glanced at my watch as I was getting up. I'd been in Barry's office for just over half and hour. That's $180. I used to worry about how we were going to put three kids through college. Now, I just worry about how we're going to pay my legal bills.

I watched the video of Meredith on my office computer last night. I cried the first time. The second time I tried to pretend it was someone else's child so I could really listen. At least now I know what they did to her.

It took a week to set up the supervised visitation, so by the time the day finally arrived, I hadn't seen Meredith for thirty-seven days. Nothing about that felt right. Not that anything about supervised visitation is right either.

The supervised visitation room at the courthouse is crammed with a fraying green plaid love seat, a worn blue corduroy chair, a dented bookshelf with a couple dozen well used board books, and three cardboard boxes filled with toys and games. Most of the toys are appropriate for children under the age of five. One tattered poster adorns the wall: a picture of a cat hanging from a branch with the words "Hang in There" underneath. I wonder if it was hung by one of the supervisees. Meredith and I were fortunate to find a deck of Uno cards on our first visit.

Meredith walks into the room accompanied by Paula, the volunteer from Safe Haven. Paula spends most of our visits sitting in the corner of the room, leafing through magazines, and pretending not to listen to my conversations with my daughter. I wonder if Paula rotates her outfits on a weekly basis, because she seems to be always wearing the same thing, a chunky wool sweater, a long flowery skirt, and Birkenstock sandals with socks. Maybe that's her "Thursday outfit" or maybe the colors change and I'm too self-absorbed to notice.

I give Meredith a long hug. I'm getting used to the new Meredith. She seems taller. She's definitely thinner. She's always been the most serious of our children, but now it's more pronounced. She never laughs when we're together.

"Ready for Uno?" I say.

"Sure."

"Let's sit on the floor. I'll deal. How is school this week?"

"Fine."

"What are you studying?"

"It's still the ocean. We have to pick a sea animal and make a poster."

"What did you pick?"

"Killer whales."

"Really. Why?"

"Because they're cute like dolphins, but they're bigger and meaner. The other sea creatures don't mess with killer whales. Uno."

When she wins the first game of Uno, the corners of her mouth turn up a little. It looks more like a grimace than a smile. Does she feel guilty when she beats me? I deal again. I think back to the good times we used to have playing Uno in front of the fireplace at our house. It was almost always the three kids and me.

The hour with Meredith goes by too quickly. Paula never hurries us out, but I feel bad making her stay late. James raps before opening the door when he arrives to pick up Meredith. We smile politely at each other. Meredith pushes the cards together into a neat pile, wraps a rubber band around them, and places the pack on the top of the bookshelf. She doesn't look at James. She climbs into my lap for another long hug and then walks by James and out the door.

"I'll call you later," he says and waves from the doorway. I don't get up. I'm too drained.

Paula is packing up her magazines. "I probably shouldn't say this, but I'm sorry you're going through this. You seem like a good mom. And I can tell your daughter is very attached to you. I'm so used to supervising visits for dads who have no idea what to do with their kids. It's painful to watch. This is my favorite hour of the week."

"Thanks." Surprisingly, her words give me a boost of energy and I'm able to get up from the floor. "Why do you do this?"

"Well, I'm retired. I signed up to volunteer at Safe Haven because my first husband was an abusive son of a bitch. Good riddance. I needed something to do and I wanted to give back to the community. My second husband was a good guy. Lost him to bladder cancer three years ago."

"I'm sorry."

"Yeah. Me too. I have a confession to make. After our last session, I looked you up on the internet. I read the article in the *Gazette* about what happened with your daughter."

I can't meet her eyes. I pretend to look for something in my purse.

"Anyway, I read the article and I thought, 'There has to be another side to this story.' You don't seem like the kind of person who would do anything to hurt your child."

I look up. "I'm not and I didn't."

"You want to talk about it?"

"I... I really can't."

Paula's face hardens.

"It's just that my lawyer told me not to."

"I won't say anything to anyone. You just seem like you could use a friend."

"Thanks. Maybe—maybe some other time."

Paula turns off the light and closes the door and then utters a quick goodbye before she strides quickly toward the exit. I know how much it probably cost her to say that to one of the defendants she monitors and I feel bad. But my family's future is more important than her perception of herself as an amateur counselor. I can't trust anyone I don't know well.

It's almost five o'clock when I get back to the shelter. Betsy is just locking my office door when I walk in.

"Hey, I wasn't sure when you'd be back, so I figured I should lock up. I'm getting ready to head home."

"Thanks. Anything happen while I was gone?"

"We got some good news this afternoon."

"I'm always up for good news."

"We found Melanie a Section 8 apartment today. She and Cameron are moving out tomorrow."

"That is good news."

"It took a while to line things up, but it came together earlier this week. Melanie's going to be working part-time at Price Chopper and Cameron will be full-time at the children's center."

"That'll be much better for him than hanging out here."

"That's for sure."

"Does she have any plans for a GED?"

"Barbara's been talking to her about that. We're hopeful."

"That's great. Thanks for telling me. I want to stay in the loop." I power up my computer.

"You going to be here long?"

"Probably a few hours. I have a lot to catch up on."

"How'd it go with Meredith?"

"I don't know. I can't read her. I wish I could ask her about what happened. What if she actually believes what the police told her?"

"Give her a little credit."

"She's only eight. You wouldn't believe that interview. It's like the police were trying to brainwash her."

"Then you'll have a heart-to-heart with her when this is over."

"What if it's too late by then?"

"It won't be too late. You're her mother."

"She probably thinks I abandoned her."

"Then it may take some time to get her trust back."

"I just want to talk to her about it."

"Be patient. This can't go on forever." Betsy reaches over and pats my shoulder.

"Thanks, but—what it if does?"

"It won't."

"Thanks again for giving me a place to stay."

"No worries. You're the easiest roommate I've ever had. You work all the time so you're hardly ever home. You barely eat, so you don't mess up the kitchen. We can keep doing this as long as you need."

"What happens if a real guest wants to use your guest room?"

"They can stay at a hotel."

"You're a good friend."

"I know. Don't work all night."

When I let myself into Betsy's log cabin it's after eleven o'clock. The inside lights are out, but the porch light is still on. I don't want to wake Betsy, so I quietly pull the door shut behind me. One of Betsy's three cats rubs up against my legs as I hang up my coat. I use the glow of the wood stove to make my way across the living room to the guest room. I don't turn on the bedroom light until the door is shut. Another cat is curled up on my bed. As usual, I let him stay. I figure it was his bed before I took it over. Besides, I like the company and he doesn't seem to mind when I cry.

In the morning, James and I meet at Jasmine's office. We've been to see her every week except the Friday after my arrest. She has helped us navigate our new family dynamic. We're such a mess that we need her to guide us through even the most mundane decisions. But if that's what it takes to get our family through this, then we're lucky to have someone fill that role.

"How are you coping this week, James?" Jasmine says.

"Well, it's certainly challenging being a single parent. It's not fair that I'm being punished by the court because of what Sarah did."

"What exactly did I do?" I say.

"Well, for starters, you pissed off the police. Then, you left Meredith at ballet. If you'd brought her home, that idiot would have never called the police and our family would be normal right now."

"Now wait just a minute, mister. If you want to start assigning blame, why don't we talk about who left an eight-year-old by herself with a police officer who was out for blood."

"Is it useful to assign blame here?" Jasmine says. "Let's step back a minute. There are a lot of places we can put blame—the police, Meredith, the 'idiot' who called the police. The more important question is whether you want to come through this with your family intact. Do you?"

We both nod.

"It's important that you each understand how this situation is impacting the other. Why don't you start, James?"

"I feel like I'm the laughingstock of the legal community," James says.

"You may actually be getting more sympathy than ridicule, but I understand why you might feel that way," Jasmine says.

"And I'm afraid I'm going to lose all my clients."

"Is that a realistic fear?"

"I don't know, maybe."

"What else?"

"None of the soccer parents look me in the eye anymore when they come to pick up their kids."

"So, you're feeling publicly embarrassed and professionally threatened."

"That sums it up."

"How about you, Sarah?"

"I don't want to downplay what James is going through, but he needs to take that feeling and multiply it by ten. Once a week I go to the grocery store. I see people I've known for years. They used to stop and talk. Now, they wave and act like they're in too much of a hurry. Nicki Sanders actually got into a longer line with her groceries so she wouldn't have to stand behind me."

"Maybe you're reading too much into it?"

"I don't think so. They all think I'm a child abuser. At least James is only the husband of a child abuser. It's nowhere near as bad."

"Okay. Assuming you're right and they are avoiding you, maybe it's just because they don't know what to say."

"If they didn't believe the article it would be easy. How about 'sorry this is happening to you, I don't believe a word of it'? The problem is people believe what they read."

"She's right," James says. "Before this experience, I used to assume that what was in the paper was at least close to the truth. Unless you've been through this or have someone close who has, you don't have a clue."

"Okay. Let's come back to that later. How are things going with the children?"

"I'm having a hard time doing all of my jobs and all of Sarah's. I don't feel like I'm doing any of it well," James says.

"At least you get to be with them," I say. "Do you have any idea what it's like to be ripped away from your family?"

"James, nobody expects you to take over Sarah's role perfectly," Jasmine says.

"Of course not," I say. "I'm doing my best to support you from the sidelines. But it's hard to be at the house by myself."

"What do you mean?" Jasmine says.

"I usually go in and clean on Monday or Tuesday. I do laundry. I vacuum. It's so quiet. Whenever I'm in the kids' rooms, I get so sad. I want them to be there. I smell their pillows before I wash their sheets. They're growing up and I'm missing it."

"That must be hard for you. This is an incredibly stressful situation. For both of you. How's the court case going? Any end in sight?"

"Not really," I say.

"We've only had one status conference. Nothing will happen now until after depositions," James says.

"The status conference was frightening," I say.

"Why?" Jasmine says.

"The courtroom was packed with people. It was bad enough standing up in front of the judge when the courtroom was empty. I was so ashamed that everyone was looking at me."

"I went with you," James says. "I was right there."

"I know. And I appreciate it. I don't think I'd be getting through this without you."

"It's super that you guys are trying to support each other through this," Jasmine says. "It sounds like you're on the right track. You just have to avoid blaming each other for a situation that is much bigger than you. Blaming only makes it worse."

She's right, as usual, but I can't help but mentally catalog my negative feelings even if it's not fair to vent. I do think James should have known better, just like he should know we don't buy whole milk. The words we had in front of Jasmine this morning were the closest thing we've had to a fight in almost two months. Partly because we don't see as much of each other, and partly because I'm too tired to fight. Somehow all the things we used to fight about seem trivial. I miss James because he used to be my best friend, but I don't miss the fights we seemed to be having with too much regularity. I don't sleep well in Betsy's guest bed, but I have a feeling I wouldn't be sleeping no matter where I was spending my nights. Sleep is for people who have control of their future.

After counseling, James and I talk in the parking lot. "What are the kids doing this weekend?" I say.

"Nothing much. Since soccer is over and the girls aren't doing ballet anymore, we'll probably just hang out and watch TV. None of the girls' friends have been calling for play dates, and I don't think I can handle having other kids over right now."

"I get that. By the way, did you remember to take pictures of the kids in their Halloween costumes?"

"I forgot. Besides, Camille's the only one who went trick-or-treating."

"How come? They've been planning their costumes since August. I made sure you guys had everything you needed."

"Meredith couldn't get her makeup right. I tried to help her, but she said it wasn't the way you do it. She wanted this white face with blood at the corners of her mouth. You know, like you did for her last year.

Anyway, right before we were supposed to leave she washed it all off and announced she was going to stay home."

"How come Nick didn't go?"

"He'd been on the fence all week. He said it would depend on which of his friends were going. He decided at dinner that he was going to stay in and watch a horror movie."

"I can sort of understand Nick not wanting to go. He's at that in-between age. But Meredith... did you try to talk her into going?"

"Of course. But, we both know how stubborn she is."

"Oh, yeah."

"Anyway, I took Camille around the neighborhood for half an hour, but it didn't seem like her heart was in it. I suspect it wasn't the same for her without Meredith."

"That's sad."

"Yeah. Anyway, I'll call you later to figure out what time you should pick up Nick and Camille."

As I am driving back to the shelter, I think about my visit with Meredith yesterday. I had forgotten to ask her about trick-or-treating. I wonder why she didn't tell me that she'd chosen not to go. I kick myself for not asking her more questions. How could I have forgotten something so important?

It seems to work best when I spend time with Nick and Camille separately. On Saturday, Nick and I go for another short hike. It gives us something to do while we talk. Not that he talks much. I don't know what we'll do when it gets too cold for hiking.

I pick up Camille when I drop off Nick. I see Meredith in her bedroom window watching Camille get in the van, and I get a lump in my throat. I inhale and exhale deliberately so I won't cry in front of Camille. As Camille is buckling up, I notice that her hair is a mess.

We spend a few hours at Betsy's. I borrowed some books and games from the shelter, so we play Candy Land and Chutes and Ladders. Camille reads to me. While I'm detangling her hair, she tells me all about the "game" she and Meredith are playing with their dolls. They each have an alter ego American Girl doll. Apparently, Meredith's doll was very bad, so they're building her a jail with cardboard boxes and drinking straws. I suggest to Camille that maybe a time-out would be a better punishment for the disobedient doll, but apparently Meredith really wants to build the jail. How do I talk to Meredith about this without discussing the case?

It kills me when I have to bring Camille home. She's six years old. I should be with her all the time. Brushing her hair before school. Kissing her good night. Just hugging her. She never asks why I don't live at home any more. She seems to have accepted whatever explanation James gave her. I guess, in this day and age, it's not unusual for parents to live apart. Sadly, I'm relieved I don't have to talk about it with her. I'm not sure what I would say.

The shelter board is meeting on Tuesday. The agenda I received by email listed only two items: 1. Annual fundraising drive; and 2. Legal issues: Director. Barry has told me not to discuss my criminal charges with the board. He's going to come to the meeting to explain my dilemma and hopefully buy me some more time. What if they fire me?

CHAPTER 18

Karen Driscoll
Wednesday, November 7, 2012

I was supposed to be working the three-to-eleven shift today, but I have to be at the State's Attorney's Office for a deposition at one o'clock. Department policy is that uniformed officers wear uniforms for depositions, so I have to be dressed. The chief said to just sign in when I'm done with my deposition. The good news is I'll get some overtime today. The bad news is I have to do a deposition in the Sarah Bennett case. I hate depositions.

I'm not really worried about it. I've done a lot of them in the past few years. The first time I had to do one, I was really nervous. It turned out it was nothing. The whole thing took ten minutes. But, as I've gotten more responsibility over the past few years, my depositions have gotten longer. I had one child abuse case where the lawyer questioned me for two and a half hours. Then, the next week, the offender took a plea deal.

I've only had to testify in trials twice. In some ways, I liked it better than depositions. It was scary being in the courtroom in front of all those jurors, but I felt more prepared. For both trials, the state's attorney made me come into his office the day before to get ready. I knew the statements inside and out. He told me what questions he was going to ask, what information was most important, and what kind of questions to expect from the defense attorney. It was like I had a part in a play.

For depositions, all the prosecutors ever do is tell us to review the case file and bring it with us. Sometimes, they tell us not to guess if we can't remember an answer. That's it for preparation.

I brought the case file home and reviewed it this morning. Then, I took Arlo for a long walk up Creek Mountain. I figured Arlo was going to be cooped up for close to twelve hours and he deserved some exercise.

I arrive for the deposition exactly at 1:00. The secretary buzzes me in and points in the direction of the conference room. Tamara Goodwin and Barry Densmore are already in there. I hear Tamara laugh as I approach.

I take a deep breath before I knock on the door. I hate lawyers.

"Come on in, Karen," Tamara says. "Have a seat. Anything you and I need to talk about before the deposition?"

"I don't think so."

"Great. Let's get started," Barry says. There's a digital recorder in the center of the table. He turns it on and positions it with the mike in front of me. Barry and Tamara both have legal pads in front of them. Tamara's is blank. Barry's has notes scribbled on the left side only.

"Raise your right hand, please," Barry says, raising his own hand. "Do you swear to tell the truth under the pains and penalties of perjury?"

"I do."

"How long have you been a police officer?"

"I was certified by the Vermont Criminal Justice Council in 2007. So five years."

"You graduated the police academy?"

"That's correct."

"How many weeks was that?"

"Sixteen weeks."

"When did you start working at MFPD?"

"Right after graduation."

"What did you do before the police academy?"

"I was in school."

"Do you have a bachelor's degree?"

"No. I have an associates in criminal justice."

"From where?"

"Community College of Vermont."

"Do you have any college-level courses in child development?"

I have to think for a few seconds. "I took Psy 1010 at CCV."

"Anything specific to child development?"

"No, I guess nothing specific."

"Did you have any experience working with children prior to becoming a police officer?"

"No."

"For the record, do you have kids?"

"No."

"Okay. I assume you've had training in interviewing children since graduating from the police academy?"

"That's right."

"Tell me about it."

"Well... in 2010, I attended a four-day training on forensic interviewing."

"Who sponsored the training?"

"I don't remember. I think it was offered by the state. I'd have to look at the certificate."

"Anything else?"

"Yes. I went to two other trainings on interviewing children."

"What were those?"

"I'd have to look at my records."

"Give me an idea."

"They were shorter, but similar. How to talk to kids. How to get them to talk to you. That kind of thing."

"Okay. I'd like you to get copies of any records you still have. Certificates. Whatever. Can you get them to Tamara this week?"

"Sure," I say. I really don't see why my training records are relevant, but Tamara isn't objecting and I don't feel comfortable arguing with Barry while I'm being recorded.

"Okay, so let's talk about September 8, 2012. What were you doing that day?"

"Excuse me?"

"The day of Meredith Bennett's interview. What were you doing?"

"It was my day off. I got called in."

"Okay, what were you doing?"

"Before I got called in?"

"Yes."

"I don't see why it's any of your business." I roll my eyes at Tamara. She just shrugs and looks down at her notepad. "And I don't remember."

"Try. It was a Saturday. It would have been about ten o'clock in the morning."

"I told you I don't remember."

"Let me give you a minute." He sits, hand steepled and eyes closed, as if he's meditating or maybe even praying.

I remember the incident with Arlo and the skunk treatments I had to do during that time frame. I don't see how it's relevant. Usually I know why a defense attorney is asking a question, but this question doesn't seem important. When I get tired of the silence, I say, "I've thought about it. I still don't remember."

"Okay. If it comes back to you during the deposition, please let me know."

"Fine."

"Who called you at home?"

"Officer Langford."

"And what exactly did he tell you?"

"I don't remember exactly."

"Try. This is extremely important."

"I can't. Because I talked to him again when I got to the PD, I don't remember what he told me on the phone and what he told me in person."

"Okay. What information did Officer Langford give you prior to your interview with Meredith Bennett?"

"Just that there was a witness. I think he said the mom turned the van around and the kid ran into the road, grabbed the door and the mom kept going."

"Anything else."

"I really don't remember."

"Is your conversation with Officer Langford recorded?"

"No."

"So, why did you think Meredith was dragged?"

"She said she was."

"No. I have a transcript of that interview." He pulls a thick stack of papers from the middle of the pile in front of him and slaps it on the table. "Meredith never once used that word. You used it three times. Why were you so convinced she was dragged?"

I'm feeling assaulted.

"I wasn't convinced of anything. I was doing an investigation. We had an eyewitness report. I was asking questions. That's my job."

"So let me ask it this way. Why did you use the word 'dragged'?"

"I guess someone said the kid was dragged."

"Who?"

"I don't know. Dave Belkin."

"Did you talk to Mr. Belkin before you interviewed the child?"

"No. It was a few days after."

"Okay, so who told you she was dragged?"

"Well, the only person I remember talking to was Officer Langford, so it must have been him."

"Okay." Barry nods and makes a check mark on his notepad. I really don't see the point of his questions. The kid agreed she was dragged. It's not like I forced her to say it.

He spends another ten minutes asking questions about Meredith's demeanor. I'm not sure why he's doing this either. The whole interview is recorded. He can just watch the DVD and see her demeanor. I have to admit that she didn't seem happy to be there, but she wasn't acting like she was scared. I've seen kids who are scared. Meredith just seemed like she wanted to go home.

"Were you wearing a uniform when you interviewed Meredith Bennett?"

"Yes."

"Including the firearm?"

"Yes. I always wear my service weapon with my uniform."

"And the nightstick?"

"Yes, it's all standard."

"So, you got called in on your day off. To interview an eight-year-old. Yet you took the time to put on your uniform and all its regalia?"

"I was going to work. It's what I wear to work."

"Even when you're interviewing a child?"

"Yes."

"Was the issue of attire discussed at any of your trainings on child interviewing?"

"Not that I can recall." I don't remember any specific directives on the subject. I know at least one of the trainings talked about creating "child-friendly" interviewing places, sometimes called Child Advocacy Centers. But Vermont is a small state. Right now, the only place resembling a Child Advocacy Center is in Burlington. We don't have a special place to interview children at the PD. Barry seems to be able to read my thoughts.

"Where did you interview Meredith Bennett?"

"Interview Room 2."

"Is that a room that you use to interview suspects?"

"Sometimes. If they're not in custody. Usually it's just witnesses."

"Describe Interview Room 2 for me."

"It's just a room."

"Anything on the walls?"

"You mean like art?"

"Sure."

"No."

"What's it got for furniture?"

"A desk with a computer. Three chairs."

"What kind of chairs?"

"Metal office chairs."

"It's not a very friendly room, is it?"

"Probably not."

"But it's not supposed to be, is it?"

"Not really."

"Because you don't want suspects getting too relaxed, right?"

"I guess not."

"So, why did you choose to interview an eight-year-old in an interrogation room?"

"It's the best room we have with recording capability." The trainings beat into us the importance of making recordings, so that children don't necessarily have to testify at trial.

"Did it occur to you that a child might find that room intimidating?"

I'm not sure how to answer this question. If I say yes, I'm admitting that it is intimidating. If I say no, then I'm admitting I missed an important message in the training. This is why I hate lawyers. They box you in. I opt for the middle ground. "I wanted to make sure the interview was recorded. I used the best room available for that purpose. We're a small department. We don't have a designated child-interview room."

"Did you consider waiting until a more friendly environment could be arranged?"

"No."

"Why not?"

"Because there wasn't time."

"Was the child leaving town?"

"Not that I know of."

"So, why did you need to interview Meredith right away?"

"I find people remember best when it's fresh in their minds."

"You interviewed Dave Belkin two days later, right?"

"Yes."

"So, you could have interviewed Meredith Bennett two days later as well, couldn't you?"

"I suppose."

"You waited four days to arrest Sarah Bennett, right?"

"Sounds about right."

"So, it wasn't a matter of protecting Meredith, was it?"

"That was part of it."

"What was the rest of it?"

"I don't know. I just wanted to get it done."

"At the risk of traumatizing a child?"

"She didn't seem traumatized to me."

"And you're qualified to make that judgment how?"

"I've interviewed lots of kids."

"Isn't it true that the real reason you wanted to interview Meredith that day was that you were afraid that, once the parents realized you were conducting a criminal investigation, they wouldn't let you talk to her?"

"I just wanted to get it done."

"You had met Sarah Bennett prior to September eighth, hadn't you?"

"I'd met her on at least one prior occasion."

"At least one?"

"Well, I clearly remember one."

"When was that?"

"A few weeks before this case, I think."

"And how did you meet her?"

"I went to the shelter where she works."

"Why were you there?"

"We were looking for evidence of a crime that had been committed earlier that day."

"Who is 'we'?"

"Myself and Sergeant Patterson."

"What happened at the shelter?"

"Nothing."

"What do you mean by 'nothing'?"

"Just that. She wouldn't let us in."

"Did she say why?"

"She was protecting the guy that robbed the Quik Stop."

"Did she say that to you?"

"No, she said something about privacy and getting a warrant."

"Did that offend you?"

"No."

"Who was the guy she was allegedly protecting?"

"I'm pretty sure his name is Bryce Anderson."

"Was he charged with the crime?"

"No." I get the feeling that Barry already knows the answers to all the questions he's asking.

"Why not?"

"Because we couldn't find enough evidence."

"But you think that if you'd searched the shelter you would have found it."

"Probably."

"You had a problem with that, didn't you?"

"Look, I wouldn't say I had a problem with it, but I don't understand it."

"Why didn't you get a warrant?"

"We tried. The judge wouldn't give us one."

"But, if Ms. Bennett had given permission for the search, you wouldn't have needed one, correct?"

"That's my understanding."

"She made you mad, didn't she?"

Right now, Barry is the one who's making me mad. "No, sir," I say, trying to show no emotion. This room is starting to feel hot. My service weapon is digging into my side and my night stick is feeling uncomfortable on my leg.

"Isn't it fair to say that you didn't like Sarah Bennett when you met her on that occasion?"

"I don't like the way she handled that situation, but I don't know her enough to like or dislike her." It seems like an answer that's close enough to the truth. Barry seems to accept it. He makes another check mark on the notepad in front of him.

"Let's talk about your affidavit of probable cause for a minute. Are you supposed to redact the names of minors and sex crime victims?"

"Yes."

"Is there an official protocol about that?"

"I believe so."

"But you didn't redact Meredith Bennett's name, did you?"

Uh oh. "Did I forget?"

"I don't know. Did you forget? Or did you do it intentionally to get back at Sarah Bennett?"

Shit. "I didn't realize I'd forgotten," I say. "Until just now."

Barry looks at me like he's disgusted. "Did you ever interview Sarah Bennett?"

"No, I did not."

"Did you try to interview her?"

"I asked her to come in for an interview, but she said she wanted to consult a lawyer. Then, you called and told me not to question her."

"Did you try to question her after that?"

"No."

"And did she make any statements to you?"

"Just the one statement that's in my report."

"What was that?"

I pick up my copy of the arrest report so that I can read what I wrote. "Go easy on me."

"And you're sure those were her exact words?"

I think back to when I arrested Sarah Bennett. I'm pretty sure. If it wasn't exact, it was close enough. I answer, "Yes, I'm sure."

"Isn't it true that her exact words were 'Please don't treat me like a criminal.'"

"I don't think so."

"And isn't it true that she said those words in the context of you putting her in handcuffs at her place of employment?"

"No."

"Then, when did she allegedly say those words to you?"

"When we first arrived, before she knew she was going to be arrested."

Barry scowls. "What did you say when you got to the shelter?"

"I told her that we were there because of the incident with her daughter."

"Did she say anything in response?"

"That's when she said, 'Go easy on me.'"

"She didn't say, 'You need to speak with my lawyer'?"

"She might have said something about her lawyer. But she also said, 'Go easy on me.'"

"And you're sure about that?"

"Yes. I'm sure."

"But, whatever she said was referring to the handcuffs, wasn't it?"

"I didn't take it that way."

"So, when you arrested her, you made your report sound like she confessed, didn't you?"

I can feel the heat rising in my face. This guy is accusing me of falsifying evidence. "Look, I wrote it the way I remembered it."

"Did anyone else hear her say those words?"

"Officer Langford was there to assist with the arrest if needed. He might've heard them. I don't know if he was close enough."

"Okay. Is the conversation recorded in any way?"

"I don't believe so."

"Don't you have a microphone on your lapel?"

"I do. But we've been having trouble with our cruiser recorder, so it wasn't picked up."

"How convenient."

I don't respond to that. I know he's just trying to bait me. Tamara looks uninterested. She's just scribbling notes.

Barry questions me for a while about my interview and measurement session with Dave Belkin. Then, the deposition is over. Tamara doesn't ask any questions. The state's attorneys almost never do. She also didn't make a single objection. That's not unusual either during depositions. It's much different than a trial.

As soon as the recorder is turned off, the lawyers start acting friendly again. I don't know how they turn it on and off so easily. Personally, I think they're all like Jekyll and Hyde. I'm exhausted, but I still have to go work an eight-hour shift.

I'm on evenings again the next day when I see Joe Langford.

"Did you have to do a deposition in the Bennett case?" I say.

"Yeah, I did it yesterday morning. It felt like a waste of time to me," Joe says.

"I know that feeling. I was in there for an hour and a half."

"I didn't get it that bad, but the defense attorney spent ten minutes trying to get me to remember where I first heard the word 'dragged.' Who cares? The kid said she was dragged, right?" Joe says.

"She did to me."

"That's all that matters as far as I'm concerned." Joe looks around cautiously before lowering his voice. "By the way, I got your back on that arrest statement."

"What do you mean?"

"Just that I told them I remembered it the way you wrote it."

"You talking about 'go easy on me'?"

Joe nods, looking me directly in the eye for the first time I can ever remember.

"Isn't that what she said?"

"As far as I'm concerned." He winks then salutes and walks back toward the entrance where the patrol cars are parked.

I'm left wondering what that conversation was all about. Was he telling me that I got it wrong and he perjured himself to cover my back? Or was he telling me he didn't hear anything, but that he made his deposition match my report? Maybe all he meant was we heard it the same way.

I remember back to the deposition. Had Sarah Bennett been referring to the handcuffs? Maybe. When I wrote the report, I was feeling pressured. I had most of the report ready, but I needed to add the details of the arrest. I had trouble with the computer. I must have forgotten to take out Meredith's name. I added the last few lines and then rushed it over to the State's Attorney's Office. I thought I'd gotten it right, but maybe I didn't. There's not a big difference between what I said and what Barry Densmore said. I wonder if Joe was within earshot when I cuffed her. I guess it doesn't really matter now. I signed my report under penalty of perjury. Then I swore to it in a deposition. If I admit that I made a mistake, I'm doubly screwed. Besides, if I was wrong, there's no way they can prove it. There's no recording. The more I think about it, the less concerned I am. The statement is hardly a big deal. It's not like I said she said, "I'm sorry I tried to hurt my kid." Besides, there's plenty of other evidence against her. There's a witness and the kid herself. I have no doubt Sarah Bennett is guilty. Maybe once the depositions are over, she'll take a plea deal like everyone else.

CHAPTER 19

James Bennett
Tuesday, December 11, 2012

It's been almost exactly three months since Sarah was arrested. It's been three months since I slept with my wife. It's been three months since Meredith made it through a night without a nightmare. It's been three months since Sarah cooked dinner, and we ate it while it was still hot. It's been three months since my family was all together at the same time.

Strangely, we've gotten used to most of it. It wasn't even that weird when I took the kids to The Hearth Restaurant for Thanksgiving dinner. There was no way I was going to try to cook a turkey.

Even though we used to fight a lot, it was comforting to share a bed with my wife. Before she had to leave, I used to think sometimes that she was my worst enemy. Now, I realize that she was also my best friend. It's been lonely without her. We still talk every day, but it's not the same. We used to chat, telling stories about things that happened at work or with the kids while we cleaned up dinner or rode in the car. We were partners and lovers. Now, talking to my wife requires a phone call or an appointment. Most of our conversations are about the logistics of getting the kids where they need to be and, of course, The Case. Not surprisingly, there's no sex.

My wife has been through hell. We both have. But it seems like every conversation quickly becomes about what's happened to her and Meredith, and how awful Officer Driscoll is. She's like a broken record. Frankly, I spend my whole day at work dealing with other people's problems. I'd like to talk about something else sometimes.

I also wish I knew what to do for Meredith. I haven't told Sarah how bad it really is because I don't want to worry her. There's nothing she can do. I had hoped that once Meredith was allowed to see Sarah every week, she would get better, but she hasn't. Every night I hear her. Sometimes she cries out and wakes up. Then I hear her getting up to use the bathroom. Sometimes she whimpers for long periods without waking. When that happens, I go in and wake her. I just give her a hug and tuck her back into bed. I don't know what else to do. I've asked her to tell me about her nightmares, but she refuses. I suspect that she'd talk to Sarah if she could. I always check on her before I go to bed. Frequently, she's still lying there awake at eleven o'clock, staring at the glow-in-the-dark stars that Sarah painted on her bedroom ceiling.

At least she doesn't cry as readily as she did in the beginning. At first, she barely ate anything. One night, I raised my voice a little because she'd left most of her dinner on her plate. I didn't even yell. I just sternly told her she needed to eat her dinner. Tears started streaming down her cheeks. Quietly she said, "But Daddy, I didn't take it, you put it there. And I'm not hungry." The old Meredith would have been defiant and argued about the applicability of the family rule: you take it, you eat it. Actually, the old Meredith would have eaten her dinner. It worries me. She has definitely lost weight. Her teacher said that she's still sad at school. I think she used the word "listless." Apparently, during recess the other third-grade girls have been building fairy houses with sticks and leaves they find on the playground. Meredith used to join them, but she doesn't anymore. Mostly, she stays by herself.

I know that Sarah is right that Meredith needs counseling. But I also know that Barry is right that it's legally risky. I remember reading about the case of a daycare worker in New Jersey who was accused of molesting dozens of children because psychologists, believing that the kids were abused, convinced them they were. We really don't need another witness added to the state's list because some so-called expert puts the wrong spin on my daughter's dreams. What we need is for this to end so we can get her the help she needs.

I hate to admit this, but the couples counseling has been helpful. It's nice to have someone to talk to. The past few months have been so hard, but Jasmine always reassures us that we're doing the best we can with a difficult situation. Her message seems to be that right now we're in crisis and we need to get through it. But if we want our marriage to survive in the long run, when the crisis is over, we need to make the marriage our priority. The question is whether we really want our marriage to survive. I think the answer is yes. I wouldn't bail on Sarah right now. I'm not that much of a jerk. But I also realize that Sarah and I are going to need to make some time just for each other. We need to take a vacation together.

Alone. Or maybe just a long weekend. I'm pretty sure the first step to fixing our marriage is paying some attention to each other. After this is over.

I've also been talking to the mother of one of the boys on my soccer team. Kristy Duschene is Jared's mom. She called the house after she saw the newspaper article to say how sorry she was. We ended up talking for an hour. She's a good listener. I didn't tell Sarah that she called. At first, I just forgot to mention it, and then I was afraid Sarah would think it was more than it is. Kristy and I talked a few times after soccer practice. Then, when the season was over, we started emailing. She started by sending me a bad lawyer joke to help cheer me up. I sent her one back. It's become a sort of contest. There are lots of bad lawyer jokes out there, so this could go on forever. We're not even really friends, but I don't want Sarah to think there's something going on. There isn't and Sarah has enough to worry about without thinking I might be cheating on her. It's just nice to have someone to talk to who isn't depressed and obsessed. I'm pretty sure Kristy is divorced. I've never seen Jared's dad at any of the soccer games and I don't have his email on my soccer contacts list. I haven't asked Kristy about her marital status because I don't want to give her the impression I'm looking for anything more than friendship.

We have to go back to court this afternoon for a status conference. Sarah comes to my office and we walk over to the courthouse together. The status conference itself lasts about five minutes. The attorneys tell the judge that they've completed the depositions. Barry says he expects that he will be adding a forensic psychologist to his witness list. The judge gives him two weeks to provide the name of the expert. Barry also says he'll be filing a motion to dismiss in the next week. The judge gives him two weeks for that too and sets a hearing for the end of January, six weeks out.

Afterward, Sarah and I meet with Barry in one of the conference rooms.

"We have some decisions to make," he says. "First, I want you to know that this is a winnable case."

"That's good to hear," I say.

"I've been out to the scene with my investigator," Barry says. "I deposed that guy Dave Belkin. He'll be a terrible witness for the state. The reason he got so much of it wrong was that he didn't actually see it. He couldn't have. He was looking in his sideview mirror from four hundred yards away for most of it. While he was driving. And approaching a major intersection. It turns out he thinks you did a U-turn because he went from looking straight on to looking in the mirror."

"Oh my God! This whole thing is based on a guy who didn't actually see it? How come they didn't mention the mirror in the police report?" Sarah is shaking her head. "My life has been ruined because that idiot didn't really see what happened."

"It should be easy to prove you didn't turn the van around," Barry says. "There wasn't even enough room for a U-turn. I can get my investigator to make a video of your van turning in that space. By the time I'm done cross-examining Dave Belkin, we should be able to put his testimony in doubt. All we need is reasonable doubt. But for the record, I can't make any promises. Any time you give a case to a jury, there's a chance they'll convict."

"Are they allowed to leave stuff like that out of the police report?" Sarah says. "It hardly seems fair."

"They're not supposed to," Barry says. "But it's not unusual. They're supposed to include all exculpatory information in the affidavit of probable cause. By that I mean the police report is supposed to include anything that might weigh against your guilt. Instead, they have a habit of only including the facts that help their version of events. That's why I told you at arraignment it would likely only get better as we dug deeper."

"But if they're not supposed to do it, why do they get away with it?" Sarah says.

"Even I know the answer to that one," I say. "Immunity."

"That's right. In the case of the police, it's qualified immunity, but it still makes them hard to sue," Barry says.

"Is it possible I could sue them?" Sarah says. This is the closest to happy I have seen her in months.

"You have to prevail on the criminal matter before you can even think about it. Right now we need to focus on getting this case dismissed if we can. But we still need to be ready in case this thing goes to trial. Which brings me to the next point. I want to hire an expert. I've already spoken to a forensic psychologist in New Jersey who can testify that Meredith's interview was unduly suggestive. That way, if this thing goes to trial, we can use him to try to quash Meredith's subpoena. If that fails, we can use him to discredit her if she says anything against you at trial."

"Are you saying Meredith might have to testify in front of a jury?" Sarah says.

"I'm hoping it won't come to that," Barry says.

I think I've known all along that it was a possibility, but it seems to be registering with Sarah for the first time.

"I won't allow it," she says.

"If this goes to trial, you may not have a choice. The state's attorneys can subpoena anyone they want. If they want to make her testify, they will. Unless we can get the subpoena quashed."

"How do we do that?" Sarah says.

"My expert, Dr. Lapitas, will testify that her testimony was tainted by the suggestive nature of the questioning, and that anything she says is unreliable. He'll also talk about how traumatized children are when they're forced to testify against their parents. We'll try to convince the court that, on balance, keeping Meredith out of the courtroom will best serve justice. I can't guarantee it will work, but it's our best bet."

"How much will this cost?" I'm well aware of the costs involved with expert testimony. I just never expected I would be the one paying for one.

"Dr. Lapitas will need a ten thousand dollar retainer. He charges a hundred and fifty dollars per hour for reviewing a case and writing a report. It's two hundred and fifty per hour for court testimony, plus travel. Which brings me to another point. We've gone through most of the first ten thousand dollars you gave me for a retainer. Marcy is preparing last month's statement for you. I need another ten thousand to get this through the motion to dismiss. If we win on that motion, you could end up with money back. If we lose, and you decide to take it to trial, I'll need more."

"How much more?" I say.

"I generally require fifty thousand dollars up front for a trial this complicated. I don't go into trial unless I'm prepared. Preparation takes time and time equals money."

Sarah and I look at each other. I suspect we're thinking the same thing: *We don't have $70,000.*

"When do you need the first twenty thousand?" I say, thinking about our home equity.

"As soon as you can get it together. I can't ask Dr. Lapitas to get started until he gets paid."

"Is there anything else that can be done to get this dismissed before we start spending that kind of money?" Sarah says. "We're talking about a lot of college tuition money." She looks at Barry and then me.

"I can go back to the prosecutor and try to get her to dismiss it. She might be more receptive now that she's seen me depose her main witnesses. If she's thinking objectively, she has to know by now that there are some holes in her case. The problem is that, once they take a case, prosecutors rarely change their minds. I might be able to get her to offer you a much better deal, but I doubt I can get her to drop it completely."

"What kind of deal are we talking?" I say.

"I can probably talk her down to probation and counseling. I might even get her to agree to a deferred sentence," Barry says.

"What does that mean?" Sarah is chewing her lip.

"Well, either way you would be on probation for a year or two. You'd have to report to a probation officer and attend some type of counseling, probably anger management and parenting. If I can get a deferred, after a few years the conviction would be erased."

"But both of those mean pleading guilty, right?" I say.

"That's true."

Sarah is starting to cry. "But I didn't do anything. And if I plead guilty, I probably lose my job. Not to mention, everyone will think I assaulted my daughter."

"I know. That's why I haven't been pushing you in that direction. I'm going to be honest with you. Most of my clients are guilty of something. My job is to get them the best deal possible. And convince them to take it. But, sometimes the system screws up and innocent people get dragged into it. For some of those people, taking a deal is still the best option. The system is set up to reward people who make plea deals. Whatever direction we go with this, it has to be your decision. There's a chance I can get the judge to dismiss the case. If that fails, there's a good chance I can win at trial. Again, no promises. And it's going to cost. The two of you have to decide how you want to proceed. Unless we're going to make a plea deal, it's time for me to talk to Meredith, figure out what kind of witness she's going to be, and get Dr. Lapitas reviewing her interview."

We thank Barry and promise to get back to him in the next few days. Then, Sarah and I walk back to my office so we can continue our discussion in more comfortable surroundings.

"I don't want Meredith involved in this," Sarah says as soon as the door is shut.

"What do you mean? She's already involved."

"I mean, I don't want Barry interrogating her. I don't want her testifying. I want her to go back to being a normal eight-year-old girl. This shouldn't be happening to her."

"I agree, but it is. The question is what's best for our family considering all the circumstances. Are you willing to plead guilty to something you didn't do?"

Sarah is staring at me, wide-eyed. Tears start to form. "I don't understand why there isn't another option."

"I don't know, but I trust Barry's assessment of the situation. Look, we both lose a lot if you make a plea deal. Obviously, you more than me. It looks bad for our family and it would affect both of us professionally. I think we should let Barry talk to Meredith and see what he thinks. Anything she says to him is confidential. Then we'll have a better idea what to expect."

"Has Meredith said anything to you about what happened?"

"Not really. And I haven't asked. I'm afraid that if I say anything to her, she'll tell someone and I'll be accused of influencing her testimony. The last thing we need is me getting disbarred."

"It's just too much to put on an eight-year-old. I'm sure Barry's a nice guy, but he's not trained to talk to children any more than that idiot police officer was. She did a lot of damage to Meredith. What if Barry makes it worse? I only see her once a week, but from what I see, Meredith is hurting, probably blaming herself for what's happening to our family."

I wonder if I should tell Sarah about Meredith's nightmares. Probably not.

"I don't want her to feel any worse than she already does," Sarah says. "She needs to talk to a therapist, not a lawyer."

"I agree that what's best for Meredith is staying out of this. The problem is that what's best for the rest of us may be putting her in the middle. What do you want to tell Barry?"

"Let's tell him to keep Meredith out of this as long as possible, but that we want to go forward with the expert and the motion to dismiss," Sarah says.

"In other words, let's commit to another twenty thousand dollars to try to get a dismissal?"

"Will he be okay with that?" Sarah says. "Are you okay with that?"

"Yeah, that sounds like a plan. And, don't worry about Barry. He'll do whatever we decide, even if he disagrees. If we say keep Meredith out of it, he will."

"Okay. Now for the twenty-thousand-dollar question. Where do we get the money?" Sarah says.

"The bank. Just like everyone else."

"We don't have that kind of money in savings."

"No, but we have the equity in our home. The house is worth at least two hundred thousand and we only owe about ninety at this point."

"I guess there's no other choice."

"Nope. And it makes sense to see if we can get a line of credit with at least seventy thousand dollars so we don't have to go back again in another month if we go through the first twenty without getting a dismissal."

"You're probably right. And here I was hoping we might pay off the mortgage before we retire."

"At least we have enough assets to cover the bill."

"What do people do when they have no way to pay for a lawyer?" Sarah says.

"I guess they plead guilty."

CHAPTER 20

Tamara Goodwin
Friday, December 21, 2012

I'm writing a memo for the judge when our secretary tells me Barry Densmore is here and wants to see me. It's ten o'clock and my memo isn't due until four thirty, so I figure I might as well see what Barry wants.

"I hope it's not a bad time. I was in the building filing my motion to dismiss in the Sarah Bennett case, so I thought I'd hand deliver your copy and see if you had a minute to talk."

Barry hands me a stack of papers.

"I can give you a few minutes, but I have a deadline this afternoon."

"Fair enough. I won't take much of your time. I'm hoping when you read this motion, you'll realize how weak your case is. I'm asking you again to consider a dismissal."

That again.

"Why would I do that, Barry?"

"Because it's Christmas and you want to spread some holiday cheer."

His smile reminds me of a barracuda. One who had braces as a child.

"Nice try. Any other reason?"

"Because your only witness didn't actually see what happened because he was looking in his sideview mirror as he was driving away. Surely that caught you by surprise during depositions."

He's right. The guy is going to make a terrible witness. But I will lose my bargaining position if I admit that, so I shrug. "I also have the kid."

"Maybe, maybe not. She's young. You never know how she's going to do at trial. And you know juries don't like prosecutors who make kids testify needlessly. Plus, our expert will testify that Officer Driscoll coerced her in the interview. You don't want to put that kid on the stand."

"Look, the woman dragged her kid behind a van. Any jury is going to think that was excessive punishment. They'll hold it against her, not me."

"First of all, she wasn't dragged. She ran. Second, you have to prove that the mom knew she was there. That's going to be hard, mainly because she didn't."

"There's enough circumstantial evidence."

"I disagree. Look, I just want you to read this motion carefully. We can prove that your witness got most of the facts wrong. He was wrong about the distance. He was wrong about the direction of the van. He was wrong that it changed direction. He was wrong that the kid was dragged. Now that we know about the mirror, we know why he was wrong—he didn't see most of it. It's a dog of a case. Especially if I can keep the kid out of it."

"It's not as weak as you make it sound."

"I'm just asking you to take a hard look at your evidence. I realize you may well win on the motion to dismiss. But, this is not a case you want to take to trial. I'm not saying that a jury is going to acquit in two minutes, but I'd be surprised if it takes more than ten. And that's likely to be months from now. What this family needs most is to put this behind them."

"So get your client to plead guilty. She can do counseling and put it behind her."

"Are you offering to drop the jail time?"

"Sure."

"What about dropping the felony?"

I pause to think about it. I'd rather take the felony conviction and dismiss the misdemeanors, but I also don't want to take a weak case to trial.

"Fine. But she'd have to plead to the more serious of the misdemeanors."

"I'll let my client know about your revised offer, but I doubt she'll take it. She's adamant she didn't know the kid was there. And I'm pretty sure if she pleads guilty, she'll lose her job and jeopardize her career."

Defense attorneys always say that people are going to lose their jobs, but it's almost never true. Besides, it's not my problem. If I worry about the collateral damage in all my cases, I won't be able to do my job.

"That's my best offer," I say. "And it's conditional. I'd rather not have to respond to your motion if your client is going to make a deal."

"I understand. I'll call her today. If you don't hear from me by Monday afternoon, you can assume she's not interested. I really do appreciate the better offer, but the truth is, I doubt she'll take it. Not if there's a chance the judge will dismiss the charges."

"Whatever. Let me know."

Barry and I wish each other a Merry Christmas before he heads out.

I finish the memorandum I'm writing after lunch. It's a routine motion to dismiss. According to Rule 12(d) of the Vermont Rules of Criminal Procedure, defendants can challenge whether the state has enough evidence to proceed to trial. It's mostly a way to weed out any case too weak to justify a trial. The process is stacked heavily in favor of the prosecution. In order to win, all I have to do is prove I have evidence on each element of the crime charged. Usually, I just attach copies of the witness statements. If there's a bit of evidence that's missing, I can get an affidavit from the witness. Or, if they're not cooperating, I can have them served with a subpoena. The memo I just wrote was for an aggravated domestic assault case. The defendant threatened his wife with a paring knife. The defense attorney argued that the knife wasn't a deadly weapon. It was a slam dunk for me and a long shot for the defense. Sometimes I'm not sure why defense attorneys file motions like that. I think they're just hoping the prosecutors will be so overwhelmed that we'll forget to respond, and the defense will win by default. I can't say it never happens. Just not often, and never with me.

I have a few hours until the end of the day, and I'm curious about what's in Barry's motion, so I decide to read it. The gist is that Sarah Bennett had no intent to harm her child, that at first she had no knowledge that the child was there, and that when she became aware, she took appropriate steps to ensure the child's safety. Barry attached portions of the deposition of Dave Belkin and affidavits from Sarah and James Bennett.

I have to admit that Dave Belkin was inconsistent in his statements, and the whole mirror thing is a problem. But I know his sworn statement will get me through the motion to dismiss. For purposes of the motion, the court has to consider the evidence "in the light most favorable to the state."

James Bennett's affidavit says that, when he arrived a few minutes after the incident, he spoke to his daughter. She said she was not injured and that she had run after the van. She never told him she was dragged, and he saw no signs of her having been dragged. In addition, she was standing approximately one hundred feet from the dance studio. This is, of course, inconsistent with Belkin's 200 feet and his deposition testimony that the child did not move from where she was standing in the time before her father arrived. James Bennett is probably lying, at least about the distance.

In her affidavit, Sarah Bennett denied turning the van around. She said all she did was drive away, and that once she realized what the kid was doing, she was afraid that if she braked too suddenly the child would trip and be hurt. She mentioned Crocs sandals, and said she slowed the van gradually to avoid injuring the child. I don't believe a word of it. I have to admit it's a good explanation. It explains most of the evidence. They must have worked hard to come up with it. However, there are two things it doesn't explain away. First, why was the van door open? People don't drive with the door open. It had to have come open while she was moving. Second, if she didn't think she was guilty of a crime, why did she act guilty when she was arrested. Innocent people don't say, "Go easy on me."

Barry's motion makes no mention of the kid's interview. According to Karen Driscoll, the kid admitted she was dragged and said the mom told her to let go of the van. That trumps Barry's arguments. All I have to do is submit a copy of the kid's recording and I'll win the motion. Then, they'll make a plea deal. My written response isn't due for two weeks, so I put Barry's paperwork on my desk with a yellow sticky note to remind myself of the date. I probably won't have time to look at it again until after Christmas, and maybe not until after the new year.

Tonight is a big night. Owen is going to meet my parents. We met at the gym and have been dating about a month. He called me a few days ago.

"What are you doing Friday night?" he said.

"I have a family thing. Every year my parents have an open house for Christmas. I pretty much have to go."

"Sounds like fun."

"You want to go?" I said, without thinking. I instantly regretted my impulsiveness.

"Sure."

"Really?"

"Why not?"

"It's going to be my family and my parents' friends and neighbors. Lots of old people."

"You trying to talk me out of it?"

"No. I just don't want to scare you off."

"Why would it scare me off?"

"I don't know, because the last time I brought a date to this thing was sophomore year in college. They might think we're serious."

"I can handle old people. Besides, maybe we're getting serious."

I'm a little nervous when Owen shakes my father's hand. I know they're sizing each other up. I told my mother a little about Owen on the phone, so it wouldn't be a surprise when I brought a date. She says hello, but she's so busy with the arriving guests and bringing out food that she doesn't have time to grill him. That's a relief.

It's a good party. My mom has put out tons of food as usual. Everybody seems to have brought wine and liquor. There are at least a hundred people, most of whom I only see once a year.

Owen is a hit. He's handsome and polite. Everyone acts impressed that he's a math teacher. I'm embarrassed when my cousin Annie holds a sprig of mistletoe over our heads. Owen just laughs and kisses me in front of my whole family.

The party gets crowded by eight o'clock. There are kids everywhere. My older sister has three. My brother has two. Most of my cousins have at least one. I'm the baby of my family, born seven years after my brother. I suspect I was a mistake though nobody would ever hint at that. I'm one of the few single people left in my generation. That is, if you don't count my cousin Heather. She's been divorced twice, and she's only two years older than me.

The kids are loud. They're playing under the dining room table and running circles around the house. A couple of them are sliding down the banister.

"I can't believe the parents aren't doing anything to stop them," I say. "They're awfully loud and out of control."

"That's what kids do, especially when they're excited," Owen says. "Don't you spend time with your nieces and nephews?"

"Not much."

"Do you like kids?"

"Sure. Of course. It's just that my sister lives in Boston. My brother lives in New Hampshire. I was busy with law school and now I have a very demanding job. I haven't spent much time with any of them."

"I see. As long as you're not one of those women whose career is so important that she never wants kids." He grins.

I'm not sure what to think. Is he teasing me? Or is he actually one of the few men I've met recently who wants to have a serious relationship?

"How about another eggnog?" I say.

CHAPTER 21

Nicholas Bennett
Monday, December 24, 2012

This is going to be the worst Christmas ever. My mom's not here. Which means all the things my mom usually does to make Christmas special aren't happening. Like, she always makes tons of Christmas cookies. I like the cutout cookies shaped like Santa and bells and trees and stuff that are sprinkled with colored sugar. Those are the best for dipping in hot chocolate. I also like the nutty ones that are covered in powdered sugar. They remind me of snowballs. This year, the only Christmas cookies in the house are the ones from the supermarket bakery. They're okay, but it's not the same.

Also, as long as I can remember we've always made gingerbread houses for Christmas. Everybody in the family gets to make and decorate a house. My mom buys bags of candy for the decorations. When they're all done, we put them together and sprinkle the whole thing with coconut and powdered sugar and make a snowy village. Then we get to eat the leftover candy. Every year it's the same, but a little different. When my sisters were younger, they made messy houses. Last year Meredith did much better. Camille, not so much. But it doesn't matter because this year we're not even doing it. My dad doesn't know how to make the house walls. And nobody remembered to get the candy for decorating.

It wasn't the same getting the tree without my mom either. We went to the same place we always go—Fender's Tree Farm. When my mom goes, we take our time. We pick three or four that look good and we vote. While my dad saws down the winner, my mom gets out hot chocolate and cookies. This year, the whole thing took about five minutes. No voting. No hot chocolate. No cookies. My dad pretty much picked the tree while we watched. Plus, it was cold and Camille forgot her mittens. The three of us went back to the car and waited while my dad cut the tree and tied it on the roof.

Decorating the tree was just weird. The ornaments were the same ones we always use, but something was missing. I thought it was just that my mom wasn't there. After we were done, I realized that we were also missing the tacky Christmas music that my mom always plays while we decorate the tree. She likes to sing along.

Nothing against my dad, but he just doesn't know how to do Christmas like my mom. Fortunately, it looks like my mom did most of the Christmas shopping. Over the past week, presents have been appearing under the tree. Not as many as last year. Hopefully, my grandparents will bring some more. They got here from Florida a few days ago. They're staying at the Marriott. They said it's because my grandpa has trouble with stairs. I think it's also because my mom's not here.

After dinner (frozen pizza again!), we watch *The Polar Express*. It's a good movie as long as you only watch it once a year. Then, when my sisters have gone to bed, I text my mom to see if she's still up. She calls my phone a minute later.

"What did you do tonight?" she asks.

"Nothing really."

"Did Daddy remember to read *Twas The Night Before Christmas*?" That's another one of our family traditions.

"Nope."

"Oh well. We can read it next year."

"Mom, can't you just come over to open presents in the morning?"

"Oh Nick, I wish I could. More than anything. But I'm not allowed to see Meredith."

"I know, but Mom, it's Christmas! We can make Meredith leave!"

"How do you think Meredith would feel if she didn't get to be there for Christmas?"

"Yeah, but I'd rather have you than her. Besides, this is all her fault. I hate her."

"Please don't say that. It's not her fault. There are a lot of people who are to blame for this, but Meredith is not one of them. She did something she shouldn't have, but she doesn't deserve what has happened any more than you and Camille."

"Whatever."

"No. Not whatever. Think about how you'd feel if you were Meredith. Remember the time you almost set fire to the tree house?"

"Yeah." I don't like to think about it. I was trying to light candles, but the matches kept blowing out. So, I lit a piece of paper, but it burned my finger, so I dropped it and this box caught fire. I didn't know what to do, so I ran for my dad. He brought the hose out and put out the fire. There are still burn marks on the wall.

"You knew you weren't supposed to have candles out there, right?"

"Yeah."

"But you did it anyway."

"Yeah."

"It's no different, Nick."

"Whatever."

"Look, I'm sorry, sweetie. This will all be over soon. Then, we can have things normal again. I promise we'll spend next Christmas together."

I hate it when she calls me sweetie, but I let it go. "Are you sure?"

"Yes, I'm sure."

I get up the guts to ask the question I've been wanting to ask for months.

"Mom, are you going to jail?"

"No, Nick. Why would you think that?"

"I read it in the paper. It said you could go to jail for fifteen years." She takes a few seconds before she answers.

"That's just what the paper says to make things sound more exciting than they are. I'm not going to jail."

"Okay," I say.

"The police made a mistake. The thing about this country is that you're innocent until proven guilty. I'm not guilty, so as soon as we're able to show they made a mistake, this will be over." I wish I believed her, but if the newspaper couldn't tell the police made a mistake, then the judge might not either.

"How much longer is this going to take, Mom?"

"I don't know. The problem is that nothing seems to happen quickly."

"Okay."

"I'll see you tomorrow afternoon. Grandma and Grandpa are taking Meredith over to their hotel so that I can see you and Camille for a little while."

"I wish they could just have Meredith go live with them so that you could come home."

"That wouldn't be fair to Meredith. Besides, they're going back to Florida in another week. Try to get to sleep soon. I'm sure your sisters will be up early to open their presents. You need your beauty rest."

"Yeah, right."

"I love you, Nick."

"Yeah. Good night, Mom."

When I wake up, my iHome says it's 4:37 a.m. That's actually late for me on Christmas morning. I go down to the living room to see what Santa brought. It looks mostly like it's supposed to. The stockings are filled with stuff. There's more presents than there were last night. I count the presents. It looks like I got three gifts from Santa this year. My sisters each got four. I hope that means I got the tablet I asked for. There's a box the right size. It's kind of a big thing. By big, I mean expensive. So long as I got it, I'm okay with my sisters getting more presents than me.

The family rule has always been you can check out your stocking as soon as you're awake, but you have to wait until the parents are up before you can open any presents. I'm dumping my stocking on the floor when Camille comes down the stairs.

"Did he come?" she asks.

"Yeah. Where's Meredith?"

"Upstairs."

"She awake?"

"I think so."

Camille empties her stocking and we both sort through the loot. After a while, we have piles of candy and little toys on the floor. It's still dark in the living room, but we don't turn on a light. If my mom was here, we would go up and jump on my parents' bed, and then my mom would get up and light the Christmas tree.

I plug in the tree lights, but I decide not to get my dad. He's not the one who gets up early with us. I notice there's lots of needles from the tree on the floor. The water bowl on the tree is empty. I think my mom uses a watering can to fill it, but I don't know where it is. I go and get a glass of water from the kitchen and pour it in the bowl. Unfortunately, I spill some on the presents. I make three more trips to fill the bowl. The wrapping paper on a few of the presents near the base of the tree is bubbling from where I spilled.

The sun starts to come up and I hear my dad moving around upstairs. By the time he comes down, light is coming in through the living room windows. That's when I notice the mistakes.

First, the Santa presents are wrapped in the same wrapping paper the family presents are wrapped in. Second, there are price tags on some of the stuff in the stockings. Santa does not shop downtown at Ben Franklin. The elves are supposed to make all this stuff.

Don't get me wrong. I don't believe in Santa Claus. I've known it's the parents since fifth grade. I just haven't told anyone I know. I figured I was more likely to get what I wanted if they thought I still believed. But Meredith's still in third grade, and Camille's only in first. I'm sure they still believe. I don't want to ruin it for them.

Camille is showing Dad the stuff she got in her stocking. I see a price tag on her chocolate Santa, so I pick it up and scrape it off. I'm about to put the Santa back in her candy pile, when she sees me.

"Hey, that's mine," Camille shrieks.

"Here. I was just looking." I hand it to her.

She looks at me like I was trying to steal it. My dad gives me a funny look. Do they really think I was trying to steal her candy? I know I have a reputation for torturing my sisters, but come on. I look at the piles checking for more price tags. When no one is looking, I scrape off two more. If I dump Meredith's stocking, I'll get in trouble. If I don't, she'll probably notice the price tags. Meredith is way more observant than Camille.

My dad goes into the kitchen to make coffee. Camille goes up to get Meredith. As soon as they're gone, I dump Meredith's stocking. I check each item for a price tag and then put it back in the stocking. I'm half done when my dad walks into the room.

"Nicholas, what do you think you're doing?" he says.

I'm about to explain when Camille and Meredith appear on the stairs.

"Nothing," I say.

"It's Christmas. Don't you think you could give it a rest for one day? Put that stuff back and give Meredith her stocking."

I quickly put the stuff back into the stocking. I see one price tag, but there's no good way to scrape it off. Hopefully, Meredith won't notice.

Meredith is really quiet while she looks at her stocking. She looks at each item and then carefully sets it aside. Camille is jumping up and down. "Hurry up, Em. I want to open presents!"

My dad is just sitting on the couch drinking his coffee. He looks like he'd rather still be in bed.

"Can we open our Santa gifts?" Camille says.

"Yeah, go ahead." My dad gets up and goes into the kitchen. I can hear him getting another cup of coffee.

Camille tears into the wrapping paper. I get the box I hope is my tablet. Fortunately, it's the one I wanted. I take it out of the box and look to see what's included.

Meanwhile, Camille has all four of her Santa gifts unwrapped and lined up on the floor. Meredith is just watching.

"Ooooh, I love them!" Camille is holding up matching outfits for her and her American Girl doll. She dances in a circle and then runs upstairs to get her doll.

She comes back, grabs one of Meredith's presents, and shoves it at her. "Open it, open it. I can tell from the outside it's the same thing. Come on!"

Meredith unwraps the present. She smiles, but she still looks sad. Camille is right. It's a matching outfit set. I have to admit they're kind of cute. Camille disappears for a minute and then comes back wearing her new outfit. She dresses her doll and then dances some more.

My other Santa gifts are smaller. A case and a keyboard for the tablet. Pretty cool setup. I'm not complaining about what I got. I just wish my mom was here to see them. Of course, she probably was the one who bought them. But still.

Camille forces Meredith to unwrap the other three Santa gifts. It's more doll stuff. I don't get it, but Camille seems excited.

"Wear your outfit! Wear your outfit!" Camille says.

"I will later. I want to stay in my pajamas right now. It's Christmas, so I don't have to get dressed," Meredith says.

I think about the mistake with the wrapping paper. There's Santa paper spread around the living room. I don't want my sisters to notice that it matches the rest of the paper, so I gather it all up and bring it to the trash can in the kitchen. My dad looks at me funny.

"Thanks," he says.

"Whatever," I say.

CHAPTER 22

Karen Driscoll
Tuesday, December 25, 2012

I literally offered to work Christmas day. The chief asked everybody when he was making the holiday schedule. Most of the other officers have kids, so I figured they'd want the day off. Besides, we get time and a half for working the major holidays.

My mom called a week ago.

"You coming to dinner at Aunt Susan's on Christmas?" she said.

"I can't. I'm working."

"Who works on Christmas?"

"We have twenty-four-hour coverage, so somebody has to work."

"But, you worked last Christmas."

"Did I?"

"And Thanksgiving."

"So?"

"You don't have to avoid the family, you know."

"I'm not avoiding them."

"Most of them don't care."

"But you do."

"You're still my daughter."

"And Dad does."

"It's Christmas. You could stop by when you get off work."

"Thanks, but I think I'll pass."

"You can always change your mind."

"I'll think about it," I said, knowing I probably wouldn't.

Christmas is slow. Pete Greene is the only other officer working the day shift with me. I spend most of the shift cruising around the streets. It turns out to be a sunny day in the mid-thirties. All the businesses are closed except the Quik Stop, the Mobil Market, and two other gas station/convenience stores, so there's very few cars. There's actually quite a few people out walking around, probably walking off Christmas overeating and enjoying the warmer temperatures.

We get dispatched to the hospital to deal with a violent patient, probably one of the local crazies. Pete pulls in behind me. He parks and follows me to the entrance. The emergency room doctor meets us at the door. He's gray haired and wearing a white coat over a plaid shirt and khaki pants.

"One of the nurses got him to calm down," he says.

"Who is it?" I say.

"The nurse or the patient?"

"Both," I say.

"The patient is Darrell Hastings. He's one of our regulars."

"We know him," I say.

"He's not usually violent. I think he's worked up because of the holiday."

"Probably. He assault anyone?"

"No, nothing like that. One of the nurses called you guys because he was clearly distressed and escalating, starting to swear."

"Sure. That's what we're here for."

"Anyway, Kelly went in to talk to him and got him to take a sedative."

"Kelly Hunter's working today?" I say.

"Yeah," he looks at me funny. "I don't think Darrell's going to cause any trouble here. We're trying to get someone from the counseling service to come talk to him."

"Do you want us to hang out?"

"If you don't mind waiting a few minutes."

"Sure."

Pete and I hang out by the nurses station. It's quieter than usual in the emergency room. The nurse at the station entertains us with a story about this pregnant woman who comes in every day thinking she's in labor.

"She should be showing up any minute now. It's usually about this time."

"One of these times, she's actually going to have the baby," I say.

"True. But she's not due for another month."

A round, petite woman walks quickly into the waiting area. "I'm with the counseling service," she says, pulling off gloves and a hat.

"Come on in. He's in Room 3," says the nurse.

She heads straight for the room. A minute later, Kelly Hunter walks out. She's blond with short curly hair and blue eyes. The scrubs with penguins on them would look ridiculous on anyone else. On her, they're cute. It's the first time I've seen her since last summer. She smiles brightly when she sees me.

"I thought I heard your voice," she says.

"I see you're working Christmas too," I say.

"Comes with the territory," she says. "I was away at Thanksgiving." She shrugs. "How've you been?"

"Fine."

"Are you seeing your family later?"

"Maybe. You here all night?" Why did I ask that? I'd rather not know.

"No, I'm done at three. Then we're driving down to Boston to spend a couple days with Shelly's parents."

"Oh." There's a pregnant pause. Pete has turned his attention from the nurse at the station and is watching me.

"It's good to see you," Kelly says.

"Yeah. Do you guys still need us?" I gesture in Pete's direction.

"No. Darrell's much calmer, and now that the counseling service is here..."

"Okay. Call us if that changes." I make eye contact with Pete and point toward the exit.

"Hey, Karen?" Kelly says.

"Yeah."

"Merry Christmas."

"Oh. Yeah. You too."

I finish up a little after 3:00 p.m. I'm really not up for dinner at Aunt Susan's. They probably haven't even started eating yet, but they're not expecting me, so nobody needs to know I could have made it.

When I get home, the sun is starting to sink behind the pine trees at the edge of the property. Arlo gives three deep barks to acknowledge my arrival. I quickly change into jeans, lock my gun, and grab my parka. There's just enough time take a short walk along our dirt road before the winter darkness makes it too hard to see the slippery patches. Now if I could only stop thinking about Kelly.

CHAPTER 23

Sarah Bennett
Thursday, January 25, 2013

I'm a nervous wreck. Today is the hearing on the motion to dismiss my case. I truly hope today is the end of this nightmare, but at the same time, I'm afraid to be too hopeful. It will be so good to kiss my children good night. It's been four and a half months. I've completely forgotten where we were in the Percy Jackson book I was reading to the girls. Maybe tonight we can get back to it. I asked Barry last week about our chances. He said he thinks it's fifty-fifty that the judge will dismiss the case. I wish I knew whether that guess was pessimistic or optimistic.

We've been waiting for weeks to see if the prosecutor was going to subpoena Meredith for this hearing. Barry thought it was unlikely, but he wanted us to know it was possible. This past week was the worst. I kept staring at my phone, wondering when James or Barry would call and say they'd gotten the subpoena. I probably called James three times a day to see if anything had happened. I took my cell phone with me to the bathroom. I checked my voicemail every time I left my desk. We never got a subpoena, so Meredith is at school right now.

The temperature outside is twenty below zero, so James and I drive the three blocks from his office to the courthouse. Even dressed in a long wool coat, scarf, and hat, I feel the cold sink into my bones just walking from the parking lot to the entrance. We meet with Barry in one of the conference rooms.

"What's going to happen?" I say.

"I don't know," Barry says. "We'll see what Tamara does."

"How long is this going to take?" I feel like I'm blindfolded, making my way through a maze.

"Probably not long. The court set aside an hour in case there was evidence, but since Meredith wasn't subpoenaed, I doubt we'll need it."

I want to ask more questions, but there's a rap on the door and someone says, "The judge is ready."

We file into the courtroom. Barry and I head to the counsel table. James sits behind us on the other side of the railing. Other than the clerks at the front of the room, the only person present is the prosecutor. She looks young and innocent seated at the counsel table. Looks are deceiving. I remember how ruthless she can be.

The judge enters and we all stand briefly.

"State of Vermont versus Sarah Bennett," the clerk says. "Attorney Densmore for the defense. Attorney Goodwin for the state."

Everyone waits for the judge to start. "It looks like we're here for a hearing on the defense motion to dismiss under Rule 12(d)," he says. "Mr. Densmore, this is your motion. Do you plan to present any evidence?"

"It's possible that I'll have rebuttal evidence if Ms. Goodwin presents evidence. If not, we'll rely on our written submissions. I do, however, wish to make legal arguments in this case."

"Very well. Ms. Goodwin?"

"The state does not have any witnesses, Your Honor. We too will rely on our written submissions."

"All right. The evidence in this motion is closed. Mr. Densmore, your argument?"

"Thank you, Your Honor. As more fully described in our written motion, the state cannot meet its burden of proof in several respects. I'd like to start with the felony attempted domestic assault. First, and probably most importantly, the state has no evidence of intent to harm the child. In order to make a case for attempted domestic assault, the state must show that my client either intended to harm her child, or that she acted knowing that there was a significant likelihood that child would be harmed. I think a close examination of this case will show that the state has not met its burden for purposes of this motion. In her affidavit, my client not only denies any intent to harm the child, but she also denies knowledge of the child's actions for most of this unfortunate incident." Barry sits.

"Ms Goodwin?"

"There's rarely direct evidence of intent and this case is no different. But, the state does have significant circumstantial evidence that, at the very least, the defendant knew that her actions were putting her child at significant risk of serious bodily injury. I think there's no dispute that, if the child had gotten caught under the van, she could have been killed or seriously injured."

The judge nods. He's watching the prosecutor, giving her his full attention. She makes eye contact with him before going on.

"And there is plenty of evidence that the defendant knew of her child's predicament. First, the child was in the road when she turned the van around. She had to have seen the child. Second, the child opened the door on the moving van. She had to have known of the danger to the child when the door opened. Yet, despite being aware that her daughter was in the road and had grabbed onto the moving van, the defendant continued to operate the motor vehicle with the child hanging on for two hundred feet. The child was dragged by the van. The defendant could have stopped the van. Instead, she told the child to let go, and kept driving. Fortunately, the child was able to safely let go and get to safety. Another citizen who witnessed the event was concerned enough that he stopped to check on the child. But, the defendant didn't even stop to check on her own child. She was so focused on punishing the child that she just left her there. That's the state's evidence of intent."

The prosecutor sits down. It's so hard to listen to her describe with such certainty a series of events that never happened. Barry is immediately on his feet.

"Mr. Densmore?"

"As detailed in our written submissions, unfortunately, the state has most of the facts wrong. In her affidavit, my client has given a complete description of what happened. The van never turned around and the door was open before she started driving. The distance was approximately one hundred feet and the whole thing was over in five seconds. There was no intent to harm the child because there was no knowledge that the child was there. This version of events is corroborated by the affidavit of the child's father who arrived minutes later. The state is relying wholly on the written statement of David Belkin and the interview of the minor MB.

"First of all, Mr. Belkin is completely unreliable as a witness. He didn't see what happened because he was looking in his sideview mirror from about a quarter mile away. We've attached an affidavit from my investigator that proves there wasn't enough space on that road for the van to have made a U-turn as described by Belkin. He got that wrong, just like he got most of the rest of it wrong, because he didn't actually see it.

"Your Honor, try walking backwards while looking in a mirror. It's confusing. I don't blame Mr. Belkin for being confused. I do blame him for making sworn statements about something he didn't see. I've also attached excerpts from Belkin's deposition, where he fully described his vantage point. It explains why many of his statements are inconsistent.

And then there's the two hundred feet. Belkin didn't come up with that number on his own. Officer Driscoll suggested it to him. Then, she took him back to the scene and asked him to measure. It's no surprise he measured out two hundred feet, given that's the number he was told in advance. But that doesn't mean that's what happened. In fact, there's plenty of evidence that it's not what happened.

"Second, if this case proceeds beyond this motion, the defense will present expert testimony that the child's interview was tainted by the suggestive nature of the questioning. But for purposes of this motion the matter is moot because the interview with MB is hearsay and therefore inadmissible. The Rule 804a hearsay exception only applies to interviews of children under ten in cases involving sexual abuse. This case does not involve sexual abuse. So, what the state is left with is nothing. Definitely not evidence of intent beyond a reasonable doubt."

"What do you say to that Ms. Goodwin?"

"The child's interview is a sworn statement. For purposes of this hearing, the state can rely on sworn statements."

"No, it's not a sworn statement," Barry says. "At no point in the interview did the interviewing officer have the child swear to tell the truth. The officer asked one question designed to determine if the child understood the difference between truth and untruth, but she never elicited any promise from the child to tell the truth. The officer didn't even explain to the child the importance of telling the truth. She's eight years old. She could have provided a sworn statement, but she didn't. I have here a transcript of the child's interview if the court would rather not have to watch the DVD submitted by the prosecution."

The judge nods and holds out his hand. Barry walks forward and gives him a copy. He drops one on the prosecution table before he sits down. The prosecutor is glaring at him.

The two attorneys basically repeat the same arguments with regard to the other two charges. Barry is adamant that there was no knowledge, and that knowledge is a requirement for the state to go forward. The prosecutor argues that there is circumstantial evidence.

When they are done, the judge says, "I want to take time to review the submissions. I'll issue a written decision. Anything further?" I guess that means I'm not going home today. At least there's still hope this will end soon.

"No, Your Honor," the prosecutor says. Barry just shakes his head.

Court is adjourned. The prosecutor gathers her things and walks out quickly without looking in our direction.

"Why does she seem mad?" I say to Barry.

"Because she knows she made a mistake, and I took advantage of it."

"How's that?"

"When she filed her motion response, I realized she thought Meredith's interview was admissible, and that she didn't need to subpoena her for the motion hearing. I could have made that argument in our papers. Instead, I waited until after the evidence was closed to pull it out so it would be too late to realize her mistake."

"What does that mean?"

"We won't know until we get the judge's decision, but at least Meredith didn't have to testify today."

"Thank you. I don't know what I would have done," I say.

"How long until we get a decision from the judge?" James says.

"Depends on how busy he is. Anywhere from a few days to a few weeks. He's been averaging about two weeks."

"What are our chances? Really?" I say.

"I can't say. The hearing went well for us. But, judges usually side with prosecutors. I guess I still give it fifty-fifty."

I have my weekly visitation with Meredith this afternoon in the courthouse, so there's not time to go back to work. I call my mother and tell her about the hearing. Then, I check in with Betsy, who says that things are under control at the shelter. Betsy wants to know about the hearing, so I repeat everything I told my mom. I still have time to kill and I don't want to spend it at the courthouse, so I walk up the street to get a Diet Coke from the convenience store. After walking a hundred yards in the arctic temperatures, I opt for hot coffee instead. I get a chocolate milk for Meredith.

As usual, I'm waiting in the supervised visitation room when Meredith comes in with Paula. When I hug her, I don't want to let go. I'm so relieved she didn't have to testify today. The thought of what could have happened terrifies me.

When I finally release her, she looks at me funny. "Why are you all dressed up, Mommy?"

"I had an important meeting this afternoon." I'm afraid to say more because Paula is sitting in the corner. I wonder if telling Meredith I was in court would constitute discussing the case with her.

"What kind of meeting?"

"Adult stuff. I got you a chocolate milk."

"No, thanks."

"Is chocolate milk still your favorite?" I say.

"Yeah. I just don't feel like it."

"Okay. You want to play?"

Meredith goes over to the bookshelf to retrieve the Uno cards.

"They're not here," she says.

"Someone probably put them in one of the boxes. Don't worry, we'll find them."

We look on the top of the boxes of toys, but the cards are not near the top of any of the three boxes.

"I don't see them." Meredith sounds panicked.

"They're probably here, we just need to look harder." I dump one of the cardboard boxes on the floor. Together, Meredith and I put each item back in the box. The Uno cards are not in the first box.

We repeat the process for the other two boxes of toys, but don't find the cards. Meredith is stiff, arms by her sides. There are tears in her eyes and on her cheeks, but she is not making a sound.

"Let's look behind the bookcase. Maybe they fell." She doesn't move. The Meredith I remember would have been searching for the cards in all parts of the room or would have found a substitute activity. I don't know this new Meredith.

I pick her up and hug her to my chest. "Oh, my baby girl, it's going to be all right," I whisper in her ear. "I love you so much."

Paula looks at me quizzically, and I realize that she's concerned because she can't hear what I'm saying. I stop whispering and just hug Meredith. After a minute I say, "The cards may still be here, but if they're not I'll go and buy a new pack tomorrow, if we still need them."

"I like playing Uno with you," Meredith says, misunderstanding my meaning.

"Well then, let's look some more and, if we can't find them, I promise I'll get some cards."

The cards are not behind the bookcase. Nor do we find them anywhere else in the room. "I'm going to buy some cards tomorrow and keep them in my purse at all times," I say. "It makes sense. You never know when you might need Uno cards."

Meredith nods slightly. She's no longer crying, just blinking fast.

"How about the face game?" I say. It's an activity I've used many times with the kids while waiting at car repair shops and doctor's offices.

Meredith's nod is almost imperceptible. I get a notepad and pen out of my purse. We settle onto the couch together, thighs touching. I just want her close to me right now. I draw a circle on the pad and hand it over to Meredith. She draws a set of eyes and hands it back to me. I add eyelashes and hand it to her. She adds ears and then it's my turn.

We finish two faces before I feel Meredith's body relax.

"How was school this week?" I ask.

"Okay."

"What happened?"

"Nothing."

"What are you studying?"

"I dunno."

"Are things okay at home?"

"Sure."

I give up on conversation, but we draw a total of eight faces before James shows up to take Meredith home. I give her another long hug off the ground before handing her over to James. He slides her down, takes her hand, and leads her from the room.

I'm unable to stop myself from crying. Paula just says, "I'm sorry," and shakes her head as she leaves the room. While I try to compose myself, I look through the faces that Meredith and I have drawn together. I realize that none of them are smiling.

Friday is the third day of the cold snap. A series of snow showers last week made everything look white and clean. Icicles hang from the eaves of the older downtown buildings. Our town looks deceptively beautiful from the warm side of a window. The temperatures are not expected to get above zero again today and they're still well below when James and I arrive at Jasmine's office.

It's starting to feel like the only thing James and I do together is go to marriage counseling. I'm tired of it. And I know we're supposed to be trying to hold our marriage together, but all I want to talk about right now is Meredith.

"She's not okay," I say. We've been seated for a minute and I'm already crying.

"None of you are okay right now," Jasmine says. "This whole thing has been really hard on all of you."

"No, it's worse than that. She's like a flower that's been picked. It feels like she's dying slowly." I tell them about Meredith's reaction to the missing Uno cards and the sad faces.

Jasmine furrows her brow. "James, what do you think about Meredith? You see her more. Is it always that bad?"

James is quiet for what seems like a minute. Jasmine is patient, so I follow suit. Finally, he answers. "It's never good and sometimes it's pretty bad. She hasn't been herself since this whole thing started."

"Of course, I can't offer an official diagnosis, but from everything you've told me over the past few months, she may well have been traumatized by the police interview and no-contact order, and now she's depressed. Explain to me again why this child is not in counseling."

"Meredith is the principle witness against Sarah. We don't know what she might say to a counselor. She was convinced to say some incriminating things by the police. We're going to try to get the police interview excluded and keep Meredith off the witness stand. We don't want there to be any other witnesses putting words in Meredith's mouth or testifying about what she says."

"But, what about confidentiality?" Jasmine says.

"There are exceptions. And we don't want to have to litigate the issue. If there's no counselor, there's no issue to litigate," James says.

"Wow, so what you're saying is that the system that's purporting to protect this child essentially discourages getting her the help she needs."

"Yes," James and I both say.

"How are the other two children doing?" Jasmine asks.

"Nick seems okay," James says. "He doesn't say much."

"But that's partly the age he's at," I say. Jasmine nods.

"Camille was hit pretty hard in the beginning," James says. "She really missed Sarah those first few weeks. But now it's almost as if she likes that she gets Sarah's undivided attention every week."

"I can see that," Jasmine says. "Some kids adjust quickly. It's probably no different for her than if this were a divorce situation."

"I'm glad *she's* adjusted," I say. "I sure haven't. Camille's turning seven next week. I made party invitations for a few of her school friends, and James is going to handle the party." Jasmine smiles at James. "When Camille asked if I was going to be at her party, I told her that I'll be out of town for work. I lied to her. God, I hate this. It means I'm not even going to see her on her birthday."

"Why did you lie?" Jasmine asks.

"Because it's more important that Meredith is there," I say. "James and I talked about it. He could have taken Meredith somewhere else and I could have run the party, but it didn't feel right to exclude Meredith. Besides, I'm not sure how the other parents would feel about leaving their kids with me."

Jasmine is clearly contemplating the dilemma. "But why not just tell her the truth?"

I'm having difficulty swallowing, so James answers. "Because she's too young to fully understand what's going on, and we don't want her to blame Meredith for her mother's absence."

Jasmine nods. "How much longer is this likely to drag out? I really think we need to get Meredith into counseling."

"Hard to say," James says.

"We're waiting for a decision on the motion to dismiss," I say. "There's a chance it will be over soon."

"I hope so for all of your sakes, especially Meredith's."

CHAPTER 24

Karen Driscoll
Monday, January 29, 2013

I stop by the State's Attorney's Office to drop off some cases for the afternoon arraignments. I'm orienting one of the new officers.

"Tamara, I want you to meet Tad Hastings. He started at MFPD today, so I'm showing him around."

"Nice to meet you, Tad. Welcome to the jungle. Karen, what the hell were you thinking when you interviewed the Bennett kid?"

"Um... excuse me?" I say. Tad slowly backs away. I wish she hadn't lit into me in front of the new guy.

"You didn't get her to swear to tell the truth."

"I thought all we had to do was show they understood the difference between the truth and a lie. That's what I remember from my training," I say.

"That might have been fine if it was a sex assault or an L and L. There's a statutory exception for sex cases, so all you have to show is an indicia of reliability. But this was a regular assault. I needed to either have a sworn statement or put the kid on the stand."

"So, why didn't you put her on the stand?"

"Because I didn't realize you didn't swear her until it was too late."

"That's not my fault. You could have listened to the recording." I can't believe she's trying to blame me.

"No, it's my fault. For assuming you knew how to do your job. How hard would it be to make the kid promise to tell the truth? It only takes a few seconds. You should do it in every case. Just like you get the adults to sign sworn statements."

"It's harder than you think. There's a lot to remember. And you never know how long you'll get with these kids. Look, I got her to tell everything her mom did. That ought to count for something."

"Yeah, it counts. As long as the judge doesn't dismiss the case."

"How could he dismiss it? It's solid. We have a witness who saw everything."

"Apparently there are problems with your witness. Lots of them."

"What kind of problems?"

"Let's start with the fact that he was looking in a mirror. And he was a quarter mile away."

"So?"

"You mean you knew about that and didn't put it in your report?"

"What difference does it make? He was clear about what he saw. And he signed a sworn statement."

Tamara is shaking her head.

"I really don't see what the problem is," I say. "The judge found probable cause. It's my job to write a report that shows probable cause. I did my job."

"You're wrong. Your job is to investigate and build strong cases. You have to think further ahead than probable cause. It doesn't do me any good to get probable cause if the judge dismisses the cases later. Or worse, if I lose at trial."

"Why would you lose?"

"Because your witness is weak and they have evidence you got things wrong."

"Are you suggesting that Sarah Bennett is innocent?"

"No, of course not."

"Good. Because I have no doubt that Sarah Bennett is guilty."

"Neither do I."

"They're all guilty. We wouldn't arrest them if they weren't guilty."

"I know. It's just that I don't like surprises."

I introduce Tad to the two other deputies, Sanjiv Singh and Brett Peterson, and the state's attorney, Fred Dutton. After we leave the office, Tad says, "They all seemed nice, except maybe that Tamara. Do we work with her a lot?"

"Oh yeah. She does all the domestics, but don't worry, her bark is worse than her bite."

"Do we work *for* them?"

I laugh. "They'd like to think so, but we really don't."

"So, how come she can talk to you that way?"

"It's just the way she is. It's a lawyer thing. They go to law school and pass the bar exam and they think they know more than everybody else. Just wait, the defense attorneys are worse."

"So what exactly is our relationship with the prosecutors? A couple of them came to the academy and gave lectures on legal issues, but nobody explained how it works."

"You want to know how it works?"

"Yeah."

"Okay, here's what you do. Listen to what they tell you about the law. They usually know the law better than we do. Usually."

"Okay."

"But when you need to decide how to handle a situation, trust your gut. We know people better than they do. And they have no idea what it's like to be on the front line."

"What happens if we don't do what they tell us?"

"That's the thing. Nothing really."

"Can they do anything?"

"They can yell at us, like she just did. They can decline our cases."

"Isn't that bad?"

"Do you really think she's going to walk away from a child abuse case just because I forgot to swear the victim?"

"Would she?"

"No. They want to nail these people as much as we do."

"Do they ever decline our cases?"

"Sure. All the time. But they're almost always the cases we weren't sure about to begin with. Besides, you can affect what they do by the way you write your report."

"How?"

"If you want them to take a case, when you write your report, make sure you put in all the details that show guilt. Really convince them. If you're not convinced yourself, write it more in the middle."

"Okay."

"The prosecutors like to think they're in charge, but we have a lot of power too. You just need to learn not to let them get to you."

CHAPTER 25

James Bennett
Thursday, February 14, 2013

I thought I would pull my hair out if I heard the song "Firework" one more time, but I got through Camille's birthday party last week. Sarah got each partygoer a set of fairy wings and a wand. The girls danced in the living room. Thank God Sarah gave me a list of things to do with them. I just wish she hadn't been crying when she dropped off the goody bags at my office.

Now I have to deal with Valentine's Day. I never know what I'm supposed to do. This year is especially tricky. I haven't slept with my wife in five months. I pick up a card and a bundle of flowers at the grocery store and decide to drop them at the shelter. I know I've made a good choice because Sarah smiles when I walk in the door of her office. It's not a joyful smile, but her dimples show and she looks genuinely pleased to see me.

"Happy Valentine's Day," she says and meets me in front of her desk. We hug and share a lingering kiss. For that brief moment in time I feel connected. I enjoy the feeling of my wife in my arms. I almost forget that our life is in shambles. Almost.

After a minute, she goes back around the desk and I settle into her guest chair. She pulls a card and a small box of chocolates from her purse.

"For you," she says. We both open our cards. Before her name Sarah has written, *"Thank you for standing by me during what I hope will be the worst time in our marriage. I'll love you forever."* I should have written something more on her card. I just signed it, *"Love, James."*

"Did you give the kids their valentines this morning?" Sarah says.

"Sure thing." The truth is that I'd almost forgotten. The kids were getting ready for school when Nick pulled me aside and reminded me it was Valentine's Day.

"Did they like the cards I made?"

"Yeah. That was a nice touch. Of course they liked the little baskets of candy too. You know that technically Meredith's card was a violation of your conditions of release, right?"

"I know I'm not supposed to communicate with Meredith, but it's Valentine's Day. Would they really put me in jail for making my kid a valentine?"

"I don't know. I'm just reminding you."

"This whole thing is ludicrous." Sarah slams her desk drawer. "How's Meredith?"

"She's no worse," I say. "You can see for yourself this afternoon when you visit. I was thinking... do you want to go out to dinner for Valentine's Day?"

"I don't know," Sarah says.

"We could try to find someone to watch the kids. Remember, it was our homework assignment from Jasmine before this whole thing started."

"I appreciate the sentiment. I really do, but I still hate going out in public. This town is so small you never know who you're going to run into. I always feel like people are judging me."

"When do you think that will get better?"

"When my name is cleared."

"No matter how this turns out, there will always be people who judge you. You can't avoid everyone."

"I know. But I'll feel better when the people we know realize I didn't do this thing. Besides, aren't our finances a little tight right now?"

I nod.

Just then, Sarah's phone rings. "Excuse me a sec." Her face turns white. "We'll be right there," she says and hangs up.

"What's going on?"

"That was Barry. He just got a written decision on the motion to dismiss. He wants to talk in person."

Damn. I know that if it were good news, he would have just told her on the phone. That's what I'd have done. Sarah is shaking.

"I think I should drive us over there," I say. She nods and grabs her purse from her desk drawer. I wish I could think of something to say to help prepare her.

"Whatever it is, we'll cope. Whatever it is, it isn't over," I say. Her clenched jaw and pained eyes tell me she knows what I'm expecting.

When we arrive, Barry sees us immediately. We haven't even settled into our chairs when he says, "The clerk just emailed me the decision. There's good news and bad news."

"Good first, please," I say. Sarah nods.

"The judge dismissed the felony charge."

"I take it the bad news is that the other two charges are still pending," I say.

"That's right."

"Can we have a copy of the decision?" I say.

"Of course. You can read the whole thing later, but the gist is that the judge felt there was insufficient evidence of intent for the felony, since Meredith's interview was inadmissible and that Belkin guy's testimony was inconsistent."

"So, why didn't he dismiss the whole thing?" Sarah says.

"Well, I'm still scratching my head on that one," Barry says. "I think he's a baby splitter."

I nod, but Sarah looks confused. "He's a judge that doesn't like to make difficult decisions, so he splits things down the middle even if it makes no sense," I say.

"Baby splitter? Like the Bible story?" she says.

"Not exactly," I say. "More like if you can't decide who should get the baby, you cut him in half anyway. It's an ugly analogy, but with some judges it's apropos."

"Oh. That's awful."

"Ironically, the judge relied on your affidavit, Sarah, to support the remaining charges," Barry says.

"My affidavit? How?"

"In the decision, he says you admitted that you continued to drive briefly after you became aware of Meredith's predicament."

"What?"

"Remember, in your affidavit we explained how you were afraid to brake too suddenly, so you slowed the car gradually."

"Of course. I was so afraid she was going to fall under the wheel if I did anything sudden. She was wearing Crocs. You thought it was important to tell the whole story."

"Well, the judge used it as justification for upholding the remaining charges. He said that a jury could find beyond a reasonable doubt that you acted recklessly and negligently. He also said you essentially admitted knowing you had acted recklessly when you said, 'Go easy on me.'"

"But, I never said that. And if I'd stopped too quickly she might have been killed!" She is already wiping tears from her cheeks with the back of her hand.

"Look, Sarah, we know all of that," I say. "Meredith may be alive because you did the right thing."

"The judge was looking for a place to hang his hat," Barry says. "He wanted to keep some of the charges. If it hadn't been that, he would have found another reason."

"But why?" Sarah is shaking.

"Judges don't like to dismiss charges. Tamara made a mistake by thinking Meredith's interview was admissible. He probably felt he had no choice but to impose consequences for that mistake, but he didn't want to punish her by dismissing the entire case."

"This isn't a game. It's my life."

"I know. But the people who work in the system get so desensitized that they lose sight of that. Some judges are better than others. I get the sense that this judge is biased toward the prosecution."

"So, what happens next?"

"We go back for a status conference the week after next to talk about whether the case is going to trial. We're in better shape now that the felony is gone. I can try to make a deal if you want. If not, we need to start getting ready for trial."

"I want a trial. As long as Meredith doesn't have to testify," Sarah says.

"We have Dr. Lapitas lined up. I have a forensic report from him saying that Meredith's interview was unduly suggestive. He says the interview will have tainted her testimony. He also quotes studies on the impact on children who have to testify against their parents. If they subpoena Meredith, we'll move to quash. But there are never any guarantees. We already know we're dealing with a baby splitter. In some ways those are the most dangerous judges."

"When are we likely to get trial dates?" I ask.

"I'm pretty sure that all the March trial dates are taken. Bob Jasper has a week-long civil trial. If we're lucky, we can get dates in April. Otherwise, May or June. I think this will be a three-day trial."

"Why so long until the trial?" Sarah asks.

"The court is busy."

"But I've been away from my family for five months. I just want to get home."

"Now that we're only looking at misdemeanors, I can file another motion to amend the conditions of release. We might have a better chance of getting rid of the no-contact order now."

"Do you think the judge might do it?" I say.

"I don't know," Barry says, "but it won't hurt to ask again. I can file a motion early next week. But before I do that, are you sure you don't want to make a deal? With the felony gone, I might have a chance at getting you a deferred sentence. The court always makes time for changes of plea. We could get in to see the judge for that within a few days."

"Remind me what a deferred sentence is," Sarah says.

"You plead guilty and get probation for a year or two. After you successfully complete probation, the charges get dismissed. You get a clean record. So far, Tamara hasn't offered that, but she might be more amenable now that she realizes what the judge thought of her star witness."

"But I have to plead guilty to something I didn't do?"

"Yes, but we might be able to do an *Alford* plea."

"What's that?"

"When you say that you're only pleading guilty because you don't want to suffer greater consequences. Sometimes prosecutors will let people do that."

"I'm having a hard time with the idea of pleading guilty. And if I go that route, there's a good chance I'll lose my job. Not to mention the damage to my reputation."

"I get that. And I'm willing to take this to trial, but there's always a chance of losing. You need to be aware of the risks. Do you want me to try to make a deal?"

"Probably not. Not yet anyway. James and I need to talk about this. I'm so overwhelmed right now. I was hoping that this would be over when we got the decision. I need to process this."

"Of course. Just let me know," Barry says.

"Barry, thanks for getting rid of the felony. Good work," I say.

"You're welcome. Sorry it wasn't better news."

On the way back to her office, Sarah is silent. "Do you want to go somewhere and talk?" I say. "We could go home. The kids won't be there for a while."

"Okay."

I pull into our driveway and we walk silently into the house. As soon as we're inside, we both stop, not sure where to go. Not sure where to start. I pull Sarah to me and hold her. She clings as if I'm a life raft. After a minute, she pulls away. She takes my hand and leads me to our bedroom.

There's no joy in the sex that follows, but there is comfort and release.

"Thank you," she says when she's lying beside me with her hand on my chest.

"For what?"

"For helping me forget for a few minutes. It's the first time I've forgotten what's happening. Usually, it is the first thing I think of when I wake up and it's with me all day."

"I'm sorry," I say.

When I get back to the office, I have a valentine email from Kristy. It's not a romantic greeting, just an animated cartoon of a bear giving hugs with a caption that says, "Happy Valentine's Day." I don't feel right sending her a valentine, but I feel the need to acknowledge her email, so I call her cell. Or maybe I just want to talk to someone other than Sarah about today's disappointment.

Kristy answers immediately.

"Thanks for thinking of me on Valentine's Day," I say.

"Of course I thought of you. I think about you a lot," she says. I don't admit it, but I think about her often too. I tell her about the ruling in Sarah's case.

"Oh James, I'm so sorry. What will you do?"

"We'll probably keep fighting. It's what Sarah needs to do. But personally, I'm tired of fighting the system."

"I don't blame you. This has been hard on you. Is there anything I can do?"

"Not right now. Just keep listening."

"Whatever you need, James. All you have to do is ask. You know I'm not super busy with my business right now."

"Thanks. It's good to not feel so alone in this."

CHAPTER 26

Tamara Goodwin
Thursday, February 14, 2013

Owen is taking me out to dinner for Valentine's Day. He arrives at my apartment with a bouquet of bell-shaped pink flowers that I think are lilies. He looks awesome in Chinos, a button-down shirt and a tweed wool jacket. His hair is damp and freshly combed, so I'm guessing he came from the gym. When I see him, I'm glad I put on a black tailored miniskirt and a silk blouse. He wouldn't tell me where we're going, so I wasn't sure how to dress.

I give him an enthusiastic kiss and then put the flowers in water.

"Are you going to tell me where we're going yet?" I say.

"Wouldn't you rather be surprised?"

"I generally hate surprises, but I can wait."

"Well, I guess you'll find out in a few minutes anyway. I have a reservation at Chez Marie."

"On Valentine's Day? I'm impressed."

"I made the reservation a week ago."

"Wow. You're a true romantic."

"Does that surprise you?"

"No. It's just that most men are inept when it comes to Valentine's Day."

"I'm not most men."

"You sure aren't."

Our table is ready when we arrive. The restaurant is dimly lit, but I can see it only holds a dozen candlelit tables. All are set for two tonight. A small fire crackles in the stone fireplace. Owen orders a bottle of Merlot.

"To us," he says and raises his glass.

"Happy Valentine's Day," I say. I decide it's a good time to give him his gift. I really didn't know what to get him, but I wanted to have a gift, so I got him a pen. It was fairly expensive. I got it at the stationery store downtown. I replaced the blue ink cartridge with a red one. I also got a card. Inside I used the pen to write in red ink, *"Now you can think of me every time you correct math homework. Love, Tamara."*

"It writes red?"

"Yeah."

"Cool. Definitely a step up from a Bic. Thanks."

"You're welcome. Thanks for inviting me here. I've wanted to go here since I moved to town."

"Me too, but I needed a special occasion."

"I see why people like it."

"You haven't even tried the food."

"I'm sure it's great."

We order food and chat about the other restaurants in town. Not surprisingly, Owen likes the places that have big portions. We both sip our wine at the same time and there's a moment of silence.

"How was your day?" I say.

"The usual. Although, this might interest you. I caught these two juniors sipping peppermint schnapps in the boys' bathroom after school."

"You're kidding."

"Nope. It was a travel-sized Listerine bottle, so it was only about a shot."

"But it was on school property. And they're underage."

"I know. The craziest part is that I know the two boys. They're both good students, not particularly popular. I wouldn't have expected it from them. But, you never can tell with kids. Hopefully, this will turn out to be the only slip on the path to a successful life for both of them."

"What did the school do?"

"They called the parents. Both boys were suspended for the rest of the week. The school policy is they'll be allowed to return to classes next week as long as they've begun counseling."

"And the police were involved, right?"

"No."

"Why not? It's a crime to drink underage."

"If we got the police involved, they would have records. They'd be in the system. These are kids from good families looking at topnotch colleges. We don't even know if there's a problem. We're talking about a couple of ounces of schnapps. The only reason I noticed was it was the wrong color for Listerine and they were acting funny about it. There's no reason to screw things up for them just because they did something stupid."

"There's stupid and then there's criminal."

"Kids experiment all the time. They try to get away with things just to see if they can. If it happens again, we'll deal with it differently. But it probably won't."

"But that's not the school's call to make. You guys should have reported it and let the State's Attorney's Office decide whether to prosecute."

"Fortunately, our policy is more flexible. We want to encourage kids to get help. If I'd caught them selling marijuana in the bathroom, we absolutely would have called the police. But there's a spectrum of behavior and not all of it warrants legal consequences. There wasn't even enough schnapps to get buzzed."

"Wow."

"Are you telling me you never tried alcohol when you were in high school?"

"Actually, I didn't."

"Really?"

"Not until I was twenty-one." I'm lying. When I was in high school, my best friend and I did some sampling from her parents' liquor cabinet one night while they were out. We got tipsy and felt terrible the next morning. I can't tell this to Owen because he'll say it's the same thing, in some ways worse.

"Well, Ms. Goody Two-shoes, we know these kids better than you do. We're in a better position to decide appropriate consequences. Obviously, I shouldn't have mentioned it. I hope you're not going to go off and get your boss involved."

"Don't worry. I understand it's a confidentiality issue. I'm not going to say anything. I just don't get why you guys don't have a zero-tolerance policy on this."

"We do. It's not like we looked the other way. We just don't think that prosecuting people for every minor mistake is the solution. Let's change the subject. How was your day?"

"I lost a motion in the Bennett case today."

"Is it a big deal?"

"You know what? Let's not talk about work anymore. I just want to enjoy being with you tonight."

"Works for me. Let's talk about all the fun stuff we're going to do this summer. I have two months off and I want to do a lot of hiking."

CHAPTER 27

Nicholas Bennett
Tuesday, March 5, 2013

Things just keep getting worse. The season is almost over and I haven't been snowboarding once. We usually get family passes to Bear Glen, but this year my dad said that, because my mom couldn't help out, he didn't want to buy passes. He promised we'd still try to go a few times after the court stuff was sorted out. The court stuff is still not sorted out.

I also remember that my parents promised us we would go to Disneyland this year for April break. I'm twelve and I've never been. At some point, I'm going to lose interest. Well, maybe not for a few years, but still. My grandma died and left my dad some money last year. That's when they promised the trip. They said that Grandma Anna would want us to use the money in a way that we could have good memories of her. Now, my dad is saying we can't take any trips because the court case is costing a lot of money. He also says we can't make any plans for April because there may be a trial. How's that going to make us remember Grandma Anna?

My dad never used to talk about money. The other night, I wanted to get pizza, but he said it was too expensive and that I'd have to just have frozen pizza. There's nothing special about frozen pizza. We have it at least twice a week. I have a feeling that money is the real reason we haven't been up to the mountain yet this year. My dad has turned into a cheapskate.

My mom is really tense. I still talk to her every day. We usually FaceTime at bedtime. And we text while I'm riding the bus home. My mom always asks me about my day. It irritates me, but at least she asks. She always asks about my sisters too. That's even more irritating.

My dad says he isn't sure if he's going to be able to coach soccer this spring. He says it will depend on the trial. I really don't get that. My dad has always been the coach. Mr. Baxter has always been the assistant coach. It will suck if he's the head coach this year. He always plays his son and his son's friends more than everyone else. My dad's much more fair about playing kids.

My sisters are really getting on my nerves. Meredith never wants to do anything anymore. I went in their room the other day because I was bored. Meredith was just laying on her bed. I asked if they wanted to play Wii Mario Kart. It's much better with more people. Camille screamed at me to get out, but Meredith didn't say anything. I had to play Wii by myself. Again.

CHAPTER 28

Tamara Goodwin
Friday, March 15, 2013

I rarely hear from Owen during the day because he's busy with his students, so I'm surprised when he calls midmorning.

"You're not going to believe this," he says.

"What?"

"I got tickets for the Grace Potter show at Higher Ground this weekend."

"That's great. I thought it was sold out."

"It is. Has been for months."

"So, how'd you get tickets?"

"This guy I know. His grandmother died, so he has to go to Minnesota for the funeral."

"That's too bad."

"Yeah. I'm just lucky he offered me the tickets. Anyway, we could go up to Burlington on Saturday afternoon, have dinner, and then go to the concert."

"I told you I have to work this weekend."

"Yeah, but it's Grace Potter. In a small venue. And you can't be working all weekend."

"I should. I'm swamped with new cases and I have a two-day trial starting on Tuesday."

"So, you're working on Saturday night?"

"No, but I'm planning to work all day and I'm meeting the victim early on Sunday morning to do trial prep. I need a good night's sleep. I was hoping we could go out to eat around here and watch a movie at my place."

"But now that we have Grace Potter tickets, you're going to change the plan, right?"

"I'd love to, but I've done nothing to get ready for this trial. I can't go in there unprepared. I'll look like an idiot. And it's not fair to the woman who got beaten by her husband."

"So, you're not going with me?"

"Can't you go with Chap?"

"Yeah, but I'd rather go with you."

"Me too, but it's a bad time."

"Is it ever a good time?"

"Look, things go in cycles around here. April and May are going to be crazy. Hopefully, that means that the summer will be slow."

"You work more than anyone else I know."

"Maybe."

"And that's not even taking into account the calls from the police at two o'clock in the morning."

"Sorry."

"So, why don't you get a job with normal hours?"

"Because I love my job."

"You could probably make a boatload working for a law firm and not have to work as hard."

"Believe it or not, this job is fun."

"Fun?"

"Yeah. It's a challenge. Like a game of chess. Or Risk. But more complicated because there are variables you can't plan for. You have to be able to think fast."

"Well, have fun working while I'm at Grace Potter."

"I'd rather be going with you, but I can't."

After we hang up, I consider calling back and changing my mind. Maybe it won't take as long as I think to get ready for this trial. Who am I kidding? If I don't work all weekend, there's no way I'll be ready.

The problem is I really don't want to blow this thing with Owen. He's the first guy I've been with since college that I may be in love with.

That's not completely honest. I'm pretty sure I'm in love with him. I'm just waiting for him to say it first. My birthday is coming up. Maybe he'll say it then.

In the meantime, I need to focus on the trial. I'll make it up to Owen the weekend after.

As if I didn't have enough on my plate, the Sarah Bennett case is turning out to be a thorn in my side. When I took it, I thought it would be run-of-the-mill child abuse case. Of course, that was before Barry Densmore got involved. I was pissed that the judge dismissed the felony count. It's not like I needed the felony. I had already offered to dismiss it as part of a plea deal. What pissed me off was that Barry outmaneuvered me. He realized I made a mistake and took advantage of it. If I had been in his shoes, I probably would have done the same thing. But it still sucks to lose.

After we got the ruling in that case, we went back a couple of weeks later for a status conference. I had expected Barry to talk about a deal before the hearing. Instead, he stayed in the gallery with his client until the case was called. I'm guessing Barry thinks that, because he got the felony thrown out, he can win this at trial. Not without a fight. If this goes to trial, I will give it everything I've got, even if it means I don't get to see Owen for a week. I do not want to lose to Barry again.

The first question from the judge was whether the case was definitely going forward.

"The state is prepared for trial, Your Honor," I said. I always say that, whether I'm ready or not.

"The case is not going to settle, Your Honor," Barry said.

"Well, then. I see that the defense filed a motion to review the conditions of release. You want to lift the no-contact order, is that correct, Mr. Densmore?"

"Yes, Your Honor. Mrs. Bennett has been residing outside the family home since September. The no-contact order has had a negative impact on the entire family, especially the juvenile, MB."

"I see. What's your position, Ms. Goodwin?"

"The state opposes any modification to the conditions of release. The no-contact condition was imposed for good reasons that haven't changed."

"That's only true if the state subpoenas MB," Barry said. "The defense will not be calling her."

"Ms. Goodwin, will the child be testifying?"

I hadn't thought about it before then, mostly because I assumed the case would settle. Dave Belkin might be enough to carry the trial, but there were serious issues with his testimony. I might need the kid to win.

"The state is planning to subpoena MB, Your Honor," I said.

"Then the defense will be filing a motion to quash, Your Honor," Barry said. "We have an expert forensic psychologist lined up."

"I'll expect a written motion, but can you tell me what the grounds are?" the judge said.

"Basically, our argument is two pronged," Barry said. "First, the child's testimony was unduly influenced by the police interview. Second, the child will be further traumatized if she is forced to testify."

"It sounds to me like the motion to modify and the motion to quash are inextricably linked. I'm going to deny the motion to modify conditions for now. I'll revisit the issue at the time of the motion to quash. How much time do you need for your expert?" the judge said.

"I think we should set aside half a day, Your Honor."

The judge looked at the clerk seated in front of the computer. "When is the soonest we can find half a day?"

"I have the morning on Wednesday, April twelfth." That was good. Six weeks out was plenty of time to prepare and plenty of time for them to change their mind about a trial.

"Very well," the judge nodded. "And how long do the attorneys anticipate for the trial?"

"I'll need a day and a half for the state's witnesses," I said.

"I'll need at least a day as well," Barry said.

"We'd better set aside three days for the trial then. Can we find three days in May?" The judge looked at the clerk again. The clerk nodded yes.

"Let's put this on for jury draw on May ninth. You'll get notices by email. In light of the issues raised today, I'd like to appoint a guardian ad litem for the child."

Barry was on his feet quickly. "I have to object, Your Honor. There's no authority for a GAL in a case like this. We're not in family court and it's not a sex abuse case."

"Do you have any authority prohibiting me from appointing a GAL?"

"No, Your Honor. But, I'd respectfully urge you to consider the circumstances. The child was already traumatized by her interview with the police. The family does not want her further damaged by inept interviewers."

"Well, I want an independent perspective, so I'm ordering it."

"If you won't change your mind, will you at least allow the father to be present for the interview? To support the child."

"That's fine, I suppose. Ms. Goodwin, you have a week to subpoena the child. Mr. Densmore, you have two to file your motion."

The whole thing sounded ridiculous. How is the kid going to be damaged by an interview with a GAL? I'm sure it was just more of Barry's tactics.

Testifying is a bigger deal, but kids testify all the time. I realize it's not ideal, but they get through it. We do what we have to do to get convictions. It's all about the greater good. Sometimes you have to make a kid testify to protect society from the bad guys. Every time we convict a bad guy, it's much less likely some other kid will be harmed.

I don't know much about this expert psychologist, Dr. Lapitas. I didn't take his deposition because I didn't want to have to pay his hourly rate to do it. It means submitting paperwork to central office for approval. Besides, I don't like to waste money on cases that are not going to trial. I thought this case was going to settle. Lapitas is probably like all the other defense experts I've encountered. You pay them enough money and they'll say whatever you want them to say. I'm actually glad I didn't depose him because now I'll get to cross-examine him at the motion hearing for free. The Bennetts will have to pay for him to come up here. I can get a sense of him before the trial.

Of course, Barry may just be pretending to gear up for trial so that I'll make him a better deal. The truth is that the whole process is about posturing. It's just like any other negotiation. The more the other side thinks you're coming from a good bargaining position, the better the deal you can make.

I sent out the subpoena right after the hearing. Then, I made a call to DCF. It occurred to me that nobody from DCF had been in contact with me about this case. In most cases involving serious child abuse, there's a family court case that parallels the criminal court case. It seemed unusual that I hadn't heard anything, and I wondered why. Mostly, I wanted to make sure the case doesn't get thrown out because I failed to turn over a file. I got Samantha Burnham on the phone. She's one of my favorite DCF investigators. She comes across as compassionate, reasonable, and confident. I liked having her as a witness in a couple of my other cases.

"What can you tell me about Meredith Bennett?" I said.

"Who?" Sam said.

"Sarah Bennett's kid."

"Oh."

"You know her?"

"I know who she is. What do you want to know?"

"Do you guys have a file on her?"

"Just the intake generated when Karen Driscoll made the mandatory report."

"Did anyone from DCF talk to the kid?"

"Nope."

"Why not?"

"The supervisor didn't validate the report."

"That's strange."

"Not really. Everybody here knows Sarah Bennett. She works with DCF as part of her job. Nobody believed she would assault her child, and we figured it was probably just a misunderstanding."

"A misunderstanding?"

"We deal with out-of-control kids all the time. It's what we do. Most of the time it's not the parents' fault."

"But sometimes."

"Sure. Anyway, the supervisor thought the case would get dismissed after you reviewed it."

"But it wasn't."

"Then, when you took the case, she said if it turned out Sarah got convicted, we could open a file. Otherwise, nobody wanted to waste the resources. You know how busy we are. Other than this incident, we have no reason to open a file on this family."

I thanked her and hung up. I should have realized it was a matter of resources. The state government is so strapped that it's hard for people to do their jobs. DCF is notoriously short-staffed. That makes it even more important that I get a conviction in this case.

Earlier this morning, I sent out an email to all the other deputy state's attorneys asking about Dr. Lapitas. Barry was required to send me a copy of his curriculum vitae when he listed Lapitas as a witness. His credentials are impressive on paper. He has a Ph.D. in psychology and has published articles in various journals. He participated in many studies including one on the use of leading questions in child interviews. I'm already thinking about how to cross-examine him. If I'm going to win this trial, I absolutely have to win the motion to quash. If the kid is not allowed to testify, I have a weak case. Now I want to know what Dr. Lapitas' weaknesses are.

Fortunately, the other deputies are quick to respond. Unfortunately, the responses indicate that Dr. Lapitas is good. Too good. Three deputies tell me they had judges refuse to let kids testify after Lapitas testified as an expert. Apparently, he cited several studies showing that children's memories are frequently altered by the use of leading questions in an interview. I need a way to attack those studies. I ask the other deputies to send me any material they still have from their hearings and make a note to study the transcript of the kid's interview I got from Barry. I probably should have gotten my own transcript before the motion to dismiss, but I didn't want to waste the resources. Just one more challenge of working for the state.

I'll spend some time with the interview after my trial next week. I'm sure it's not bad in terms of leading, but I need to be extra prepared for this hearing. Barry may have won the last battle, but I am still planning to win the war.

CHAPTER 29

Sarah Bennett
Wednesday, March 20, 2013

Six months down, two months to go. But who's counting? I really don't understand why this is taking so long. Barry says there are cases that have been pending for longer and that we're lucky to have gotten trial dates in May. I don't feel lucky. I feel like a puppy left tied to a tree in a thunderstorm. I just want to go home. We don't have to go back to court again until April when we have the hearing to find out if Meredith has to testify. Now it's all about waiting. And wondering. And trying not to get my hopes up.

When I saw Meredith last week, things were the same. I'm so worried about her. I'm afraid she'll forget how to be happy.

My visits with Nick and Camille still feel unnatural. Since it's been too cold to be outside, it's been hard to come up with things to do. We usually just hang out at Betsy's. At least it's better than supervised visitation.

Thanks to Barry, I still have a job. At the board meeting in November, he convinced the board that the case against me was weak. He told them he had advised me not to discuss the case with anyone, including the board, while the charges were pending. I think it helped that Barry is a friend of Blaise Rutherford, the chairman of the board. Blaise is the president of the local bank and sits on more boards than anyone I've met. He never misses a meeting.

At the January meeting, Janice Higgins tried to bring up my criminal charges, but Blaise simply asked me if the charges were still pending. When I told him we were still waiting for a hearing on the motion to dismiss, he told Janice to drop it. I was thankful.

I wish I could have come to tonight's board meeting and told them it was all over and that I could get back to focusing my energy on the shelter. After we read the minutes from the last meeting, the board wants a full report on the fundraising drive. Unfortunately, the news is not good—we're fifteen percent behind where we were last year at this time. I hand out a fact sheet showing how many solicitations we sent out and how many donations we've received to date. I explain the data.

"I suspect contributions are down because people no longer view this as a reputable charity," Janice says. "If they have to choose between two charities, people choose the one they trust."

"I don't think that's the issue," I say.

"Of course you don't. You're the reason the shelter has a black cloud," Janice says.

I meet her bitter stare and try my best not to sound defensive. "People are still feeling the recession. All the nonprofits are feeling pinched. If you look carefully at the report, you'll see that the number of donations is ahead of where it was last year at this time but that people are giving less. That doesn't necessarily reflect negatively on us. It's just the economy."

"Convenient excuse," Janice says.

"The important question is how we're going to make up the difference," Blaise says, rescuing me. "We still have a budget to meet."

"We may need to do some creative fundraising," I say. "Summer is a good time for outdoor events. Maybe we can have a walkathon or something. Let's think about it. In the meantime, I'm planning to send a second round of donation requests to the previous donors who have not yet given this year."

"What about the grants that we depend on? How certain are they?" Bill Harrington asks.

"They're likely to be renewed," I say. "As long as we get in our applications for next year on time. I've got one application due this month and another in May. Don't worry. I know how important these are. They pay the salaries of some key people. Without them, we'd be short-staffed."

We spend some time discussing fundraising ideas, but table the discussion after Blaise points out that it doesn't make sense to put a bunch of time into an event that only raises $500.

The meeting is nearing an end when Bill asks the question I've been dreading. "What about your court case? Is it over? I haven't seen anything in the paper."

I feel like every person in the room is studying me, waiting to judge. "No. It's not over."

"Where do things stand?" Blaise asks.

"The judge dismissed the felony. We have trial dates in May for the other two charges."

"There's going to be a trial." Janice pats her chest. "That will look good in the newspaper. I can just see it: 'Director of the Murdoch Shelter convicted of child abuse.' I guarantee *that* won't have a positive effect on the fundraising."

I can feel the heat in my face. "It wouldn't have a positive effect on my family either. I didn't ask for this and I don't deserve it." I study the faces of the board members. I don't sense any glimmers of compassion. Mostly they look blank, fixed, except for Janice, whose eyebrows are raised and lips are pursed. I want to tell them what happened, make them see that I'm being persecuted. But I'm not supposed to talk about the case.

"Look, I love my job and I care a lot about the shelter. I would never intentionally do anything to harm it. Just like I love my kids, and I would never intentionally do anything to harm them."

"If you care so much about the shelter, maybe you should step down," Janice suggests.

"But I didn't do anything wrong."

"If that's the case, why didn't the judge dismiss all the charges?" Janice asks.

"I don't know."

"He or she must think you're guilty."

"You have no idea what you're talking about. You have no idea what it feels like to be accused of something you didn't do. You have no idea what it's like to have the weight of the system bearing down on you. None of you do. And I hope for your sakes that you never find out. Because if you did, I doubt you'd be so quick to judge." I can feel the tears welling in my eyes. "Excuse me."

I go to the bathroom and lock the door. I study my face in the mirror. I hardly recognize myself anymore. I look ten years older than the woman I remember from six months ago. I shouldn't have lost it in front of the board. It was unprofessional. But I'm so tired of holding my tongue. I want to tell them they're stupid for believing what they read in the paper. I want to tell the prosecutor what an idiot she is. I want to tell the judge to get a backbone and do the right thing. Most of all, I want to tell Karen Driscoll to go to hell and stay there so she can never damage another family the way that she has damaged mine. But I'm not allowed to say anything to anyone because it might jeopardize my case. When this is over I'm going to tell every one of them what I think of them.

When I've recovered, I head back to the meeting room. Everyone except Blaise is gone. He's waiting by the door, a long black overcoat draped over his left arm.

"Are you okay?" he says. "Stupid question."

"At this point it's all relative. I'm still here. Some days that's the best you can do."

"Do you want to take a leave of absence? Under the circumstances, everyone would probably agree to it. Of course, it would be unpaid. You know how tight the budget is."

"I appreciate the offer, but I'm better off working. First of all, my legal bills are unbelievable."

"I can imagine."

"Second, what would I do with myself? Right now my job is the only thing keeping me sane. If I sat around and thought about how unfair this whole situation is, I might go crazy."

"Fair enough. For the record, I don't think there are many people on the board who question your dedication. It's just that most of them don't know what to think. Or how to act. This whole situation is so outside the norm for them."

"Why are you different?"

"I've been listening to Barry's stories for twenty years. And I've been around long enough to know there are two sides to every story."

I nod. "What happens, God forbid, if I get convicted of these charges? I'd like to think it can't happen, but I know from what I've read on the internet that it does. More often than people realize. What I mean is, am I going to lose my job?"

"Let's cross that bridge later. Obviously, there are people like Janice on the board who will want your head. But I, for one, would like to think that the people on this board are more open-minded than that."

CHAPTER 30

Karen Driscoll
Monday, March 25, 2013

I just got the "Officer of the Year" award. It's not a huge deal, but it was kind of cool. I got a plaque. I got my picture in the paper. There was an article in the *Gazette*.

> MFPD Detective Driscoll is Officer of the Year
> by Manny Rodriguez
>
> Middleton Falls Police Detective Karen Driscoll is the Rotary Club Officer of the Year. The award is given annually to a police officer in Adams County who exemplifies excellence. Driscoll joined the department in 2007. She worked patrol for several years before becoming the primary investigator for child abuse cases in 2010. According to Rotary president Ted Newman, "Detective Driscoll was selected because of her demonstrated dedication to protecting children." MFPD Chief Harold Higgenbottem said, "We are lucky to have Officer Driscoll as the lead child abuse investigator. These are some of the toughest cases we get. Officer Driscoll has worked hard to learn techniques for handling them. She has gotten results that make Middleton Falls a safer place for children." Driscoll is a 2003 graduate of MFHS.

I wasn't sure how the other officers were going to react to the article. The day after the paper came out, I had just finished some paperwork at the barracks when Tim Bartlett and Sergeant Patterson walked in.

"I see you got a promotion," Tim said. "Not only Officer of the Year, but now you're a detective. I didn't know we had detectives."

"I didn't tell him I was a detective," I said. "Manny Rodriguez just made an assumption."

"Who'd you pay to get the award?" Tim said. "We know you didn't sleep with Ted Newman."

"Well, we know *you're* not going to get any awards for sleeping with anyone. You still paying for sex?" I said.

"You're just jealous, Bartlett," Patterson said. "Congratulations, Driscoll."

"Thanks, sarge. I didn't even know I'd been nominated. I was pretty surprised," I said.

"Well, you've had your name in the paper a lot during the past year," Tim said. "That probably helped."

"Definitely," said Patterson. "The Rotary guys don't know anything about law enforcement. They know what they read in the paper and what the chief tells them."

"I guess all that brownnosing paid off," Tim said.

"That's not fair," I said. "I'm a brownnose because I went to a training nobody else wanted to go to?"

Tim shrugged. "The Bennett case didn't hurt either."

"Yeah, you were on the front page with that one," Patterson said.

"Here, let me get the door for you, Your Majesty," Bartlett said. "Make way for the officer of the year." He bowed as I walked through the door.

My mom even called the day after the paper came out.

"I saw that article. In the paper," she said.

"It's really not a big deal," I said.

"Oh. Okay. Well, congratulations, anyway."

"Thanks."

"I'm surprised, you working with kids. I thought you didn't want kids."

"I like kids. I just probably won't have any."

"No, probably not. Unless you meet a man you like enough. One who doesn't have a problem with your history. And can put up with you being a cop."

"Mom. That's not going to happen."

"I guess not. You can't blame me for wanting grandkids."

"Ted will probably have kids."

"It's not the same. You're my daughter. I really don't understand why you decided to be a police officer. No man is going to want a wife who's a cop."

"That's okay. I don't need a man."

"I guess you don't. You still with that woman?"

"I told you. We broke up last summer."

"Oh. Anyway, Dad says congratulations too."

"What are you guys up to?"

"You know. The same old stuff. Take care of yourself."

I got a notice this morning from Tamara Goodwin that I have to attend a motion hearing in a few weeks in the Bennett case. When I call Tamara to ask what the hearing is about, she says they're trying to keep the kid from testifying. She wants to make sure I'm there in case she needs me. I guess the case is going to trial. I better tell the chief that he needs to keep me off the schedule for that morning. What a waste of time. I don't understand why Sarah Bennett doesn't just make a plea deal. I heard the judge threw out the felony. That must mean the two misdemeanors are solid. She should plead out and save us all the trouble.

CHAPTER 31

James Bennett
Thursday, March 28, 2013

L ast week I wrote a check for $50,000 to Barry Densmore. That has to be the largest check I've ever written. It depleted our recently opened home equity line of credit. I don't know what I'll do if Barry needs more money for the trial. There's no more equity to tap. I guess we'll have to start selling things. Of course, that's easier said than done. I have a feeling we would take a loss on the house if we had to sell it right now. Both our cars have liens. We don't really own anything else that people would want to buy.

Today, the guardian ad litem is coming to our home to interview Meredith. Barry says there's no authority for a GAL in a case like this. If Sarah gets convicted, it could be grounds for an appeal. Of course, that doesn't help us now. Barry and I talked about what the limits of the interview should be. I've also thoroughly read the report prepared by Dr. Lapitas. I'm now aware of how the type of questions can influence the answers, something I had not thought about much before, even though I'm trained to ask questions.

Our conundrum is that this person, some guy who's a volunteer with almost no training, can make the difference between whether or not Meredith has to testify. He can help keep her out of the courtroom. On the other hand, if he's as unskilled at questioning children as Officer Driscoll, he could potentially do more damage both to Meredith and to Sarah. I'm struck by how naive the Vermont court system is in granting this degree of responsibility to laypeople. But, we have to work with the court order. So, according to Barry, my role should be to appear cooperative unless the guy does anything suggestive. Even then, I need to be gentle with him. We want him on our side.

I pick up Meredith early from school. The GAL is supposed to be at the house at two o'clock. That should give him plenty of time to talk to her before the other kids get home on the bus at three thirty.

I'm not sure how to explain this man to her. His name is Keith Bumpus. That's all I know at this point. I'm aware that kids repeat things, so I don't want to say anything that might jeopardize the case or scare her.

"Why did you pick me up early, Daddy?" Meredith says as we are walking from the school to my car.

"Well, sweetie, there's a man coming to our house to talk to you."

"Will you be there?"

I cringe. "Of course. I promise to be with you the whole time."

"What does he want to talk about?"

"He wants to talk to you about what happened last year with Mommy."

"Is he a police officer?"

"No. He's just a man who works for the court."

"Can we ask him to let Mommy come home?"

"I think he's going to be the one asking questions. You should just do your best to answer."

When we pull in Keith Bumpus is waiting in the driveway. He's sitting in his Prius, reading something in his lap. After we're out of my car, he gets out. He looks about seventy years old, with a mop of white hair and bright blue eyes, made larger up close by glasses. He walks with a slight limp. "Keith Bumpus," he says and extends his hand.

"James Bennett." We shake.

"And this must be Meredith. Nice to meet you both."

Meredith is clinging to my leg, something she hasn't done in several years. I invite Keith into the living room. He takes a seat on the chair. Meredith and I head for the sofa. She has her body pressed up against my side.

"Meredith, I'm here today to get to know you a bit. That's all. Is that okay?"

Meredith snuggles closer, but doesn't answer.

"My job is to talk to kids who are involved in the court process to make sure that things aren't any harder for them than they have to be. How are you doing?"

Meredith wrinkles her forehead.

"You don't need to be afraid of me. I really am here to help you if I can. Do you understand?"

Meredith still doesn't answer. She's staring at the wall.

"Meredith, it's okay to talk to Mr. Bumpus," I say. "And I'm here if you need me."

Keith nods approvingly. "That's right, Meredith. We can talk about anything you want. And you should call me Keith. I just want to get to know you a little. Did you just come from school?"

She doesn't respond. Keith keeps trying for about fifteen minutes. He tells her about his hobbies and tries to get her to talk about what she likes to do, but Meredith won't talk to him. Finally, he gets up as if to leave.

"Meredith, why don't you wait for me upstairs in your room," I say.

She gets up and looks directly at Keith. "Please let Mommy come home," she says softly and then runs up the stairs. We hear the bedroom door shut.

"Is she always that hard to talk to?"

"Only since the police interview. She used to be a normal eight-year-old."

"Is it worth trying to talk to her again on a different day?"

"You're welcome to try, but I can't offer much hope. The only person she talks to these days is her sister."

Keith nods. "I need some advice on this one. I've never been so stonewalled by a kid before and I've been doing this for five years."

"What got you into it?"

He laughs. "I'm a retired engineer. I don't play golf, and I was looking for something worthwhile to do."

"Well, thank you. I'm sorry this was a wasted trip."

"That's okay."

"Please call me if there's anything else you need."

As soon as he pulls out of the driveway, I go up to the girls' room. Meredith is lying on her bed.

"Why didn't you talk to him?" I say.

"I was afraid."

"But he seemed like a nice man. He wasn't going to hurt you."

"I was afraid I would say it wrong again."

"What do you mean?"

"Nick says it's my fault that Mommy can't come home because I ran after the van and then I said it wrong last time. I didn't know what I was supposed to say."

I sit down on her bed and gather her to me. "Oh sweetie, it's not your fault Mommy can't come home. None of this is your fault."

"But I ran after the van. I knew I wasn't supposed to."

"Of course not. It was dangerous. But that doesn't make the rest of it your fault. This whole thing is too complicated to explain. But the one thing you have to remember is that you are not to blame."

"I just want Mommy to come home."

"We all do." I realize that the only way Meredith will survive testifying is if Sarah is acquitted. If Sarah is convicted, Meredith will blame herself. She's too young to have that much pressure on her. And she's too young to understand the nuances of the situation. She was already led to agree with things that didn't happen. What will stop it from happening again?

"How about you and I go downstairs and have ice cream for a snack. We don't need to tell Camille and Nick."

"No, thanks. I'm not hungry."

CHAPTER 32

Tamara Goodwin
Wednesday, April 3, 2013

I wish I knew how many trials I'm going to have this month. Owen wants to go away for a week. He called me last night. I was still at the office getting organized for today's jury draw.

"I'm almost afraid to ask, but what are the chances of you getting the third week in April off?" he said.

"I don't know. Why?"

"It's school vacation week."

"It must be nice having a teacher's schedule."

"My uncle has a cottage on the beach on Cape Hatteras. It's off season so nobody's using it. You want to go?"

"You mean a week and a half from now?"

"Yeah."

"It's not much notice."

"I guess not."

"We're drawing juries tomorrow and I didn't black out the dates."

"Is that a 'no'?"

"No. It's a 'that sounds great, so I'll do my best.' What would we do?"

"Beach stuff. Walks in the sand. Kayaking on the sound. Did I mention the cottage is right on the water?"

"I like the sound of that. How would we get there?"

"It's about a twelve-hour drive."

"So a long weekend isn't an option?"

"I don't want to spend two days driving to get two days on the beach."

"Gotcha. I'll work on it and let you know tomorrow night," I said.

I really want to go to Hatteras. Walks on the beach with Owen sound fabulous. I'd even enjoy the long drive, just being with him. We could really get to know each other with all that time to talk. I still feel bad about missing the Grace Potter concert last month, but it was worth it. Probably. I won the trial at least.

It was a domestic case involving a fifty-year-old mechanic who assaulted his forty-year-old wife of twenty years. It wasn't a hard case to win. We had photos of her injuries—two black eyes, a deep cut on her scalp that required stitches and an "Indian sunburn" on her arm. I worked with her for months trying to keep her on board and ready to testify. She confessed he'd been abusing her for most of their marriage. I charged him with a felony based on "substantial disfigurement." According to the law, black eyes count, even if they're temporary.

The wife looked bad in the photos, but none of her injuries were life threatening, so I had offered to dismiss the felony if the defendant pled to a misdemeanor. I'm not surprised he took it to trial. He didn't think she would have the guts to testify against him. We both knew that, without her testimony, I had nothing. I called her every day for two weeks leading up to the trial, just checking on her. And I spent most of the weekend prepping her.

Not only did she show up for trial, but she was a very convincing witness. She cried when she described the assault. She talked about other incidents during their marriage. I guess she'd finally had enough. Too bad she waited so long. If she had gotten out sooner, she might not look like an old woman.

According to the court staff, the defendant looked shocked when she walked into the courtroom. Then, he actually looked hurt that she was telling on him. He, of course, testified that he never laid a hand on her and that she made up the assault to get a better divorce settlement. I didn't believe a word of it, but I know defendants always make stuff up to try to get out of criminal charges. Juries aren't always as savvy. Fortunately, it only took the jury about an hour to convict him on all counts. The judge had him taken into custody and set the sentencing for the following week.

When he was taken away in handcuffs, the wife cried. I assumed it was the stress of the trial. I let her know that she had done a great job testifying and thanked her for all she'd done.

A week later at the sentencing, I asked for two to five years to serve, figuring I would get at least a year. I referred to the long history of abuse and reminded the judge how badly beaten she had been. The defense asked for probation. Then, the wife stood up to read her statement. As the victim, she's entitled to make a statement at the sentencing. She begged the judge to give her husband probation and talked about how he was a good man who just needed help with his problems. She said she never would have cooperated with the prosecution if she had thought he would end up in jail, and that she would not be able to live with herself if "this good man" spent time in prison because of her.

Wow. My first thought was that I made a tactical error in not calling her every day between the trial and the sentencing. My second thought was *How can she be such a doormat?*. I've been to trainings on domestic violence, so I understand how difficult it can be for a woman to finally take the steps needed to leave an abusive partner, but she had already left him. His case was pending for almost a year, and there was a no-contact order the entire time. Why did he still have such a hold over her?

The judge apparently took her pleas to heart because he sentenced the guy to thirty days to serve followed by probation. That pissed me off. I gave up going to Grace Potter with Owen preparing for the trial. And spent two days in court trying the case. The trial cost the state a lot of money. That case was worth more than thirty days.

I'm camped out in a conference room outside the courtroom at 8:00 a.m. with my colleagues Sanjiv and Brett. We're waiting for the monthly jury draw. Unfortunately, I have seven cases left that may still go to trial in April. If I can get them to settle, I might be able to go to Cape Hatteras. The first jury draw is supposed to start at 9:00, so we have an hour to make deals. Fortunately, there is a flurry of last-minute paperwork and all but one of my cases settle. Some months are like this. My theory is that some people can't accept responsibility for their actions until they are confronted with the reality that the problem is not going away. In other words, they are in denial to the very end. The defense attorneys always whine about us coming down too hard and getting things wrong, but in the end almost all of their clients plead guilty. In my opinion, the best defense attorneys are the ones who convince their clients to make deals early. It saves their clients money and keeps the court from getting bogged down with frivolous motions.

The jurors are waiting in the courtroom, so we do a series of plea changes in the hearing room at the other end of the building. We hit a snag when the judge seems offended by one of my deals. It's the case of a twenty-year-old guy that I charged with assaulting and "raping" his eighteen-year-old girlfriend. I don't usually do sexual assault cases, but this one got turfed to me because it was really a domestic violence case. The assault is solid, but the rape is a dog of a case. According to the girl, he struck her on several occasions and she has photos of bruises to prove it. Then, one night when he was angry, he forced her to have sex with him against her will. I am a big believer that no woman should be forced to have sex without consent. The problem is that it happened at his parents' house while they were home. And no one heard her cry out or scream. Afterward, she watched TV with his parents. She didn't mention it to anyone until two weeks later. And she stayed with him.

Apparently, the defense was going to be that she was retaliating because he broke up with her to join the navy. She admitted that he broke up with her, but denied the rest. I believe her because I get it. Sort of. But there's no way I could sell a jury on that rape. I knew that when I took the case. I only charged the sexual assault so that I would have a better bargaining position on the domestic. But the judge seems disgusted that I'm dismissing a charge that serious. I bet he was never a prosecutor. Lots of judges get appointed with no experience in criminal law whatsoever. Anyway, the girl is happy with the deal because it keeps the guy from joining the navy. The navy won't take him with a domestic assault conviction because it means he's prohibited from possessing a firearm. I'm happy because I don't have to try a case that I was probably going to lose, and there's a chance I can go to Hatteras. I don't know if the defendant is happy, but he should be because he's avoiding a conviction on a rape charge. Seems like a win-win-win to me. In a private conference with the judge and the defense lawyer, I convince the judge I have issues with the victim, and he finally accepts the plea deal.

Afterward, I stop at the clerk's office. Miranda is working the desk. That's good, she's not as difficult as Leanne.

"You got any trials this month?" she says.

"Just one. Can I ask a favor?"

"You can always ask."

"Any chance of me getting the trial dates for the second week in April?"

"Maybe. What's up?"

"I want to go away the third week."

"Unscheduled vacation?"

"Maybe."

"I'm not doing you any favors unless you spill the beans."

"Okay. Owen asked me to go away."

"The new boyfriend?"

"Yeah."

"Ooh la la."

"Can you give me dates the second week?"

"Sure. But you better follow up with a written request as soon as possible, so nobody else schedules you in."

"No problem."

"What are you going to do about your status conferences?"

"Brett and Sanjiv said they would cover."

"Okay. Consider it done. But you owe me."

"I do. Thanks."

Things are looking good for Hatteras.

After I have finished prepping for my one jury, I head into the courtroom to watch. Brett Peterson is drawing a jury against Barry Densmore.

The current case is a DUI. I used to be proud of myself when I won those, but the truth is, we *should* win them. They are so straightforward. But Barry has a way of making jurors question everything. Brett has plenty of experience, but by the time they've chosen a jury, I know Brett has his work cut out for him. Barry has several people on the jury that I would call "Doubting Thomases." He only needs one of those to get a hung jury. I make a mental note to stay away from those jurors when it's my turn.

Barry also has every juror on the panel laughing at his quips. I don't know why everyone finds him so charming.

It turns out there's not enough time to draw my jury before lunch, so court adjourns. I'm waiting for the potential jurors to exit when Barry comes and sits next to me.

"Got a sec?"

"Anything for you, Barry," I say.

"I want to try one more time on the Sarah Bennett case."

I can't help rolling my eyes. "Go ahead."

"I just want you to reconsider what the system is doing to this family. We have Dr. Lapitas lined up for the hearing next week. This defense is costing them a fortune. They're not rich people."

"So have them apply for a public defender."

"They wouldn't be eligible and you know it. But it will be a shame if they go bankrupt defending against these charges."

"Look. I've offered you a good deal. Are you trying to get a better one?"

"You know me, I'll always consider a better deal. But, no. I don't think Sarah Bennett would get through a plea colloquy. She's adamant that she did what she thought was best for the safety of her child. I just want you to consider whether you might be wrong about this. We're not talking about irresponsible parents. We're talking about pillars of the community who had a disobedient kid. Any parent knows that kids do stupid things. That doesn't make it the parents' fault every time. Unless you've been in those shoes, it's hard to judge what the right thing to do was."

"So now you're saying I'm not qualified to prosecute child abuse because I'm not a parent?"

"No. I'm saying that most parents are going to be a lot less judgmental than you are about what happened. Kids don't come with instruction manuals. You do your best. Parents know that. And there will be some parents on that jury."

"I have a solid case."

"I'm sure it looked solid when you took it. I'm just asking you to reevaluate. I've seen what a trial will do to a family. This family doesn't deserve to go through that. What if Lapitas is right that the kid was unduly pressured by Karen Driscoll? We already know Dave Belkin is an unreliable witness. What if all of this is unnecessary?"

"So, it's my fault?"

"I'm not blaming you. Not at all. You relied on what the cops told you. But the truth is, Karen Driscoll skewed the interviews, and she skewed the affidavit of probable cause. I'm not even saying she did it intentionally, just that she did it. She gave this thing momentum. And somebody on your side needs to put on the brakes. I was hoping the judge would do it, but he didn't."

"Because it's a solid case."

"No, it's not. You won't win this. You'll lose the trial, and this family will lose everything they have. How is that justice?"

"That's how it works. It's an adversarial system. I'm one of the adversaries. I have to do my best to convict. If I lose, so be it."

Barry's expression is even. I sense that he's working hard not to show his frustration. "Obviously, I'm not going to convince you. I'd like to talk to your boss about this case, but I don't want to do it behind your back. Would you like to have a three-way meeting?"

"No, you can go ahead and talk to Fred if that's what you need to do." I try to say it nonchalantly though I'm irritated. I've been prosecuting cases for three years. It's not like I'm a newbie whose boss needs to oversee her work. Barry thanks me and leaves the almost vacant courtroom.

When I get back to my office, Barry is talking to the secretary making an appointment with my boss, Fred Dutton.

My afternoon jury draw goes well. I get fourteen jurors I feel good about. I don't have Barry's skill at winning over juries before the trial even starts, but I think I do a good job making them like me, or at least not dislike me. I smile a lot and laugh heartily whenever someone tries to inject levity into an unnatural and tense situation.

The trial won't be until the end of next week, so I spend the rest of the afternoon making sure all the witnesses have been subpoenaed, and that everything is in order. I return the phone calls I missed during the day.

As soon as I draft a notice about my April vacation, I plan to call it a day. Fred Dutton knocks on my door.

"Barry Densmore came to see me today," he says.

"That was quick."

Fred shrugs. "Barry and I go way back. He doesn't come to me often, so when he does, I try to listen."

"Did he complain about me?"

"No, I wouldn't call it a complaint. He's just concerned you're not capable of being impartial in the Bennett case."

"Why would I be biased? I don't even know the woman."

"He thinks that because of the publicity the case received, and the fact that you were the one who signed off on it, you might not be able to see clearly how weak the case is. Is it true that the only witness was looking in a mirror as he was driving away?"

"Yeah."

"And that Karen Driscoll used a lot of leading questions during the interview with the kid?"

"I don't know. I haven't read the transcript yet."

"Is it possible the whole thing happened the way Sarah Bennett said it did?"

I look him in the eye. He appears to be searching my face. I'm not sure what he's looking for. "I don't see it," I say. "Her explanation is too pat."

"Look. I admit that, after talking with Barry, I have second thoughts about the case. But I'm not going to tell you that you have to dismiss it. That's not my style and you know it. You know the case better than I do and I trust your judgment. But I raised three kids and now I have two grandchildren. It's hard being a parent and I haven't met any perfect ones. I'm wondering if we can resolve this in a way that works for everyone."

I'm tired of people telling me I don't know enough just because I don't have kids yet. But obviously, I can't say that to my boss. "I offered her probation. She's not interested. Besides, the judge denied the motion to dismiss."

"Just because we *can* prosecute people, doesn't mean we should every time. Why don't you offer a deferred sentence?"

"Won't that make us look weak in the press?"

"I can handle the press if it comes to that. Don't worry. Whatever you do, I'll spin it in a way that makes us look good. The most important thing is treating people fairly."

"What if she won't take the deferred?"

"I'll leave it up to you. But you might consider dismissing it. Anyway, I'm sure you'll do the right thing."

He gets up out of my visitor chair.

"For the record, I see how hard you work here. You're doing a good job. We're lucky to have you."

"Thanks, Fred."

"Good night, Tamara."

When he's gone, I ask myself what that was really about. Does he want me to dismiss the case? That damn Barry. He's so silver-tongued that he convinced my boss that my case is a dog. But I know better. I'm not going to let Barry psych me out. I can win this case, even against Barry. And I will. Unless Sarah Bennett takes the deferred sentence. I feel like Fred didn't give me any choice but to offer that option. But, he was also clear that the decision on whether to try or dismiss was mine.

I'll call Barry tomorrow and let him know about the revised offer. Right now, I'm too pissed off to talk to him. I'm going home.

CHAPTER 33

Nicholas Bennett
Wednesday, April 3, 2013

I need new pants. Probably shirts too. I mentioned it to my dad a few times, but I keep forgetting to tell my mom when I talk to her. In the meantime, I'm hoping the weather gets warm soon so I can wear shorts to school and stop looking like a nerd.

My dad is acting strange, like he's hiding something. He decided not to coach soccer this spring. He said the trial in May is making it hard for him to make commitments. I told him not to worry about it, but the truth is that it sucks. The new coach makes us run two miles at the beginning of each practice. He's always yelling at us. He called me a girl when I missed a shot during a scrimmage. He said I needed to hustle more. When I told my mom about that she was furious. She wanted to complain to the school, but I told her that I really didn't want the attention. I made her promise she wouldn't call. She probably won't remember anyway because she seems so distracted right now. Sometimes when I talk to her, she doesn't seem to be listening.

I know she's worried about the upcoming trial. I am too. I've heard my parents talking on the phone. It sounds like the thing they're most worried about is whether Meredith will have to testify. That's pretty scary. I've seen trials on TV. I can't imagine having to testify. Based on the way Meredith's been acting, it probably won't be easy for her either. The whole thing sounds kind of screwed up to me, making kids testify against their parents, that is.

My dad's been spending more and more time in the office on the computer. I want to see what he's doing, so I sneak in there. I figure if I'm quiet enough I can see what he's doing before he notices me. I almost pull it off, but before I can read what's on the screen, he spins his chair around and grabs my arm.

"What are you doing?" he says.

"Nothing."

"Are you spying on me?" He tightens his grip on my arm.

"No."

"You were." He lets go of my arm and shoves me backward. I fall onto my butt. It hurts, and I can feel the tears coming into my eyes even though I try to stop them.

"No, I wasn't," I lie. "I was just getting some paper for a homework assignment."

He looks at me funny and then points at the stack of paper. "Get out."

I grab a few sheets of paper. As I head for the door, he turns back to face the desk. I don't know why he's so bent out of shape. It looked like all he was doing was sending emails.

I call my mom and tell her about what happened with my dad.

"Are you okay?" she asks

"Yeah."

"Does it still hurt?"

"Only when I sit down. But there are finger marks on my arm."

"How does he seem? I mean, are you afraid he's going to do anything else?"

"No. He was just mad for a few seconds."

I hear her breathing deeply, then she says, "I think you shouldn't tell anyone else."

"Okay."

"And, if the marks are still on your arm tomorrow, wear a long-sleeve T-shirt."

"Okay."

"Look, Nick, you know I don't approve of violence in any form, but our family is already under so much scrutiny. We don't need anyone else finding out about this."

"Okay."

"But, if you think there's any chance he'll hurt you or your sisters, I want to know."

"No. Don't worry about it."

"It's my job to worry. I'm your mother and I'm glad you called to tell me. I just think we should cut your dad some slack right now. He's under a lot of pressure too. Let's just get through this."

"Okay."

"Promise to call me if anything else happens?"

"Okay."
"Anything at all?"
"Okay."
"I love you, Nick."
"Okay."

CHAPTER 34

Sarah Bennett
Thursday, April 4, 2013

Barry calls me at the shelter late in the afternoon. "I talked with the state's attorney yesterday about your case," he says. "And I just got a call from Tamara." Teeny Tammy. That's what I call her in my head. She's too young and inexperienced to wield the kind of power she does. "She's still not willing to dismiss the charges, but she offered a deferred sentence."

"That's a step in the right direction," I say. "If we lose on the motion, I may have no choice."

"Unfortunately, the offer is on the condition that we make a plea deal prior to next week's motion hearing."

"How am I supposed to decide before I know what happens with the motion?"

"Tamara doesn't want to waste her time preparing for the hearing if we're going to make a deal."

"But that's not fair."

"I agree. But it's not unusual. Anyway, a deferred sentence would mean your record would be clean in a couple of years."

"But, I need to plead guilty, right?"

"Yes."

"That would be a great deal if I was guilty of something, but I'm not. And if I take that deal, I'll probably lose not only my job, but any hope of getting another job like it."

"Just think it over and discuss it with James."

"Can you tell me what are the odds we'll win on the motion?"

"I really can't."

"Just give me an educated guess."

"Fifty-fifty. But it's just a guess."

"Okay. I'll think about it."

I'd like to talk to James about this, but we hardly ever talk anymore. Every time I call his office, he's on the phone. Every time I call his cell in the evening, he's busy at home. I'm sure he has a lot to do. He's been taking care of the kids for seven months. But I'm finding he has less and less time for me.

He also stopped going to counseling. He said it's because I need the support from Jasmine dealing with my own issues. Jasmine tried to convince him it was important to keep working together, but he said he needed a break. I get that. I need a break too. This case is all I think about. I can't help thinking how I used to take my normal life for granted. Sure, James and I had issues in our marriage. Most couples do. But we were working on them. And he's proven what kind of man he is during the past seven months. He's been right here beside me during this whole ordeal. I can't blame him for wanting a little distance from this mess. I just hope we'll be able to put things back together. When this is over.

I think I have a better understanding of what used to make James so angry. It was the feeling that he wasn't in control of his own life. That's exactly how I've been feeling. It's so frustrating. I'm sure that's why he overreacted with Nick last night. We're all strung so tight.

CHAPTER 35

James Bennett
Wednesday, April 17, 2013

Today is the hearing on the motion to quash Meredith's subpoena. It was supposed to be last week, but Barry had a conflict with another case in Chittenden County, so it was rescheduled. It's school vacation week, so Meredith is at home. There's no reason for her to be here.

I've been mostly working at home this week so I can keep an eye on the children. When I have to go to the office for a while, I leave Nick in charge. It's not a great option, but I don't have a better one. He's technically old enough to babysit at twelve, and I've left him in charge for short periods before, but he still fights with his sisters sometimes, so I don't completely trust him. I made sure everyone knew how to call 9-1-1 before I left them the first time.

Sarah and I met at my office this morning and walked over to the courthouse together. We go to court together like many couples go to church.

We're waiting for Barry in one of the conference rooms when he comes in with Dr. Lapitas. The hearing is at 9:00 a.m., so Dr. Lapitas drove up yesterday afternoon from New Jersey. I'm grateful he's here, but I can't help doing the math. I assume we have to pay for his travel time. Five or six hours to drive here, plus a night in a hotel, a couple of meals. I'm sure it's all on our tab. It has probably cost me $2,000 just to get him to show up. A minimum of a half day of testimony is another $1,000. It occurs to me that we may end up owing Dr. Lapitas more than the amount of his retainer before this is over.

Lapitas is tall and thin with combed-back gray hair. He reminds me of Mr. Rogers. He's wearing a suit, but he looks like he'd be more comfortable in a cardigan.

We've barely completed the introductions when the court clerk informs us the judge is ready and that we need to be in the courtroom. Karen Driscoll is in another conference room with Tamara Goodwin. The clerk also knocks on their door to get them moving. Driscoll stares in our direction with undisguised contempt. I don't get that. What did we do to her? She's the one who attacked our family out of revenge.

Lapitas and I sit behind Barry and Sarah in the front row of the gallery. Driscoll goes to Tamara's side, but opts for the last row of the seating. Barry gets up and whispers something to Tamara, who goes back and says something to Driscoll. She glares at us as she gets up and walks out of the courtroom. As she leaves, Keith Bumpus, the guardian ad litem, comes in and sits behind Tamara. I wonder if that means he's supporting her side. A few minutes later, the judge comes in with the usual fanfare.

"Before we begin," the judge says, "I'd like to ask the parties whether there's any chance of resolving this case prior to trial. We have three days set aside for a trial in May, but as you know, the docket is crowded. I'd like to know if we've done everything possible to resolve this matter."

Tamara stands. "Your Honor, we offered the defendant a deferred sentence. I don't see that there's much more I can do."

Sarah and Barry are whispering. I can see Barry's hand on the mute button so nobody can hear them.

"Mr. Densmore?"

"Your Honor, it has been our position all along that no crime was committed here. Unless Ms. Goodwin dismisses the charges, we have no choice but to take the matter to trial."

The judge rubs his upper lip and furrows his brow. He sits silently for about ten seconds. "Very well. Let's proceed with today's hearing. Mr. Densmore?"

Barry calls Lapitas to the stand. He is sworn. Barry briefly questions him about his education and background. Lapitas has ten years of clinical experience and twenty years of experience as a professor and researcher. He has published numerous scholarly articles.

"Have you been qualified as an expert witness in Vermont before?" Barry says.

"Yes, I have."

Tamara stands. "Ms. Goodwin?" the judge says.

"Your Honor, the state has no objection to Dr. Lapitas being qualified as an expert."

"Very well. The witness is qualified."

Barry continues. "Thank you. Dr. Lapitas, what did you do to prepare for today's testimony?"

"I watched the recording of Officer Driscoll's interview with Meredith Bennett. I also read the police reports and the statements of all the witnesses. I studied the transcript of Meredith's interview, and I reviewed various scientific studies on interviewing children and memory."

"Tell us about the studies on interviewing."

Lapitas spends half an hour talking about some studies. Now that he is testifying, he reminds me more of a professor I had in college. He goes into detail about how the studies were designed. Basically, the studies show that interviewers who are given false information about events often shape children's reports to be consistent with their inaccurate beliefs about what happened through the use of leading questions and other suggestive techniques. One study concluded that thirty-four percent of children will corroborate false events that the interviewer believed had transpired. In other studies, the numbers were higher,

He also talks about a study on repeating questions during a child interview. Apparently, when children are asked yes/no questions, if the question is repeated, they're likely to change their answers, assuming that the first answer that they gave is wrong.

It's clear to me that a biased interviewer makes it likely that an interview will yield inaccurate information. I hope the judge is getting this.

"Can you apply the data from the studies to Officer Driscoll's interview of Meredith Bennett?" Barry says.

"Well, there are a multiple problems with the way the interview was conducted. First, I would characterize Officer Driscoll as an assertive and suggestive interviewer. I'll go through the particular questions that were troubling, but beyond that her entire manner did not invite dissension."

"Can you be more specific?"

"Absolutely. She was dressed in a uniform. She was wearing a sidearm and a nightstick. I would say that not only was her appearance assertive, it would have been incredibly intimidating to an eight-year-old child. In fact, there was a study on that as well. Children who were interviewed by a uniformed officer were much more likely to provide inaccurate information." He goes on to provide the details.

"Any other issues with the interview?"

"Well, there's the location. An interrogation room is scary to adults. That's why they have them. It would have had an even more intimidating effect on an eight-year-old child."

"What can you tell us about the questions asked?"

"Two things in general. First, it's clear that Officer Driscoll had a preconceived notion of what the child witnessed. If you accept Ms. Bennett's version of the events for purposes of this analysis, Officer Driscoll had inaccurate information. Second, if you disregard the initial background questions and focus on the questions designed to elicit information about the event, more than forty percent of the questions asked by Officer Driscoll were leading. Of those, more than fifty percent were misleading. That's not even counting the drawing. There were also several times during the interview that the officer repeated questions when she did not like Meredith's response."

"Can you give us examples?"

"Absolutely," says Lapitas. He goes line by line through the transcript and points out the problems. It takes a while, but the judge seems to be listening intently and making notes. It gives me hope.

"What about the drawing?"

"When Officer Driscoll was having trouble getting Meredith to talk, she decided to make a drawing to help things along."

"Officer Driscoll made the drawing or Meredith did?"

"In her affidavit Officer Driscoll refers to a drawing made by the child, but on the video what you see is Officer Driscoll making the drawing."

"Is that a problem?"

"Yes. Because the officer not only told her what the officer believed were the correct answers with the form of her questions, she actually depicted it for the child in her drawing. Children are smart. They're good at figuring out what adults want them to say. And Officer Driscoll literally gave Meredith a road map."

"So, based on your training and experience, do you have an opinion about the validity of the information provided during the interview of Meredith Bennett?"

"I do. I would say it's completely unreliable. Meredith was placed in an intimidating situation, and interviewed by an assertive interviewer, who had misinformation. All three of those things weigh heavily against the accuracy of any information provided by a child."

"And is it likely that the child's memory was affected by this interview?"

"Absolutely."

"Can you explain?"

"Contrary to popular belief, human memory does not work like computer storage. The human memory is a malleable thing. It's responsive to misinformation."

"You have more studies for us?"

"Of course. This area has been studied by psychologists for more than thirty years. It's now commonly known as the 'misinformation effect.'"

Lapitas talks about how, when people who perceive an event are subsequently given misinformation about that event, there is a substantial likelihood they will adopt that misinformation and that it will become part of their memories. He explains that even misleading questions can cause people to misremember events. He explains the results of several studies. The most surprising one showed that thirty percent of the people can be convinced to remember with confidence and details a childhood event that never happened to them after the idea is planted by a family member.

"Children and the elderly are most likely to incorporate misinformation into their memories," Lapitas says.

Next, Barry moves on to the issue of the trauma to children who are forced to testify. Lapitas describes a study done on children who testified in court. Apparently, seven months after their testimony, those children were significantly more likely to experience behavioral disturbances than children who were not involved in the criminal justice system. He also explains how maternal support appeared to have an effect on how well the child survived the ordeal.

"And do you have an opinion about how Meredith would respond to being forced to testify against her mother?"

"I have no doubt that it would be traumatizing for her."

"Why is that?"

"Not only is she being forced to testify, but for seven months, she's been denied the support of her mother. It puts her at a higher risk of adverse consequences."

"Could it possibly be an empowering experience for Meredith to help get her mother acquitted?"

"That's unlikely. The research shows that one of the things that children most fear when testifying is misunderstanding the questions and getting confused. And that's not an irrational fear. I know firsthand how easy it is to get confused on the witness stand." He chuckles and looks at the judge who nods his head and smiles.

"Plus, there's still the issue of how much her memory may have been contaminated by Officer Driscoll's questioning techniques. That may make it difficult for her to testify accurately and convincingly."

Barry asks a few more questions about the research. When he is done, Tamara has her chance to cross-examine Lapitas.

"It's possible that Sarah Bennet is lying about what happened, isn't it?"

"Yes, I suppose."

"So it's possible that Officer Driscoll did not have inaccurate information, right?"

"Yes."

"And if that's the case, the analysis changes, doesn't it?"

"It doesn't change that a large percentage of the questions were leading."

"But many of them may not have been misleading, true?"

"We can't know for sure. But regardless, they were potentially misleading."

"But, there's no way to know, is there?"

"No."

"You talked about some studies on memory. Isn't it true that time is a factor in whether a false memory will be planted?"

"Yes. That's one factor."

"Isn't it true that the longer the time between the event and the 'misinformation,'" she uses her fingers to indicate quote marks, "the more likely it will affect memory."

"Yes."

"So, how long was it between the event and Meredith's interview with Officer Driscoll?"

"I don't remember exactly, but I understand it was not long afterward."

"What if I told you it was less than an hour?"

"That might be accurate."

"Isn't it true that an interview that soon after the event is likely to affect memory much less than an interview the next day?"

"Yes, but—"

Tamara interrupts him. "Or the following week?"

"Yes, but—"

She interrupts him again. "Thank you, doctor, you've answered."

Lapitas is clearly frustrated. He looks to Barry, who just nods his head in reassurance.

"Did you interview Meredith Bennett?"

"No, I did not."

"And yet you are comfortable giving an expert opinion about the mental health of someone you've never met?"

"Well, I admit it's not ideal, but I doubt she's unlike the other children her age I've encountered or the children who participated in the studies."

"Have you ever diagnosed someone in your clinical practice without meeting them?"

"No."

"Yet, that is essentially what you're doing here today, isn't it, doctor?"

"Not exactly. I'm giving an expert opinion based on the available information."

"But, isn't it true that you can't know how Meredith will respond to testifying against her mother?"

"I can make an educated guess."

I cringe at his word choice. Tamara smiles, seizing the opportunity. "Do you really think the court should decide cases based on guesses?"

Barry stands up, but before he can object, Tamara says, "Withdrawn."

"How many times have you testified in criminal matters, doctor?"

"Twenty-seven."

"Were all of those for the defense?"

"Yes."

"And in how many of those cases did you conclude it would be reasonable for the child to testify?"

"None."

"Thank you. That's all I have."

I'm afraid her point is made, and that we made a mistake not allowing Lapitas to interview Meredith. Fortunately, Barry has a chance to question him on re-direct.

"Can you tell us why you didn't interview Meredith?"

"Because her parents didn't—"

"Objection, hearsay."

"Sustained."

"Would it have been helpful to the defense if you had been able to interview Meredith?"

"Absolutely, but I can understand the parents not wanting—"

"Objection, hearsay."

"Sustained."

"Attorney Goodwin asked you about the timing of the Meredith's interview, correct?"

"Yes."

"Does the timing of the interview affect your conclusions about its reliability?"

"Absolutely not."

"Why is that?"

"Like I said before, there are so many other issues. The assertiveness of Officer Driscoll. The intimidating nature of the circumstances. And the highly suggestive nature of the questioning. When you put that together with the age of the child, almost everything that Meredith said during that interview is unreliable."

"And could that interview have affected Meredith's memory of the event?"

"Absolutely. It's very possible, likely even."

"Thank you. I have nothing further for this witness."

The judge looks at the clock and announces a brief recess. I'm glad for a break. I could use the bathroom. Lapitas looks like he's glad to be done. He's been on the stand for almost two hours. Since we have to pay him for half a day of expert testimony, he agrees to hang out in case he's needed again. He'll drive back to New Jersey in the afternoon.

Fifteen minutes later, we are all back in our places and Barry calls Karen Driscoll to the stand.

The court clerk retrieves her from the hallway where she has likely been waiting throughout Lapitas' testimony. She strides to the front of the room, eyes focused on the witness stand, looking confident. She takes the stand and is sworn.

"Officer Driscoll, did you know Sarah Bennett prior to September 8, 2012?"

"I knew *of* her. I wouldn't say I knew her."

"How did you know of her?"

"From her job at the Murdoch Shelter."

"Did you have an interaction with Sarah Bennett in the weeks prior to the incident with her daughter?"

"I guess you could call it an interaction."

"Why don't you tell us what happened?"

"I went to the shelter with my sergeant. We had a conversation with Ms. Bennett. We left."

"Was there more to it?"

"Not really."

I can't believe Driscoll is downplaying this as much as she is. It makes her look dishonest. If she were my witness, I would have instructed her to be more forthright. Barry is taking it in stride, as if he expected it.

"Your Honor, request permission to treat the officer as a hostile witness."

"Granted," the judge says without looking up from his notes. This means Barry can now question the officer as if she were under cross-examination. It gives Barry some leeway and allows him to ask leading questions.

"Officer Driscoll, isn't it true you went to the shelter because you were in the midst of an investigation?"

"Yes."

"And you wanted permission to search the shelter, true?"

"Yes."

"And Ms. Bennett refused to allow you access, right?"

"Yes."

"And that made you angry, didn't it?"

"I wouldn't say angry. More disappointed."

"She told you to get a warrant, didn't she?"

"Yes."

"Did you try to get a warrant?"

"Yes, we did."

"And were you successful?"

"No."

"Has anyone been charged with the crime you were investigating that day?"

"No."

"Isn't it true that you blame Sarah Bennett for thwarting your investigation?"

"No."

"But it's true that you thought Sarah Bennett should have let you search the shelter, isn't it?"

"It was her right to refuse."

"You didn't like it, did you?"

"I was doing my job. She was doing hers."

"But you didn't like the way she did her job, did you?"

"I wouldn't say that."

"I'm going to show you what's marked as defense Exhibit B. Do you recognize it?"

"Yes. It's a copy of my deposition."

"I refer you to page 32, line 14. During your deposition, did you say that you didn't like the way that Sarah Bennett handled the situation?"

Driscoll is reading the pages. "I guess I did."

In my opinion, Driscoll looks like a liar who has it in for my wife. I hope the judge is getting the same impression.

"So, when Meredith Bennett came to the police station a week or so later, you were already biased against my client, weren't you?"

"I wouldn't say that."

Barry lets that go. He knows he's not going to get her to change her answer. Besides, one of the cardinal rules of cross-examination is that sometimes it's enough to get the trier of fact to question the truthfulness of the answer.

"Prior to interviewing Meredith, did you talk to anyone about what may or may not have happened?"

"Yes. I spoke with Officer Langford."

"What did he tell you?"

"I really don't remember."

"Did he tell you the van had turned around?"

"I believe so."

"Did he tell you the child had run after the van?"

"I believe so."

"Did he tell you the child had opened the door while the van was moving?"

"I believe so."

"Did he tell you the child was dragged behind the van?"

"Probably."

"So you had a clear picture of what had happened before you set eyes on Meredith Bennett, didn't you?"

"I wouldn't say it was a clear picture. I had an idea."

"And sure enough, your interview confirmed everything that you already envisioned, didn't it?"

"I also got additional information from the child."

"But again, isn't it true you confirmed everything you already knew? Yes or no."

"Yes."

"And nothing you learned contradicted what you already believed going into the interview, did it?"

"Not really."

When Barry is done, he sits down. Tamara rises for cross and asks a few questions about Driscoll's training as a child interviewer. Driscoll lists several week-long trainings.

"Did the trainings teach a particular interviewing protocol?" Tamara says.

"I have learned about several protocols in my trainings. The one I most closely follow is the NICHD protocol. National Institute for Child Health and Development."

"Tell us about that protocol."

"We're supposed to start by building a rapport with the child to get them used to talking to us. Then, we ask questions that get more specific to find out what happened."

"Is that what you did with Meredith Bennett?"

"It's what I tried to do. Sometimes when a child is particularly difficult to talk to, you have to deviate from the protocol. But for the most part I try to stick to it."

"Do you have any doubt about the accuracy of the information you obtained from Meredith Bennett?"

"Objection."

"No, I do not," Driscoll answers anyway.

"Sustained."

"That's all I have." Tamara sits down. Karen looks at the judge to see if she is excused, but Barry is already on his feet for re-direct.

"Does the NICHD protocol say anything about wearing a weapon and uniform when interviewing a child?"

"I don't recall."

"Did they talk about that at all during the trainings?"

"Not that I can remember."

"Did it occur to you that your attire might be intimidating to an eight-year-old?"

"Objection, beyond the scope of cross."

"Sustained."

"According to the protocol, you were supposed to ask open-ended questions, weren't you?"

"Yes."

"But you didn't do that, did you?"

"I tried."

"In fact, you abandoned the protocol, didn't you?"

"I wouldn't say that. You need to be flexible when interviewing children. Sometimes a script doesn't work."

"Do you understand that the script was designed to reduce the number of false accusations?"

"No, I understand the script is a tool I was given to help me do my job. My job is to investigate child abuse."

"So, you don't see a problem with deviating from the script?"

"Not at all. Especially, if that's what it takes to get kids to talk."

"Thank you, Officer Driscoll." Barry sits down.

"Thank you, Officer. You are excused." The judge nods at her.

She leaves the stand with less swagger than when she took it. I wonder if she has any clue how misguided her efforts were or whether she appears deflated because testifying is a deflating experience for anyone. She takes a seat behind Tamara in the first row of the gallery.

The judge asks if there will be any further witnesses. Barry confers briefly with Sarah before he calls me to the stand.

It's a first for me. I've never testified before. I knew that this was a possibility because we discussed it with Barry a few days ago. I was hoping it wouldn't be necessary, but I trust that Barry is making the right call.

I have questioned witnesses before in this very chair. I know what to expect and I'm a wreck. I can't even imagine how an eight-year-old would process this experience. And in front of a jury no less.

I am sworn and seated. I put on my lawyer face, but I can't stop my right leg from jiggling. Fortunately, the low wall around the witness stand keeps it from being visible to anyone but the judge.

Barry asks some identifying information and then gets to the issues.

"Did you let Dr. Lapitas interview Meredith?"

"No, we did not."

"Why?"

"Because we are trying to keep her away from the court process. We don't want her damaged any more than she already has been. She's too fragile right now."

"Have you noticed changes in Meredith's behavior since September 8, 2012?"

"Yes, I have."

"Describe those changes."

"First, I have to explain how Meredith used to be."

"Go ahead." Barry nods.

"Meredith used to be friendly and outgoing. Confident. She used to sleep through the night unless she was sick. She used to enjoy eating. Before September eighth, Meredith was a normal, happy eight-year-old girl. She had friends. She played. According to her teachers, she was popular with the other kids at school, a leader even."

"Now what is Meredith like?"

"She's nothing like she was. She barely eats. According to the pediatrician, she's lost eight pounds since she was weighed last year, but she's grown two inches in height."

"Was she overweight before?"

"Not at all. She was normal, healthy. Fiftieth percentile on the charts. Now she's below tenth percentile for weight."

"What about her moods?"

"She appears depressed."

"Objection. The witness is not a psychologist."

"Overruled. It was an observation not a diagnosis."

Barry continues. "What, specifically, have you observed?"

I'm watching Sarah's face. "Meredith suffers from nightmares."

"Did she have nightmares before September 8, 2012?"

"All kids have nightmares. She was like any kid. She had them every once in a while. I was only aware of them every so often."

"And now?"

"She cries in her sleep. Frequently, she calls out for her mother. Sometimes, she wakes up on her own. Sometimes, I have to wake her. Either way, it's a nightly thing."

Sarah's eyes are like saucers. I can see she's about to cry. Barry is unaware of Sarah as he needs to be right now.

"What else have you observed?"

"Meredith rarely smiles. I don't think she has laughed in seven months. She cries at the drop of a hat. She has little interest in anything, except cleaning and doing her homework. She has become meticulous. Her room is perfectly ordered at all times. I never have to ask her to pick up after herself. She even picks up after her brother and sister when they leave things in the living room. Last week, she made a mistake on her math homework. When she erased it, it made a smudge. She copied over the entire page rather than hand in a paper with a smudge."

"Is that big deal?"

"It took over half an hour."

"This is a change?"

"Yes. She was never as messy as her siblings, but prior to September eighth, she was a normal kid. Normal kids have to be reminded to clear their dinner dishes and pick up their rooms. Not Meredith. The only thing that interests her is being perfect."

"You have two other children?"

"Yes, Nick is twelve and Camille is seven."

"Have you observed behavioral changes in the other two children during this time period?"

"The no-contact order has affected us all. The atmosphere in our house is generally more somber. But, I have observed no significant or lasting changes in the behavior of the other two children."

"At any point, has Meredith told you what's bothering her?"

"Objection. Hearsay."

Barry clearly expected the objection. "Your Honor, there are two ways of looking at this. First, it isn't hearsay because it's not being offered for the truth. It's being offered to show what the child believes. Second, it's a Rule 803 state of mind exception. Either way it is admissible, and it's critical to the issue of whether she should testify."

"I'll allow it," the judge says.

I'm relieved because I know how important this information is. "Meredith has told me two things. She misses her mother, and she thinks it's her fault that her mother can't come home."

Sarah has her hands over her face. I can tell that she's crying.

Barry indicates he is done with direct and Tamara gets up. She has a notepad in one hand and a pen in the other. I steel myself for cross-examination.

"The first time that Meredith told you she blames herself, did you record that conversation?"

"No."

Tamara makes a check mark on her pad.

"Do you believe your wife's version of what happened on September eighth?"

"Yes."

"So, isn't it true that you are biased toward that version?"

"I guess so." Another check mark.

"You're not a psychologist, are you?"

"No."

"You don't have any specialized training interviewing children?"

"No." She checks again.

"In fact, you're a lawyer, aren't you?"

"Yes."

"You're pretty good at getting people to answer questions the way you want, right?"

"I wouldn't say that."

"But you know how to ask leading questions, don't you?"

"Of course." Check mark.

"And the conversation with Meredith wasn't recorded. So, we'll never know whether Meredith told you that spontaneously, or whether you planted the idea, will we?"

Damn it. Tamara basically just accused me of trying to influence my daughter's testimony. It's an ethical violation and a situation I've been trying religiously to avoid for seven months. Before I can respond, Tamara says, "Nothing further."

Barry gets up. "Do you blame Meredith for what's happened to your family?"

"Of course not. She's an eight-year-old. None of this is her fault."

"What was the context under which she made that disclosure to you?"

"It happened spontaneously after the guardian ad litem tried to interview her."

I am excused. I'm so frustrated because I know that Tamara just used our own expert's testimony to discredit my testimony. As I walk back to the gallery, I see that she's scribbling notes, probably preparing for arguments. In that moment, I despise her. I wonder if that's how witnesses felt about me after I cross-examined them. I suspect I was never as effective at it as Tamara is.

Neither side has more witnesses, so the judge asks to hear from Keith Bumpus. He's been sitting there listening all morning. A couple of times I wondered if he'd fallen asleep. It's hard to see his eyes through his glasses.

The judge doesn't make him take the stand, but beckons him forward to stand next to Tamara.

"Thank you for being here today, Mr. Bumpus," the judge says. "I'm always grateful for your service. What can you tell us about Meredith?"

"Unfortunately, not as much as I'd like."

"Did you interview the child?"

"I tried, but it was very difficult."

"Why is that?"

"She refused to answer my questions. I'm pretty good at getting kids to open up, but not her. She strikes me as not quite right." It strikes me how much of an understatement that is. "I think she's very shy or scared, and possibly a little stubborn."

"Do you feel that Mr. Densmore is representing the best interests of Meredith?"

"I do, Your Honor. I do not think she should testify. Based on everything I heard today and everything I observed with that child, I believe she'll be traumatized if she has to testify. Especially, if her mother is convicted as a result. The only words she said in more than half an hour were that she wants her mother back. I can't help thinking about the possible damage to this child."

Tamara's turns to face Bumpus. Her eyes are like slits. "Your Honor, I object. Mr. Bumpus' last statement is hearsay. And he's not supposed to give an opinion on the merits of the hearing."

"I won't consider the hearsay. Thank you for your time, Mr. Bumpus. I'll hear argument from the attorneys now."

The attorneys argue the merits of the motion to quash. Then Barry reminds the judge that he promised to revisit the issue of the no-contact order and they argue that as well. When they are done and the judge is gone, Tamara and Karen head out of the courtroom ahead of us. As we exit, I can see them at the end of the hall entering the staircase together.

Dr. Lapitas comes over and extends a hand. "I'm sorry that the system has treated your daughter so appallingly."

"Thank you. And thank you for your testimony today."

"I just hope it was enough to help Meredith. And the rest of you too."

My curiosity has the best of me. "What did you think of Officer Driscoll?"

"She's bad, but sadly, she's not even close to the worst I've seen. Unfortunately, the criminal justice system is full of cops just like her. They get a little training and then get tasked with doing a job that is completely beyond their abilities. It's worst in the suburbs and rural areas. At least in the larger cities there are child advocacy centers with trained psychologists for interviewers. That NICHD protocol was a good idea that failed miserably because it only works if you follow the script. But human beings don't like to be told how to do things, especially if they think they know the answers, so the cops almost never follow the script. The bottom line is that you can't teach someone to do the job of a trained psychologist in four days or even four weeks."

"She doesn't get it, does she? Officer Driscoll, that is."

"I doubt it. Which means the only way she'll change her technique is if the judges start throwing out her cases."

"Thank you again. No offense, but I hope we won't be needing your services anymore."

"None taken. Good luck." He waves and heads for the door. Barry and Sarah turn to me.

"How do you feel about the hearing?" I say.

"It went about as well as it could have," Barry says.

"What will the judge do?" I say.

"If only I knew," Barry says.

"But surely he has to see how this whole thing has been skewed," Sarah says. "I thought Dr. Lapitas was a good witness."

"He's the best. Which is why we're lucky to have him. But just like judges don't like to dismiss cases, they don't like to tie the prosecutor's hands. If the judge grants our motion, Tamara won't have much of a case."

"What are our chances?" Sarah says.

"I give it fifty-fifty," says Barry.

"I guess I have to live with those odds," Sarah says.

CHAPTER 36

Karen Driscoll
Wednesday, April 17, 2013

Based on the way Tamara storms out of the courtroom, I can tell she's mad. I feel like a puppy dog trailing in her wake as I follow her down the hall.

"What's wrong with you?" I say.

"I really wish you could have heard Dr. Lapitas' testimony."

"Why?" I start climbing the stairs with her. "What happened when I was out in the hallway? You were great for the part I saw." I figure a little flattery goes a long way with prosecutors.

"I'm afraid we're going to lose on this motion," she says.

"What did Lapitas say?"

"He basically said you skewed the interview."

"How?"

"Because you had an idea of what happened before you started."

"So? He wants me to go into an interview without having any idea what happened?"

"Apparently."

"That's stupid. How can I do my job if I don't know what to ask?"

"I know. Ridiculous, right? But he talked about all these studies on interviewer bias. He was very convincing. And I happen to know he's been persuasive with several other judges in cases like this."

"What else did he say?"

"He analyzed your whole interview. Question by question. You asked a lot of leading questions. You're supposed to ask open-ended questions with kids."

"I know."

"Well, according to Lapitas, something like fifty percent of your questions were leading and half of those were misleading."

"And that somehow makes Sarah Bennett innocent?"

"He didn't come out and say that, but the implication is clear."

"You don't think the judge will see it that way?"

"I hope not. But, one thing I've learned in this job is that you never know what a judge will do. Sometimes I see a case one way and the judge sees it completely differently."

"You know what's wrong with this system?" I say. Tamara raises an eyebrow. "People with money can afford experts who will say whatever they want them to say. And judges and juries believe it."

"And they can afford lawyers like Barry Densmore who are good at finding loopholes," Tamara says.

"It doesn't make them any less guilty."

"Of course not, everybody knows that O.J. was guilty, but he got off. I just don't want to be remembered like Marcia Clark and Chris Darden. The whole country knows how badly they got outfoxed by the Dream Team. The last thing I want is to be remembered as the prosecutor who got beaten by Barry Densmore every time."

She gets a call and I head back downstairs. Time to go punch in.

CHAPTER 37

Tamara Goodwin
Wednesday, April 17, 2013

What a crappy day. The hearing this morning was awful. I was prepared and it didn't matter. No wonder the other deputies were so sympathetic when I tried to get advice about Lapitas. I had read the summaries on the studies that Lapitas referred to. I studied the transcript of Driscoll's interview with Meredith. I figured once Lapitas started testifying I would see a way to discredit him, but it never came to me. He made it all sound so logical and scientific.

Except he's missing the big picture. Sarah Bennett is a child abuser and she absolutely should not get away with what she did. I don't understand guys like Lapitas. How can they live with themselves knowing they're helping people get away with crimes?

I wasted the whole morning in that hearing. Then I got sucked into spending an entire hour on the phone with one of my victims. I usually turf her over to the victim advocate when she calls, but I picked up the phone while our secretary was away from her desk. Once Hannah knew I was in the office, it was impossible to avoid her. Not surprisingly, she was having second thoughts about calling the police on her boyfriend. She didn't know how she was going to pay her rent. She also heard he was spending time with another woman and was afraid that, if they didn't patch things up soon, it would be too late. I don't get it. The guy is an absolute loser. She already told me this is not the first time he hurt her. She should be saying good riddance. I wasn't in the mood to listen to her. I just hope I didn't piss her off so much that she recants. I'm used to that, but it definitely makes my job harder.

By the time I'm ready to leave the office, it's nearly 7:00 p.m. I missed the 6:00 spinning class. That's been happening more and more. I'm looking forward to seeing Owen. We're spending the night at my place tonight.

I have just enough time to slip into my favorite jeans and long-sleeve T-shirt and pour myself a glass of Chardonnay before I hear Owen letting himself into my apartment. I gave him a key last month. He gave me his key a week later.

I take a big sip of the wine, feeling the instant relaxation. It must be psychological because the alcohol can't possibly get into my bloodstream that fast, but it sure helps with the stress of the day. I greet Owen in the living room. He's freshly showered from a workout at the gym. I'm jealous he had the time. We kiss and I relax against him into a hug. After thirty seconds, I feel almost normal again.

I pour him a glass of wine.

"Pasta okay?" I say. "I've got some of my mom's pesto in the freezer."

"Sounds good."

"And there should be a bag of salad in the fridge."

"I'll get it," he says.

"How was your day?" I say as I put a pot of water on to boil.

"They're having unseasonably warm weather in Cape Hatteras this week."

"You know I really am sorry."

"I know."

"It's not my fault the court moved the hearing."

"It's never your fault."

"You could have gone without me."

"Yeah. Nice romantic week on the beach. Alone."

"I'm sorry."

We sip wine in silence while we wait for the water to boil. Finally, Owen speaks.

"How can you ever make plans with your job the way it is? I wouldn't want to spend money on a vacation and not be able to go."

"For something special like that, I can file a notice with the court that I'm not available."

"So why didn't you file a notice for Hatteras."

"We're supposed to do it in advance. The Hatteras thing came up on short notice."

"Two weeks is short notice?"

"In my world, yes. And it was only a week and a half."

"Same thing," he says. Not really, but I let it go.

"The court is scheduled months in advance. I finagled the week off by asking the clerk nicely, but they didn't record my notice for a couple of days." This is a lie. The truth is that I forgot to file one, but Owen won't understand that. "By the time they did, I was already scheduled for the hearing today. I tried to get it moved, but their expert witness couldn't do it until May. That would have meant moving the trial dates, so the court said no."

"You told me all that before."

"I know. It just seems like you don't get it."

"The worst part is that for a week I thought we were going."

"Me too."

"It would've been better if you'd just told me no from the get go."

"I know. I'm sorry."

Owen is leaning against the wall with his arms crossed. He watches me while I stir the pasta.

"You want to hear about the hearing?" I say.

"Sure."

I tell him about Dr. Lapitas. Owen listens intently. It's one of the things I like best about him. He's a good listener.

"Are you allowed to tell me this stuff?" he says.

"Everything that happens in open court is a matter of public record, so I don't have a confidentiality issue."

"So, are you actually going to make the eight-year-old testify against her mother?"

"If I have to."

"But, what if this doctor guy is right, and the police told her what to say?"

"I don't see it, but if the judge buys it, he'll quash her subpoena."

"And if he doesn't?"

"Then I do my job."

"I couldn't do your job. Not if it involved putting an eight-year-old through that. She may never get over it."

"The mom can always plead guilty and avoid the whole thing."

"And what if she's innocent? Don't you have discretion to drop the case?"

"You're starting to sound like the defense attorney. Of course I could drop it, but why would I? She's guilty. They're all guilty. That's why ninety-nine percent of them make plea deals."

We set the table and sit down to eat. We really need to talk about something not related to my job.

"When do you start coaching lacrosse?" I say.

"As long as the fields are dry, we'll start right after spring break."

"Do you know how many kids you have this time?"

"Not yet. If there are too many kids, we'll try to whittle it down after the first week. Hopefully, we can take everyone."

"But you can always not play them, right?"

"Yeah, but it's bad for a kid's self-esteem to spend the entire season on the bench. If they don't have potential, I'd rather be honest with them and give them a chance to do something else. Ninth graders can be fragile. That's why I talk to them privately and give them a chance to quit."

"I guess I hadn't thought of that."

"Besides, sometimes it makes them work harder and they improve enough to get playing time. Did you play any team sports growing up?"

"Um, does the debating team count as a sport?"

"Definitely not."

"Only kidding. I was on the gymnastics team."

"That's not a team sport."

"Sure it is. It's a team. Are you saying gymnastics isn't a sport?"

"No. I'm saying it's an individual thing. You get points for your team, but you don't have to work together. You do the best you can do for yourself and that helps the team."

"So you're saying it's not a team."

"Not like a lacrosse team or a soccer team."

"If you say so."

"I bet you looked really cute in your uniform though."

"You want to see pictures after dinner?"

"Absolutely."

"Were you any good?"

"I scored some points for the team."

"I bet you did."

CHAPTER 38

Nicholas Bennett
Sunday, April 21, 2013

Spring break is over. What a waste of a vacation. The most interesting thing I did all week was play Wii. I wish I had an Xbox. I got stuck babysitting my sisters a few hours a day while my dad went to the office. I think I should have been paid. Then I could buy my own Xbox.

CHAPTER 39

Sarah Bennett
Monday, April, 29, 2013

It's been eleven days since the hearing on the motion to quash Meredith's subpoena. We're still waiting for a decision from the judge. The trial is supposed to begin in three weeks, but the jury will have to be chosen soon if there's going to be a trial. James explained that they only choose juries once a month. He expects we'll get a decision on the subpoena any day.

The waiting is the worst. I keep imagining how it would feel to be waiting for a verdict from a jury, not knowing whether they could see the truth through the spin. At least jurors aren't there by choice. There's a chance they can see the truth. I've decided that part of the problem with the system is that, by definition, the people who are most willing to judge others are least qualified to do it.

I don't want a trial. I haven't said it out loud because I'm not ready to talk about it. I know James and Barry will try to convince me, but I won't allow Meredith to testify. I will only consider a trial if Meredith is left out of it. When I heard James talk about Meredith's nightmares on the witness stand, I was angry. Not at him for not telling me. He was trying to leave me choices. I see that. I was angry at the system for creating this situation and angry at myself for being so wrapped up in my own ordeal that I couldn't see what was happening to my daughter.

I should have known. I could have found out somehow. I admit it would have been difficult to talk to Meredith, given that all my communications with her are monitored by Paula. But I should have known. The clues were there. I think I was just in denial about how bad it is. But good mothers don't have the luxury of denial.

I realize now how bad a mother I've been during these past months. Maybe I deserve this after all. If I had made a plea deal a long time ago, I could have been back with Meredith taking care of her. I could have assured her that none of this was her fault. I could have stopped the nightmares months ago. But I was being selfish. I thought it was more important to defend my reputation than it was to take care of my child. It's so ironic. I was so focused on wanting people to know I was a good mother that I stopped being one.

What the system did to my family was wrong. Very wrong. But, I should have just accepted that I would never beat them. They're too powerful. They have all the resources on their side. And I squandered most of what my family had fighting them. It was stupid and selfish.

There's still a small part of me holding out hope that the judge will quash the subpoena and that Teeny Tammy will develop a case of humanity and dismiss the charges. But every time I've dared to hope, the disappointment is even more painful. I'm pretty much done hoping. Regardless of what happens, it's time to put my family back together again.

Things at work are worse. Donations are still down and the demand for services is up. That's what happens during a recession, but I'm sure the board will find a way to blame me, especially if we don't get a renewal on one of our federal grants. I was half an hour late getting the application for a renewal filed. It was technically due by midnight. I didn't push the send button until 12:23 a.m. It was completely my fault. I shouldn't have left it until the last minute. And I shouldn't have put my head down on my desk while I was trying to get it done. I fell asleep for an hour and missed the deadline. Hopefully, the people in Washington who review these things won't notice. Afterward, I went to Betsy's house to try to sleep and couldn't.

I haven't slept more than three hours in a row in seven months. I'm so exhausted that I fall asleep for a couple of hours before midnight. Then, I'm awake for the rest of the night. I lie there thinking about how screwed up my life is and how much I would like to go back to my previously imperfect but immeasurably better life. If I'm lucky I fall back to sleep for an hour before I have to get up.

Jasmine constantly reminds me that sleep deprivation is bad for the health, but I can't stand the idea of sleep aids or antidepressants. Besides, the last thing I need is an addiction to sleeping pills on top of everything else that's going on. I've lost all control of my life during these months. I need to feel like I have choices. I choose not to take drugs. Partly because I'm afraid that if I start, it will be too easy to solve all of my problems with medication. And partly because I don't want to dull the pain.

Meredith has been in pain for the past seven months. I can't take that away, but I can at least empathize.

CHAPTER 40

James Bennett
Friday, May 3, 2013

We're pretty much tapped out financially. I haven't told Sarah how bad it is yet because I don't want her to make her decisions based on money. We just got our April bill from Barry. Based on the bills so far, it's going to take quite a bit more money to get through a trial. I know how much trials cost. And when Barry asks for another retainer, I'm not sure where we'll get it. I hate the idea of borrowing from family, but it may come to that. Sarah's parents aren't wealthy, and neither is my dad. They're all on fixed incomes and probably can't afford to give us much. Besides, it's embarrassing to be a forty-year-old lawyer asking your father for money.

I guess the worst case scenario is we withdraw the money in our IRAs. We'll have to pay penalties and taxes, but there may be enough left to cover the trial. I think it's ironic that there's a penalty exception for medical expenses, but not legal expenses. I guess the government sympathizes with people with large medical bills, but feels people accused of crimes don't deserve special treatment. Just one more way the system assumes you're guilty.

If we win on the motion to quash Meredith's subpoena, it would be crazy not to take this to trial. The state's entire case is based on a guy who was looking in his sideview mirror. The odds that Barry will win are good. Tamara isn't a bad lawyer, but she's not in Barry's league and the facts are on our side.

Sarah and I are meeting at home for lunch today. It's not something we've done often during the past months. Probably we should have done it more. Sarah wants to talk.

When I arrive at twelve thirty, Sarah's van is already in the driveway. She's in the kitchen putting away groceries. I greet her with a kiss on the cheek. There's a pot of soup heating on the stove. It's been so long since I've seen her cooking in this kitchen that it looks strange.

"Soup from a can okay?" she says.

"Fine. It's probably better for the budget," I say. I hadn't meant to bring up money, but it was the first thing I did.

"I blew through a lot of money this year, didn't I?"

"It's not your fault."

"I know. But I do have the power to stop it."

"Only if you admit to something you didn't do."

"Thank you for that."

"For what?"

"For believing in me."

I'm about to say that she would have done the same for me, but I realize I'm not sure if it's true. I've been a loose cannon for a while. We both know that, if I had been accused of abusing one of our children, Sarah might have had her doubts about me. And rightly so. I wonder how things might have been different if I had been the one to take Meredith to ballet that day. I could have just as easily been the one accused of child abuse. Hell, I might have even spanked the kid in public if she made me mad enough.

Sarah ladles vegetable soup into two bowls. She pulls a roll out of the toaster oven and puts it on a plate next to my bowl. I get the butter out of the refrigerator.

"How come you don't have a roll?"

"I'm not hungry. I have too much on my mind."

We eat in silence for a few minutes. "What did you want to talk about?" I say.

"The kids. Us."

I don't say anything, I just look at her.

"Are we going to make it?" she says.

"What do you mean?"

"Is our marriage going to survive? Is our family going to stay together?"

"Why are you asking me that now?"

"Because I have some decisions to make. We're going to get a ruling from the judge any day now. I have to figure out what's best for the kids, what's best for the family."

"What are you thinking?"

"I don't want a trial."

"Neither do I, but sometimes it's the best option."

"What if we just start over? If Teeny Tammy won't dismiss the charges, I'll get Barry to make the best deal he can. We'll put this behind us as quickly as possible and move. We're still young enough to start over."

"Move where?"

"I don't know. You choose. Anywhere but here. We were happy in Chicago."

"We were college students. It's different with kids."

"I know."

"And what about my practice? I've spent all these years building a practice and a reputation. I would have to get licensed to practice in another state and start from scratch."

"It's a lot, but it would be worth it."

"The kids would have to start in new schools."

"They're kids. They'll adapt."

"We picked this place because it's one of the few places where kids are safe no matter what."

"There are other safe places."

"What would you do for work?"

"I don't know, it depends on where we move. The most important thing is that we all get to be together and that we get a fresh start."

"Do you really want to sell the house? I thought you loved this house."

"I do. Or rather I did. I've come to the realization that everything here will only remind me of what I've been through. What we've been through. Jasmine says I have PTSD."

"I guess that makes sense."

"Apparently, it's not unusual for people who've been falsely accused of a crime. I should have realized it, but it's hard to diagnose yourself. I don't doubt that Meredith is suffering from the same thing although for different reasons. It would be good for her to start over as well."

"Wow. It sounds like you've put a lot of thought into this."

"Only since I realized it's hopeless."

"But it isn't hopeless. Sure, the system is skewed. That's painfully obvious. But I have to believe that, in the end, justice will prevail. If it doesn't, then my whole profession is a sham."

Sarah gets up, picking up both empty bowls. She places them in the sink and then turns to face me, leaning against the counter. "It's too late for justice. They've already done too much damage to us. The question is how best to pick up the pieces."

"I don't know."

"Before this happened, we had troubles in our marriage. People don't go to marriage counseling for fun. This legal mess trumped everything. And I don't blame you for taking a break from the counseling under the circumstances. But what I want to know is whether you're committed to making this work."

"Are you?" I say.

"James, you have been there for me through the worst time of my life. I loved you before and I love you still. If you're willing to keep working on our marriage, then so am I. I think we can make it, but only if we're both committed."

I don't know what to say, so I don't say anything. Instead, I get up and go to her. I pull her to me and hug her, caressing her hair. For the past seven months, I have been so focused on the court case that I haven't thought of what would happen afterward. I think I had always assumed that we would prevail, that our reputations would be cleansed, and that we would go back to the life we used to have, a lot poorer and a bit beaten up. Then, we would figure out the future of our marriage. Now, it's like Sarah is asking me if I want to get married all over again. Do I want to start over again in a life with her? She's different than she used to be. We haven't had a fight in seven months. She seems to appreciate me more. But will we fall into the same patterns? I didn't like her when we used to argue. Hell, I didn't like myself either. It's been nice not arguing with her.

"I love you too, Sarah," I say. It's not a lie, but it's not the whole truth either.

CHAPTER 41

Karen Driscoll
Monday, May 6, 2013

I have a new child sex abuse case. This time the dad was touching the private parts of his six-year-old daughter. The mom came in a few days ago and gave a statement. She said the kid disclosed to her while she was getting dressed. Like many of these cases, the parents are separated, although in this case, no divorce papers have been filed yet.

I was officially assigned the file this morning. I called the mom who brought the kid to me for an interview. The mom seems genuinely upset, like she doesn't want to believe the father would do this. Apparently, the grandma convinced her to let the police do an interview. Personally, I can tell when a parent is just trying to get a better deal in a divorce. I don't get that vibe in this case, partly because the mom said it was a trial separation, and she was hoping they were going to work things out.

The mom and the grandmother wait outside while I take Becca to the interview room. I told them it will be at least an hour. I got the impression from the Bennett case that my weapons were an issue, so before I came in, I locked my gun and nightstick in my locker. I'm sure there are people who would rather I change out of my uniform, but I don't have a change of clothes with me and it didn't seem worth taking the time to go home. Besides, neither the mom or the grandma said anything about my clothing.

Becca is a little brunette with two ponytails on the sides of her head. She's cute and seems fairly friendly. I start by explaining that it's my job to make sure kids are safe and that I need to ask her some questions to make sure she's safe. I give her paper and crayons to distract her while I ask questions. It's a suggestion I got at a training I went to last month. I have no trouble getting Becca to give me some background information. She tells me she's six, and that she has a younger brother, Zach, who's four.

She's fairly open about her school and her teachers. I ask some questions to make sure she understands the difference between the truth and a lie. Then, just to keep the prosecutors from getting pissy, I tell her how important it is to tell the truth.

"Do you promise that everything you tell me today will be the truth?" I say.

"Yes." Hopefully that will be enough to keep Tamara from jumping down my throat again.

I ask Becca a few questions about her dad. She explains that her dad isn't living with them right now because he's having a "time-out," but that she and her brother visit him and sleep over. She says it's not like a regular time-out because it lasts longer, but at least he gets company.

"Is your dad having a time-out because he was bad?" I say. She just shrugs. I wait to see if she volunteers anything else, but she just keeps drawing.

"Is that your family?" I say.

"Yep."

"A mom, a dad, a big girl and a little boy, right?"

"Yep."

"Do you like visiting your dad?"

"Not really."

"Why not?"

"My toys aren't there."

"Any other reason?"

She shrugs again.

"What do you do when you visit your dad?"

"Watch TV, read library books, mostly."

"Anything else?"

She shrugs again.

"Has anyone talked to you about good touches and bad touches?"

"Yes."

"Who talked to you about that?"

"Penny."

"Who's Penny?"

"She used to be my teacher in preschool."

"What did Penny tell you about bad touches?"

"That you should tell your parents."

"Is that why you told your mom about your dad touching you?"

The kid is drawing intently, but she doesn't answer.

"Did your dad touch you in a place he shouldn't?" Still no answer.

I need to do something to get the kid to disclose. I take a piece of paper and draw a generic picture of a child. It looks more like a gingerbread man than a kid. I explain what I'm drawing as I draw it. "Can you point on the picture to where your daddy touched you?"

She shakes her head.

"Becca, can you show me what your teacher told you was a bad touch. You can use your crayon to point."

Becca uses her crayon to point to the crotch of the generic child.

"Is that where your daddy touched you?"

She shakes her head, but doesn't answer out loud.

"Becca, did your daddy touch you like you showed on the drawing?"

This time she nods.

I knew it. I really want to get more details. "Where were you when your daddy touched you there?"

"I don't know."

"Was it in your room?"

"No."

"Was it in the bathroom?"

"No."

"Was it in his room?"

"No."

She's probably confused because the living situation is in flux. I need to ask the questions in a way that's more clear to her.

"Which house were you at when your daddy touched you?"

The kid doesn't look up from her drawing. "My daddy touched me at my house and his new house."

"How many times did your dad touch you?"

"My daddy touches me every time he sees me." That's either really bad or the kid is confused.

"Where were you when your daddy touched you in the bad way?"

"I don't know."

"Was it at your mom's house?"

"No."

"Was it at someone else's house?"

"No."

"So, it was at your dad's new house?"

"No. He lives in an apartment."

"Okay, so your dad touched you in his new apartment?"

"Yes."

"And the way he touched you was the bad way like you showed on the drawing?"

"Yes."

"And where was your brother when your dad touched you?"

"I don't know."

I feel like I've gotten as much as I'm going to get from this child. I'm convinced she was abused by the dad. She's six, so she's not going to be able to remember dates and times. I managed to get her to tell me "who" and "where." That's probably the best I'll do.

I finish up by thanking her for talking to me. Then, the grandma takes the kid outside so I can talk to the mom.

"Did she tell you?"

"Yes, she did."

"What are you going to do?"

"I'm going to take this to the state's attorneys and see what they want to do."

"What should I do?"

"It would be best if you not talk to anyone about this, especially your husband."

"But I'm supposed to send the kids to his place this weekend."

"I'll make sure the prosecutors understand the situation."

"But if I keep the kids home, he'll know something is up. If I send them over there, he may molest her again."

"Do you have any sort of court order requiring you to send the kids?"

"No."

"Then keep them home."

"What do I tell him?"

"Make up an excuse."

She nods, sighing deeply. It seems like a no-brainer to me, but some people need to be walked through everything.

"How long until you decide what's next?"

"I can't say. All I can do is present the facts to the prosecutors."

"Okay, I understand, but I have to protect my daughter."

"You've taken the first steps. I promise you I'll make this a priority."

"I can't believe this is happening. I never thought he would do something like this. I wouldn't have believed it if I hadn't heard it with my own ears."

I promise to get in touch and she leaves. I head for my sergeant's office. Patterson was monitoring the interview on the closed-circuit camera.

"What did you think?" I ask.

"She said it, alright."

"I wish she would have been more specific."

"Yeah, but she's young. In my experience, kids have a hard time with details."

"Do you think he did it?"

"Probably. She wouldn't have said it if he hadn't done something."

"There is that."

"What do you want me to do?"

"Write it up and take it up to the state's attorneys."

"Yes, sir."

"Hey, good work in there."

"Thanks."

When I get back to my desk, I have a message from Tamara, so I call her back. Apparently, she got a decision from the judge in the Bennett case. She wants to talk to me. She doesn't sound mad, so I'm guessing it's not all bad news. I tell her that I can come to her office in an hour. I want to write up the summary of Becca's interview while it's still fresh in my mind.

An hour and a half later, I'm sitting in Tamara's office. She hands me some stapled sheets.

"That's your copy. I want you to study it."

"Now?"

"No, later. But before you do another interview of a child."

"Did we lose on the motion?"

"Not technically."

"What does it say?"

"The judge denied their motion to quash the subpoena."

"That's good news."

"But the bad news is that he *sua sponte* suppressed your interview. I think you should know he came down pretty hard on you."

"But you can still use the kid to testify, right?"

"Yes. But, I can't use your interview to impeach her. If she gets up on the stand and says my mommy didn't do it, I'm stuck with it. I can't even mention your interview, much less put it into evidence as a prior inconsistent statement."

"But, at least you still have a case."

"Not one I want to take to trial. I can't beat Barry with my hands tied behind my back. He has access to the kid to prepare for trial. I don't. And now I can't use your interview to show he's fabricating her testimony."

"What are you going to do?"

"I'm going to keep playing hardball and hope that they take a deal."

"And if they don't?"

"I don't know. I may have no choice but to dismiss it."

"And she gets away with it?"

"Don't blame me. I'm not the one who used so many leading questions that the judge labeled the interview 'intrinsically unfair.' That's on you."

Tamara glares at me and I feel like I'm dismissed. I really can't respond without reading the decision. I take it back to the PD and settle in to read.

When I'm done, my first thought is that at least some of this is Tamara's fault. The judge seemed to buy everything that Dr. Lapitas said. If she'd done more to attack him or had put on an expert to counter what he said, the interview wouldn't have been suppressed. I know that Lapitas labeled almost half of my questions as leading and the judge found that the circumstances of the interview were suggestive. But surely Tamara could have done more. It's not like the Bennett interview was all that different from all the other interviews we do, and those don't get suppressed. Personally, I'm not going to take all the blame for this.

CHAPTER 42

Tamara Goodwin
Tuesday, May 7, 2013

I'm not surprised to hear from Barry a few days after the Bennett decision comes out. He shows up at my office without an appointment again. I think he does it to catch me off guard. I'm expecting him to gloat. I may have won the battle, but he won the war and I know it. For some reason, he doesn't look particularly happy.

"Any chance you'll dismiss the charges, now that we have a decision?" he says. I was expecting the question, just not the tone.

"You know me better than that. I don't give up easily. I like a good challenge."

"Even if it means making an eight-year-old testify?"

"Just doing my job." I shrug.

"Then, my client wants to make a no contest plea. Is the deferred still on the table?"

I'm surprised and definitely relieved. "First of all, I don't take no contest pleas on domestics. You can't participate in counseling if you can't admit you committed the crime." That's my stock answer. "Second, if you recall, the deferred was time limited. It expired when we had that hearing on the motion to quash."

"Come on, Tamara. You don't want to try this case. You've got nothing left."

"Then why is your client making a deal?"

"She's not willing to let her kid testify. Didn't you hear Dr. Lapitas? Kids who testify get irreparably damaged. This kid's already in bad shape. Her mother's not going to take any more chances with her mental health."

"Didn't you read the opinion? Judge Jenkins said there was insufficient evidence that the cause of the kid's problems was either the police interview or the no-contact order. He said it was possible that the damage to the child was from the mother's actions. That's why he didn't quash the subpoena or lift the no-contact order."

"Of course he said that. It never ceases to amaze me how the system protects itself from its mistakes. He's not going to admit he was wrong any more than you are. He's the one who ordered no contact. A different judge might have admitted the mistake, but apparently not Jenkins. I was hoping I was wrong about him. Guess not."

"So now we're all wrong and your client is a saint?"

"Look, I'm not blaming you for what happened to the kid. You're just a cog in a great big machine. I'm just telling you that Sarah Bennett is not going to put her child through a trial. In her words, 'I would rather admit to something I didn't do than risk any more harm to Meredith.' She's a good mom. She's doing what any good parent would do under the circumstances. If we had won on the motion to quash, we'd still be taking this to trial. But that's not what happened, and I'm coming to you to make a deal before you put a bunch of time into preparing for trial. So please, give us a break."

"I already told you—a no contest plea won't work in a domestic."

"It's not technically a domestic any more. Remember, the judge dismissed that charge."

"I'm not going to agree to a no contest, but if you can get the judge to take it, then fine. But she has to plead to both the remaining charges."

"Really? Don't you think that's a bit harsh?"

"Okay, she can plead to the reckless endangerment charge. But don't even ask for a deferred. Six to twelve months suspended with two years of probation."

"You want to saddle this woman with a record for being a good mom?"

"Are you going to go to my boss again and try to overrule me? Because he already told me it's my decision."

"I was just trying to get a fresh perspective on this case. I wasn't trying to overrule you. I was hoping you'd change the way you see the case."

"You're right, Barry. I don't see this case the same way you do. Sarah Bennett brought this on herself. Not Driscoll. Not me. And not the judge. Bennett's the one who tried to drag her kid behind her van. All we did was our jobs. We may not have gotten all the facts perfectly right, but it doesn't change what she did. I've given you the best deal you're going to get. Take it or take this to trial. I really don't care which."

Barry looks like he wants to strangle me. "I'll talk to my client and get back to you," he says and turns away. I don't understand why he's angry at me. We're supposed to be professionals, above petty squabbles. We both represent our clients. It's not supposed to be personal. Besides, if anyone should be angry, it's me. It's humiliating to have people going to your boss to complain about you.

CHAPTER 43

Nicholas Bennett
Tuesday, May 7, 2013

Saturday is my birthday. I'm going to turn thirteen. That means I'll be a teenager. Which is kind of a big deal. When I turned ten, my mom made a big deal out of it because it was double digits. In some ways this is bigger.

Except nobody seems to have remembered my birthday.

I know everyone is thinking about the trial, but you only become a teenager once. Usually by now my mom would have sent out invitations to my friends for a party. I guess there isn't going to be a party this year.

I think I can count on my grandparents to remember. They usually send cards with checks. It's better than nothing.

CHAPTER 44

Sarah Bennett
Wednesday, May 8, 2013

I'm hoping this will be the last time in my life I ever set foot in a courtroom. We were supposed to draw a jury tomorrow, but instead we're in court today for my change of plea.

I didn't sleep at all last night. I'm relieved this will be over today, but I'm afraid because I don't know what the consequences will be. I fear that this is going to be another one of those life-defining moments, but I can't see where this path will lead. There are too many unknowns, too many variables.

Barry promised that I'll be allowed to go home today. That I'll see Meredith, without someone looking over my shoulder. That I'll kiss Camille good night. That my family will be all together again. For now, I'm focusing on that.

I packed up my belongings at Betsy's house this morning. They're in the back of the van. The kids should get off the bus at three thirty. I'm planning to be there waiting for them.

Right now I'm alone, waiting for Barry in one of the little conference rooms in front of the courtroom. James is not here—for the first time since this started. He said he has an important client meeting this afternoon. He offered to cancel it, but I told him not to worry about it. There's nothing he can do at this point. I just need to get through this. I called my mom an hour ago, and she assured me for the tenth time that I'm doing the right thing, that she would do the same thing.

Barry comes into the room with some colored sheets of paper. He explains that it's the standard plea agreement form. Then, he looks into my eyes.

"Are you sure you want to do this?"

"Yes... and no. But I am going to do it."

"You mean Meredith?"

"I can't let her testify."

"I get that. I really do. It's not like me to talk clients out of making plea deals. It's just that the state has no case. We don't even know if Tamara's bluffing about putting Meredith on the stand. If I were her, there's no way I would use Meredith as a witness."

"And what if she's not bluffing? Is she going to make a deal after the trial starts?"

"Probably not. Once the trial starts, the judge would almost certainly make you plead straight up to all pending charges. And then the sentence would depend on his mood that day. They don't like to encourage last-minute changes of heart."

"Then I have no choice. I know you have a lot invested in this too. And I'm sorry."

"You don't need to apologize to me. I'm just doing my job. And my job is to resolve this in a way you can live with. This isn't about me."

"If it helps, I had a long talk with my therapist on Friday. I thought long and hard all weekend. It's time to put this behind us. We need to get back to being a normal family and we can't do that under these circumstances. Besides, we might have had to sell the house to pay for the trial," I say.

"Okay. If you're sure. Let's go over this paperwork then. The deal is that you'll be on probation for up to two years. The only condition is that you attend counseling as directed by the probation officer. It will probably be less than a year on probation. The system is so overloaded that they've been discharging people as soon as they complete their required conditions. You won't know what type of counseling is required until you meet with your PO."

"And as soon as I'm off probation, I can leave town for good?"

"Absolutely."

I sign on the line marked "Defendant." It's not a label I have enjoyed, but I suppose it's better than "Convict" which is the label I will have earned after today's hearing.

We walk into the courtroom. It's the first time I've been in the room when it has been this crowded. There are people sitting in all the pews. Lawyers in suits are huddling with clients in ragged jeans and T-shirts. I know that we will be called early because I have retained counsel. It's a mixed blessing. I have to pay for less of Barry's time, but I have to be humiliated in front of more people.

Barry gives the plea agreement to Teeny Tammy who looks briefly at the form before signing. I'm trying not to hate her. Maybe it's not her that I hate, but what she stands for—the powerlessness of being accused. It's hard to look at her because she looks so fresh faced and well rested. But I know she's like a feral dog, taking on all comers as if her very life depended on it.

We are the second ones called. Barry hands the copies of the plea agreement to the clerk and the judge. My ears are ringing. I can hear the judge, but I have to concentrate very hard. He asks me a series of questions. I listen carefully, not wanting to make a mistake. Barry has already explained that the questions are designed to make sure I am competent to plead guilty. I cannot hear my own voice—it's too loud in my head—but I can tell I am answering correctly because the judge keeps going. Then, he asks the question I've been dreading.

"How do you plead?"

I realize that I am crying. Tears are dripping down my cheeks and onto the table where I am supporting most of my weight with my hands. My legs are too wobbly to hold me.

Barry jumps in. "Your Honor, with the court's permission we will be entering an *Alford* plea. That's why the plea form indicates that this will be a 'no contest' verdict. My client maintains her innocence, but recognizes that pleading guilty would be in her best interests and the best interests of her family."

"Attorneys approach," the judge says gruffly.

Barry and Teeny go up to stand in front of the judge. I don't know whether I should sit down. Nobody has told me. I keep leaning on the table. My hands are getting numb from the pressure.

The room is filled with white noise that makes the lawyers' voices inaudible while they have an animated discussion. Teeny is slapping her pen against her notepad. Barry is red faced, hands clenched behind his back. It's unnerving that they are discussing my fate and I'm not even allowed to hear them, much less participate in the discussion. After a minute Barry returns to the counsel table.

"What was that about?"

"Apparently, the judge is not a big fan of *Alford* pleas."

"Is he going to let me do it?"

"Yes, because I convinced him that, if he didn't, we would appeal his decision on the motion to quash and keep this thing kicking around for a few more months."

"But I want to go home today. I told you I don't want to appeal."

"I know. I was bluffing. The word is that Judge Jenkins is afraid of getting reversed. Tamara was pissed because she thought it was a straight no contest, but she caved too when she realized she might have to write an appellate brief."

"Thank you."

There's no more time for discussion because the judge resumes the hearing. "Ms. Bennett, I understand that you will be pleading no contest pursuant to *North Carolina versus Alford*. Is that correct?"

"Yes, Your Honor," I say. I try to hold it back, but I cough several times. The judge waits.

"Okay then, for the record, how do you plead?"

I look at Barry who nods his head. "No contest," I say.

"Okay, you may be seated." I am relieved to no longer be supporting my weight. I sink into the chair and immediately start circling my wrists to regain circulation. The judge continues, "Ms. Goodwin, would you please recite the facts?"

"Yes, Your Honor. If this matter were to go to trial, the state would prove beyond a reasonable doubt that the defendant operated a motor vehicle knowing that her child was holding onto the door handle, thereby placing the child at risk of death or serious bodily injury."

"Do you agree with those facts, Mr. Densmore?"

"No, we do not, Your Honor." Barry stands and grabs my wrist to let me know that I need to stand as well. "My client continues to dispute having knowledge at first. We also contend that, once she became aware of the child, her actions were intended to protect the child. For the record, my client is making this deal only to avoid having her eight-year-old daughter traumatized by having to testify."

"Okay. I will accept your plea of no contest and enter a judgment of guilty. Ms. Bennett, do you wish to say anything before I impose sentence?"

I look at Barry, who subtly shakes his head.

"No, thank you," I say softly and shake my head.

"Very well. Sentence is imposed in accordance with the plea agreement. Ms. Bennett, you must report to probation before leaving the building."

"Anything further on this matter?"

Both attorneys say no and we are excused. It's over just like that. I now have a criminal record. After nearly eight months, the whole legal ordeal is over.

Manny Rodriguez from the newspaper follows us into the hall. I hadn't noticed him sitting at the back of the courtroom.

"Hey Manny, what brings you to court today?" Barry says. I can tell he is trying to sound nonchalant.

"I heard maybe there would be a change of plea. Apparently I heard right."

"Who told you?"

"Never reveal a source, you know that. Any comment for the paper?"

"Sure," Barry says. He and I had talked about this possibility a few days ago and agreed what he will say. "You may have noticed what we did was an *Alford* plea. My client essentially pled no contest without admitting guilt."

"But she did take a plea deal, right?"

"Yes. But, the *Alford* plea is a way of saying I didn't do it, but the state might have enough evidence to persuade a jury, so I'm making a deal to avoid worse consequences. In this case, the consequences my client wanted to avoid were her daughter being to be forced to testify and the cost of a trial, even though we're confident we could have won. The police got most of the facts wrong and we would have proved it, but the state offered a punishment that was essentially a slap on the wrist. Even though my client wanted to continue fighting this, under the circumstances, it made sense to just put it behind her."

Manny is scribbling in a notepad. We wait while he finishes.

"You got all that?" Barry says. "I can say it again if you want."

Manny smirks. "No, thanks. I've learned to write pretty fast over the years." He turns to me. "How do you feel about this?"

When Barry and I agreed that he would do all the talking to the press, I hadn't expected Manny to be waiting after the hearing. It's one thing to not return a phone call. It's another to say, "no comment" to his face. I feel like I should say something. "I'm just glad that this is over. It's time for my family to heal from this ordeal," I say.

Manny thanks us and we leave. He stays outside the courtroom, probably waiting to talk to Teeny.

Barry points me in the direction of the probation office.

"Thank you... for everything," I say.

"You're welcome," he says. "I just want you to know that I have a lot of respect for you and James. You faced some tough decisions and you behaved admirably. You're good people."

"Thank you."

"The only other thing I want to tell you is that time will heal this. It may not feel like it for a while, but this is the beginning of the end. You will put this behind you."

"I hope you're right."

He waves and heads for the exit.

The probation office is on the second floor. Five people are sitting on benches in the hallway. There's a clipboard on the wall under a large sign that says, "Sign in here. Wait to be called."

I write my name on the curled page. I'm still too keyed up to sit, so I pace the hallway.

Two of the bench guys are having a conversation. They both look to be about mid-twenties.

"Who's your PO?" one says.

"I have Ed. He's okay."

"Yeah, I had him last time. He doesn't give you too much shit as you as long as you don't get in trouble. This time I have Pam. She's a pain in the ass, keeps talking to my wife, trying to find out what I'm doing."

Over the next fifteen minutes, three people get called into the offices that line the halls. It appears the clipboard has taken the place of a receptionist. It is now two thirty. I just want to get home to my kids.

Finally, at quarter of three, I get called by a middle-aged woman. "Sarah Bennett?"

"That's me."

"Pam Pringle." I follow her into a small office. "Why does your name sound familiar?"

"Probably because I'm the director of the Murdoch shelter."

"You could have made an appointment if you wanted to talk about one of my clients. You didn't need to wait here in the hall."

"Actually, I'm now officially one of your clients."

Her eyebrows go up. "You got any paperwork for me. The file hasn't made it upstairs yet."

I show her the copy of the plea agreement that Barry gave me. "This is all I have."

"Reckless endangerment, with a dismissed charge of gross negligent operation. You got a drinking problem?"

"No. Alcohol had nothing to do with it."

"Drugs?"

"No. Just a stubborn kid and a mistaken witness."

"I have to admit I'm curious."

"Do you read the *Gazette?*"

"That's right, I think I remember something from a while ago. Why don't you tell me what happened?"

I have no idea whether it's a good idea to spill your guts to a probation officer. Barry didn't give me any advice on this. All I know is that for nearly eight months, I've been holding it in. I tell the whole story. It takes close to an hour. I have to give it to Pam. She's patient. She jots a few notes, but mostly she watches me and listens.

When I'm done, she says, "I'm not saying I don't believe you, but there's one thing I've learned in this job—everybody lies. So I take everything with a grain of salt. And you should probably know that the official version of what happened is basically whatever is in the police report, which should make it up to my desk sometime tomorrow."

"But the police report is all wrong. They're the ones who lied."

"Doesn't matter. You're now guilty and that police report is what we use to supervise your probation because it's the most concise description available."

"So, it doesn't matter that the felony was dismissed, and that I pled no contest to a misdemeanor?"

"A little. Your case should be in the computer by now, which means I can serve you with your official probation conditions. Let's make an appointment for next week. By then, I will have had a chance to review the file and figure out what kind of counseling we're going to require."

Pam prints out a sheet listing my conditions and reads them aloud. When she's done, I sign the page and she makes me a copy. As I leave, I see her looking at the clipboard for her next probationer.

I'm exhausted. I was hoping that by putting the court case behind me, I would feel like I was taking control of my life. Instead, I feel like it's just more of the same. Pam essentially spelled out that the system is not interested in the truth, just getting things done. What if I just made a big mistake?

It's now quarter of four. The kids are already at home. My plan to wait at the bus stop isn't going to happen. As I get closer to home, I feel better. I can't wait to see the kids. They are the reason I did what I did today. I just have to keep reminding myself it was worth it.

CHAPTER 45

Nicholas Bennett
Wednesday, May 8, 2013

My mom just walked in the door. "Mom, you can't be here. Meredith is home," I say.

"It's okay. I know. It's over. I'm allowed to come home," she says.

I can't help smiling. My mom comes over and gives me a hug. "It is so good to be here with you," she says.

"I know," I say.

"Where are the girls?"

I'm a little disappointed that she has to rush off to be with them. I haven't had much time with her for a long time. I want to ask her what happened with the court case.

My mom goes up to the girls' room. When she comes out about ten minutes later she's crying.

"What do you want me to make for dinner?" she says. I have to think. It's been so long since she cooked us dinner.

"How about macaroni and cheese?" I say. "Dad only makes the kind from a box. I'd like to have the kind you make."

"Mac and cheese it is." She smiles and it's almost like things are back to normal. Except they're not. My mom is still my mom, but it feels almost like someone put a spell on her that took away her sparkle. That's it, she's like Tinker Bell without her pixie dust. My mom always used to say stuff like that. Anyway, she's here but something's missing.

My dad gets home while my mom is cooking dinner. "How did it go? You didn't call." He gives her a long hug. It's good to see them together.

"I was busy dealing with stuff," she says and looks at me. "And then I wanted to get home to see... the kids."

My dad nods. I wonder what she was going to say. I bet she wanted to get back to Meredith. What are Camille and I? Dog poop? I want to know what kind of stuff she was dealing with. I'm not stupid. Something happened today.

The food is good. The macaroni is tender, but not mushy, and the cheese is thick and creamy, but not gooey. I should ask my mom how she does that in case she goes away again.

Dinner is quiet. I figured Meredith would go back to normal again once my mom got home, but she's the same. Camille talks a bit. My mom and dad mostly just give each other these half smiles.

After dinner, I suggest a game of Uno, but my mom says it would be better to play something else. We end up playing Slapjack, but it doesn't last long because Camille is too slow to be any good and Meredith keeps giving Camille cards from her own stack to keep her in the game. After a few minutes it's down to my mom and me. She's pretty slow too, so it's over quick.

After everyone has showered and gotten in their pj's, my mom reads to my sisters. I sit in the hallway to listen because I want to hear my mom's voice, but I don't want my sisters whining about my being there. They start reading where they left off, but Camille keeps asking questions like she can't remember what happened in the book before they stopped reading back before the court stuff. What's weird is that Meredith remembers everything and keeps reminding Camille.

When my mom stops reading and starts tucking in my sisters, I go to my own room. A little while later, my mom comes in to say good night.

"How come you're allowed to be home? I thought there was going to be a trial next week. What happened?"

She's quiet for a while. I can tell she's thinking about how to answer my questions, so I just wait.

"Well, Nick, I made a deal so I could come home."

"What kind of deal? Did you pay money to the judge?"

She smiles. "No, nothing like that. The system doesn't work that way. Although, it wouldn't be any more unfair if it did." She reaches over and messes up my hair and then pets my head. It annoys me when she does that, but I'm glad to have her home, so I don't say anything. "The deal was that I agreed to stop fighting the charges and go to counseling, and they agreed to let me come home. It's a little more complicated, but that's the gist of it."

"So, you're not going to jail?"

"Of course not. I hope you haven't been worrying about that all these months."

Of course I've been worrying about it. "No, I was just making sure. But what I don't understand is why you didn't just make a deal a long time ago. We really could have used you around here."

"I know, honey. You're right. I should have been here."

"Promise you won't leave again?"

"At least not any time soon." She kisses the top of my head.

She's standing by my bedroom door with her hand on the light switch when she says, "What do you want to do for your birthday on Saturday?"

"Let's all do something together as a family," I say. "Maybe we could go to Burlington and go bowling."

"Sounds great," she says and hits the switch.

I'm tired. The last thought I have before I fall asleep is that it's good to have things back to normal.

CHAPTER 46

Tamara Goodwin
Thursday, May 9, 2013

I had to draw a jury today in one of my domestic cases. If the Bennett case hadn't pled out, I would have had to draw two. Everyone at the court seemed glad the Bennett case got resolved yesterday. It freed up three days in May for other trials.

I'm especially glad I didn't have to go to trial against Barry. It's not fair that my boss is going to take all the credit in the newspaper, but it would have been worse if Bennett had been acquitted. I'm sure, if that had happened, my boss would have been quick to point out to Manny Rodriguez that I handled the case.

Owen said he's stopping by my place at six thirty. I offered to make dinner, but he said he will have already eaten.

He's waiting in the hallway outside my apartment when I arrive a few minutes late.

"Did you forget your key?" I say.

"No."

I unlock the door. "You want a beer or something? I think there's still wine left from last weekend."

"I can't stay long," he says and follows me into the living room. I drop my purse and sit on the couch. Owen sits on the chair facing me.

"I assumed you were spending the night."

"No. I have something I have to do."

"You can still spend the night. If you want. After you do whatever you have to do."

"Tamara."

"Yes."

"This isn't working,"

"What do you mean?"

268 | ALL ABOUT THE GREATER GOOD

"You're a great girl. I mean, woman. But I don't feel like you and I are compatible."

"Of course we are. We like all the same things."

"And I need more than you can give right now."

"It's my job, isn't it? I can change that."

"No, you can't."

"You'll see. I'm going to have much more time this summer."

"It's more than that. It's who you are."

"You just said I'm great."

He sighs. "I was trying to soften the blow. The truth is, you belong with someone else. We don't see the world the same way."

"So what? It makes things more interesting."

He shakes his head. "You're too judgmental and competitive for me. I need to be with someone who's more… compassionate. Warmer."

What the hell is he talking about? I'm a good person. Sure, I work too hard. But it's only because I'm trying to make the world a better place. "I care about people. That's why I work so hard."

"I don't think so."

Why would he say that? Owen shifts his weight and puts his hands on his knees. He opens his mouth to speak. I figure he's about to tell me what he meant, but he stops. Finally, he looks down at his hands and says, "I just don't think I'm in love with you."

But he's not sure. He's too good to me to not feel something. "Maybe you just need more time."

He shakes his head. "These past six months have been good, but not good enough."

Maybe I'm missing some facts. "Is there someone else?"

"Not really."

"Do you have a date with someone else tonight?"

"No."

"Then how come you didn't tell me where you're going?"

"I don't know. Maybe I wanted you to think I had a date."

"Where are you going?"

"I joined a volleyball league on Thursday nights."

"Are you sure?"

"About volleyball?"

"No, about us."

"Sure enough," he says. "Here's your key back." He holds out his hand. The shiny key is in his palm.

"We should have gone to Hatteras," I say, taking the key and setting it on the end table.

"It might've been fun."

"Would you be breaking up with me if we had gone?"

"I don't know. We didn't go."

"I wish we had."

"Can I have my key?"

"Sure." I fumble with my key ring until I find his key.

"You're crying," he says. "You never cry."

"I'm sorry."

"I'm the one who should be sorry. I am. Sorry." He gets up and I follow.

"I'll miss you," I say. He wraps me in a hug.

"You'll be okay," he says. "I'm sure of it. I have to go or I'll be late for volleyball." He walks to the door and glances back as he opens it. I'm pretty sure there are tears forming in his eyes. There's no question he's sad. He shuts the door with a soft click.

I sink into the couch and stare at my returned key. How did I miss the signs? Maybe there were no signs. Maybe he's just upset about Hatteras. He wouldn't be crying if he really wanted to break up with me. Maybe he just needs a little space. I'll give him some space and time to miss me. Then, I'm going to try to get him back.

I call Sherry and tell her that Owen and I broke up.

"Who broke up with who?" Sherry asks.

"It was mutual," I say. "It just wasn't working."

"Good. Because I want someone to do the Hike for Hunger with me in a few weeks, but I don't want to have to listen to you whine about Owen for eight miles. You game?"

"Sure," I say, mostly because it sounds like the kind of event that Owen will be at. It will be good if he sees that I'm not working or sitting at home pining after him. Besides, it's for a good cause.

CHAPTER 47

James Bennett
Friday, May 10, 2013

Sarah has been back in our bed for two nights. It's good and bad. The good is that I ended another no-sex streak. The bad is that I've had two nights of inadequate sleep. I've gotten used to sleeping alone. Now, whenever Sarah moves, I feel it. She says she doesn't sleep well anymore, and I believe it, based on how much sleep I got with her in the bed.

I couldn't go to the change of plea on Wednesday. It just felt wrong. I understand why Sarah made the choice she did. It's probably much better for Meredith. It may be better for Sarah too. But it's not necessarily better for me. I couldn't stand the idea of watching my wife plead guilty to a crime, even if she did make an *Alford* plea. People hear guilty, they think guilty. In some ways it would have been better to be convicted at trial. Everyone knows that sometimes innocent people get convicted. But nobody's going to understand why an innocent person would plead guilty.

I told Sarah I had a meeting with a client on Wednesday afternoon, but the truth was, I spent the afternoon in my office. I emailed Kristy and she called. We spent an hour on the phone. She gets it. My reputation is important to me. She really understands how all this has affected me.

The local paper ran a story about Sarah's plea bargain in the Thursday issue. The headline was "Homeless Shelter Director Pleads Guilty in Child Dragging Case." I saw that coming. I know Barry and Sarah tried to temper it, but let's face it, headlines sell papers. The article itself wasn't much better.

> Sarah Bennett, director of the Murdoch
> Shelter for the Homeless, pleaded guilty
> on Tuesday to a charge that she recklessly

endangered her child by dragging her behind a motor vehicle. The case was scheduled to draw a jury on Thursday, but a last-minute plea deal kept it from going to trial. Bennett was sentenced to a 2-year term of probation with a condition that she participate in mental health counseling.

According to the police report filed by Officer Karen Driscoll last September, a witness reported that Bennett turned her car around while the child ran in front of the vehicle and then drove away. When the child managed to grab the door and open it, Bennett continued driving, dragging the child for 200 feet. The 8-year-old told police that her mother knew she was there but kept driving because she wanted her to go to ballet.

When questioned about the apparent lenience of the sentence in a case involving child abuse, State's Attorney Fred Dutton said the deal was designed to make sure that Bennett's children would not be further endangered. He explained that the probation office will be monitoring Bennett's behavior and ensuring that she participates in necessary counseling. According to defense lawyer Barry Densmore, Bennett took the plea deal to avoid having her daughter testify against her.

If she had been convicted at trial, Bennett could have been sentenced to up to 2 years in jail. As she was leaving the courtroom, Bennett commented that she wanted her daughter to heal from what she did to her.

Janice Higgins, a member of the board of directors of the Murdoch Shelter, said the board would be considering whether to terminate Bennett's employment. "We gave her the benefit of the doubt when she claimed to be innocent of the charges. Now, there is no doubt. We can't have convicted child abusers in charge of an organization tasked with protecting families."

Next to the article is a picture of Sarah. It is the same one they ran when they printed the story about her becoming the director of the Murdoch Shelter. At least it wasn't the mug shot this time.

Sarah is livid when she reads the article. "How could he have twisted this so much?" she says.

"Technically, almost everything he said was true."

"And yet, he missed the whole point. Barry explained it to him. And by the way, he got my quote wrong."

I'm just glad that my name wasn't mentioned in the article this time. If I'd gone to the change of plea, I would have been on Manny's mind. He might have gotten a quote from me too. Of course, I can't say this.

"This will blow over," I say.

"Sure. But not until after I've lost my job."

What can I say? She's probably right.

CHAPTER 48

Karen Driscoll
Tuesday, May 14, 2013

I have to admit it was nice to see my name in the paper last week. On the front page, no less. A couple of the guys at the PD commented that I seem to have a knack for getting my name in the paper. I haven't heard from my mother yet. Maybe she didn't see the article.

The chief calls me into his office after lunch.

"I saw that Sarah Bennett pled out."

"Yes, sir. I was personally a little surprised. Tamara seemed to think the case was going to trial. We'd already scheduled prep time."

"Well, I just wanted to say, 'Good job.' It makes us look good when people see that our investigations result in convictions. They like to know what we do with their tax dollars."

"Thank you, sir."

"You still like doing the child abuse investigations?"

"I wouldn't say that I like them. But I'm definitely getting better at them. I'm getting a lot more kids to disclose than I was when I first started. Personally, I think it's just a matter of learning how to talk to kids."

"Well, I'm glad that you've settled in. It's helpful having someone we can count on to handle those cases."

CHAPTER 49

Sarah Bennett
Tuesday, June 10, 2013

My phone is ringing. I don't usually answer it, but I always check to make sure it's not the kids or their schools calling. Not that I get a lot of calls anymore. The name on the screen is Amelia, my sister. I haven't talked to her since the day I was arrested. I'm not sure why I accept the call.

"I can't believe you didn't tell me about what happened," she says.

"Mom told you."

"Everything. Just now. And here I was assuming no news is good news. I would have been there for you."

"I didn't want to bother you," I say, knowing it's only partly true. With hindsight, I think a bigger reason was not wanting our roles to be reversed for the first time in our lives. She's the screwup, not me.

"How are you doing?"

"I lost my job. No surprise."

"It's not the end of the world. I've lost jobs. I always find another one."

I don't bother to say the situation is incomparable. "They gave me the option of quitting, but I let them fire me so I could collect unemployment."

"At least that buys you some time."

"I guess. I'm supposed to be looking for another job as a condition of my probation."

"Any luck?"

"I haven't started looking. My probation officer is cutting me some slack." Which is an understatement. Pam has been great. She actually took the time to read the court file. She said she has two kids in high school and knows how challenging it is to be a parent. Pam couldn't understand why the case wasn't dismissed.

"How's Meredith?" Amelia asks.

"She's in counseling. James says she's eating better than when I was gone, but she's not back to normal."

"I should have realized something was up when Dad made the trip to Vermont last Christmas. I'm so sorry this happened to you guys. Let me know if there's anything I can do to help. And call if you want to talk. Anytime."

We talk for half an hour about her life in California. I'm glad to hear she's happy with her job selling radio advertising. And that she's managed to keep it for over a year. When we hang up, I realize I'm glad I took the call.

Of course, I didn't tell Amelia how bad things really are.

I use all my energy every day just putting on a good face for the kids. It seems to be enough for Camille. I'm not sure she remembers how things used to be. And Nick's so wrapped up in his teenage life that I doubt he notices much else. Meredith... well, I don't think I'm fooling her. It's a good thing the school has a summer program for kids. Hopefully, it will keep the kids from being affected by my depression when school gets out in a week.

As soon as the kids are out the door to school in the morning, I go back to bed. Not that I can sleep. My sleep hasn't gotten any better. Mostly, I just lie there. I never used to watch TV, but now I crave its mindlessness. It distracts my mind enough that I can fall asleep for while. Sometimes I even make it through an entire episode.

I used to love to read fiction. Now, I get to the bottom of a page and can't remember what it was about. The only books that hold my attention are the ebooks on trauma in children that I buy on Amazon. I need to understand it so I can do what's best for Meredith from here on.

I can't seem to stop thinking about how unfair the whole situation is. No matter what I do, the thought is always there in my mind, never leaving for more than a few seconds. I think about Karen Driscoll and Teeny Tammy a lot. It doesn't seem fair that they get to go on with their lives, oblivious to what they've done to my family. I also think about what a moron that guy Dave Belkin must be. I wonder what kind of person gives sworn statements about things that didn't happen. I get angry at the judge.

Pam is concerned about my depression. She probably should be. She's letting me continue seeing Jasmine to meet my counseling requirement.

Jasmine says I need to go forward. She keeps suggesting antidepressants. While the court case was pending, I refused to take them because I felt like the depression was situational. I knew that as soon as the case was dismissed, I would break out of the depression. Vindication would cure my ills.

The problem is that the case wasn't dismissed. I put my family through hell for eight months for no reason. I don't deserve to feel better. We could have gotten Meredith into therapy eight months ago if it weren't for my need to prove my innocence. I may not deserve what the system did to me, but I had choices. I don't deserve to feel better until Meredith feels better. Of course, according to the books I'm reading, Meredith needs me to get better so she can get better. Catch-22.

Jasmine doesn't come right out and say it, but she's been hinting that I should start exercising again and find a new job. I know she's right, at least about the exercising. But I can't seem to do either. Besides, I don't see how I could find the energy to work. I'm taking care of the children's needs. They wear clean clothes and have healthy food to eat. I even wander around the house and pick things up every day. I wouldn't call it cleaning, but right now, it's the best I can do.

DCF opened a file on my family. A twenty-two-year-old caseworker with a very high ponytail and shiny skin came to the house to interview me. I referred her to Barry and Pam. I got a letter a few weeks later saying the allegation was not substantiated. It's so ironic that DCF doesn't consider me to be a child abuser even though the rest of the world does. Thank you, Teeny!

Betsy stops by as often as she can. She says things at the shelter are going well and the new director is okay. She let me know that the grant I missed the deadline on got renewed. That was a relief.

James has been spending more and more time at work. I'm sure he's trying to make up for all the time he lost while he was a single parent. Just like I'm sure he would rather be at work than at home with a depressed wife. It's not fair to be critical given that he's the only one in the family making money right now. He's still avoiding going to see Jasmine with me. He says she's my therapist now. I should try to find another therapist to work on the couple's issues, but I don't have the energy to do any more therapy than I'm already doing. It will have to wait.

CHAPTER 50

Tamara Goodwin
Wednesday, July 17, 2013

I miss Owen. I've been going to the gym as much as I can, hoping to run into him. I want to see how he reacts to seeing me. I know I look pretty good. I've lost a few pounds, and I even managed to get a bit of a tan by eating lunch outside and sitting on my porch last Saturday afternoon while I caught up on some reading.

I really thought he would have called by now. He must miss me too. I've picked up the phone to call him a few times, but I never go through with it. I don't want to seem desperate. I'd rather have him think we're running into each other by chance. He wasn't at the Hike for Hunger. I even went to the Fourth of July parade, but I didn't see him. Maybe I should take up volleyball. No, that would be too obvious.

May and June were crazy busy at work. Last month, everyone in the criminal justice system had their annual training sessions. The court shut down for most of a week. Basically, unless somebody committed murder, we didn't deal with it. And since we have so few murders in Vermont, it wasn't much of an issue. This year the prosecutors met at Green Mountain College. The regular students were gone for the summer, so we were able to use the classrooms for our sessions. I talked to a bunch of my colleagues about Dr. Lapitas. He's universally loathed by prosecutors.

The focus of this year's training was special investigation units. Apparently, the state is trying to set up specialized units in each county to handle cases involving sexual and family violence. The problem is they haven't earmarked much money. At lunch the last day, Fred, Sanjiv, Brett, and I talked about how we're going to set up our unit. We were sitting outside on the grass under a large oak tree eating the bagged lunches provided by the state.

"According to the model, we need a designated investigator slash child interviewer," said Fred. "But there's no money to hire anyone new, so it needs to be someone already on the payroll who's willing to specialize and probably put in some unpaid hours."

"It needs to be someone with experience," Sanjiv said. "These cookies are really good. They taste homemade."

"Yeah. I agree," I said. "About experience. You want my cookie?"

"Thanks. I hear the judges are meeting at the Hyatt in Burlington and the public defenders are at the Snowflake Resort," Sanjiv said.

"Why do I doubt they're getting bag lunches?" Brett said.

"The state's just making it up to the PDs for always losing," I said. "Besides, this sandwich is good."

"There are only a couple of investigators who have any experience with kids," Sanjiv said. "Most cops try to avoid those cases."

"It's basically Karen Driscoll from MFPD and Ryan Hastings from the state police," I said.

"Which one is better?" Fred said.

"Ryan has more experience," Sanjiv said, "but he can be intimidating. He's a big guy."

"He's got three kids. He knows how to tone it down," Brett said.

"Karen's probably less intimidating because she's a woman," I said.

"I thought you were mad at her about the Bennett case," Sanjiv said. "Didn't she screw that up?"

"Yeah, but it worked out okay," I said, "and hopefully she learned from the experience."

"What about someone from DCF?" Brett said. "They've got Samantha Burnham."

"She's awesome," I said.

"They're too busy," Fred said. "They can't spare anyone."

"Let me get this straight," Brett said. "We have to convince someone to take a job that involves something nobody wants to do?"

"Right," Fred said.

"And we don't have any money to pay them, but they're going to have to work a lot of extra hours?" Brett said.

"That pretty much sums it up," Fred said. "Now the question is which one of you guys wants to be the designated prosecutor?"

Nobody volunteered. I think they all expected me to do it, but I was wary. My job may have destroyed my relationship with Owen. I couldn't take on more. What I needed was to take on less.

We dropped the subject for a few weeks. This afternoon we're supposed to have an office meeting to talk about the special unit again.

Right now, I need to get lunch. I couldn't find anything in my fridge this morning. I'm also out of cereal. I decide to run to the grocery store. I can get a salad from the salad bar and pick up a couple of other things, including Raisin Bran.

I've just finished making my salad when I look up and see Owen. He's with an athletic-looking girl whose blond hair is pulled back in a scrunchie. She's sort of cute, but something about her facial symmetry is off. They're both in shorts and T-shirts. They have a cart full of groceries and are coming toward me.

Maybe they're just friends. He doesn't see me. I can tell because he touches her arm and looks down at her, smiling. They are not just friends. If I turn quickly, he might not see me.

"Tamara."

I pretend to be startled. "Oh. Hi, Owen." There's an awkward silence. I look at their grocery cart.

"How's your summer going?" I say.

"It's half over," Owen says.

"Already?"

"The teachers have to go back early," he says.

"Are you a teacher too?" I say to the blonde.

"No. I'm a nurse practitioner," she says.

"Oh. I'm Tamara." From the way her eyes open, I can tell she knows who I am. That's good. It means Owen talks about me.

"Sorry," Owen says. "This is Jody."

"Going camping?" I say.

"How did you know?" Jody says.

"S'mores and hotdogs," I say. "Where are you going?"

"It's a canoe trip on Lake Champlain," Owen says. "We're taking a group of kids from the summer program."

"I didn't know you were doing that this year."

"I wasn't, but one of the counselors broke an ankle, so I offered to step in."

"Are you a counselor too?" I say.

"No, well, yes, I mean, just for the weekend. I volunteered to step in too," Jody says.

"I need to get back to work," I say. "Have a good trip."

Owen just nods and looks down at his Keens.

I go around the corner and stop to catch my breath. Owen and Jody must be coming in my direction. I hear Jody say, "Tamara's prettier than I expected."

"Yeah," Owen says. "She's pretty all right... pretty coldhearted and pretty closed minded." I can hear the disgust in his voice.

I need to get out of the store, but I already made my salad. If I don't pay for it, they'll have to throw it out. That's like stealing. I go to the express lane. Owen and Jody are at the back of a longer line.

I don't look back as I leave the store. As soon as I'm outside, I dump the salad in the trash.

CHAPTER 51

James Bennett
Wednesday, November 6, 2013

It's been six months since Sarah took the plea deal. Given what has happened, I'm not sure she made the right decision. Of course, without a time turner it's impossible to know whether the prosecutor would have actually put Meredith on the stand.

Sarah hasn't left the house in six months except to go to see Jasmine and her probation officer. That's not completely accurate. Once a week she drives up to Burlington to go grocery shopping. She says she feels like people are staring at her when she shops locally. I can't tell her that's crazy, because it isn't. Living in a small town has its disadvantages.

Meredith still doesn't like to be away from Sarah. She has to go to school, but she avoids all other activities that might keep them apart. They're both too skinny. I'm no shrink, but I think Meredith won't get better until Sarah gets better. I'm just not convinced that Sarah will pull out of this in time to salvage Meredith's childhood.

The question is whether I should stay on this sinking ship. I feel guilty thinking about leaving Sarah. I did make a commitment for better or worse, but it's not like she has cancer or something. She's depressed, and I don't think she's doing enough to fix it. Kristy agrees with me. She thinks it would be better for the kids to get away from Sarah. She's probably right. I know it would be hard on everyone at first, especially Sarah. But in the long run, we might all be happier. Obviously, I'm not going to do anything during the holidays.

Sarah keeps talking about leaving town at the end of this school year. She's expecting to get off probation at about the same time that the kids finish school. She keeps bringing up places we should consider moving to. I've pretty much decided I don't want to move, but I still haven't told Sarah.

Sarah and I haven't had sex in months. She doesn't seem interested and every time I touch her it feels like she's going to shatter. She's still beautiful, but she looks more like an anorexic than the woman I married.

Something happened. Kristy and I kissed. Once. About a month ago. Her kid was at a sleepover, so she suggested I come to her place to talk. I left my car at the office and walked in the dark. It's not like we were planning to do anything wrong. I just figured my family didn't need any more scandal, and she doesn't live that far from my office. We sat on the couch and drank wine. She made me laugh. It felt so good to be with someone who could laugh. I don't know what came over me. After the second glass of wine, I leaned over and kissed her. She kissed me back, but then we both pulled back.

"I can't cheat on Sarah," I said.

"That's one of the things I like about you. You're honorable. Let's just forget that happened," she said.

After that, I decided I shouldn't be friends with Kristy anymore. That lasted about a week. The problem is that there isn't anyone else who understands me the way she does. I like talking to her. As long as it isn't sexual, I don't see that it's a problem.

CHAPTER 52

Karen Driscoll
Tuesday, December 3, 2013

Things are looking up. I met someone. Her name is Kara. She's a teacher at the middle school. The chief asked me go to the school and talk about sexual assault in the health classes. He said it was because I'm used to talking to kids. I think it was because I'm a woman. And he couldn't talk anybody else into going. I am so glad I went because Kara's great. Arlo likes her too.

I've also been asked to be part of the new special investigations unit. Personally, I'm honored. They could have chosen any investigator from the county, but apparently the state's attorney himself asked for me. MFPD can't afford to have me there full time, but I'm going to be allowed to spend twenty hours per week working with the new unit. Tamara's going to be the prosecutor. There's also an administrative person who's supposed to be trying to find grants so that we can hire more people and eventually get a space of our own.

We've had a couple of organizational meetings. Tamara is pushing for a child-interview room. Apparently, there's a small room at the courthouse we could repaint. I'm sure that's a good idea, but I doubt I'll be able to use it in all my cases. The courthouse isn't open on weekends and I don't like to wait on interviews if I can avoid it.

Judge Whippet just ruled against us in the case against Bryan Pembroke, Becca's dad. Whippet is the judge in Adams County right now. Apparently, he's been a judge for a long time, but we haven't had him in our county for a few years. The problem is that Pembroke hired Barry Densmore, who used Dr. Lapitas to attack my interview.

I talked to Sanjiv about it when the decision came out.

"I'm going to dismiss the charges," he said.

"Can't you still use the kid to testify?" I said.

"I can, but I won't."

"Why?"

"Because I'm not convinced the dad did anything wrong."

"So, why did you file the charges in the first place?"

"Because your report had some choice quotes that made him look guilty."

"He is guilty."

"How do you know?"

"I believe the kid."

"Which time? She was all over the place."

"She got a little confused, that's all."

"Maybe, but you can't assume the one time she got it right was the time she said something a little incriminating."

I shrug. "She told the mom, too."

"Maybe. Or the mom told her. You need to pay more attention to what Lapitas said."

"Don't tell me you're buying it too."

"It doesn't matter. The judge bought it, which means you need to buy it."

"Okay. Whatever."

I get what Lapitas said. I'm not stupid. But Lapitas doesn't understand what it's like to try to get a kid to disclose. If I never asked a leading question, I would probably sit in the interview room watching them draw all afternoon. My job is to protect children. I can't protect them if they won't talk. If I did what Lapitas suggested, I would never file any cases.

Besides, Lapitas only gets hired in a few cases. Most people are still going to make plea deals because most people are guilty. We'll catch a lot more people doing it my way, and if we lose a case every once in a while, the world is still a better place.

CHAPTER 53

Nicholas Bennett
Saturday, October 11, 2014

I'm getting ready for my dad's wedding. He's making me wear a suit and tie. He's getting married to my friend's mother. Can you say awkward? I don't understand what the hurry is. My parents' divorce was final a week ago. When I asked my dad why he was getting married so soon, he said he and Kristy want to be together, and that it didn't make sense to keep two houses. In other words, they're getting married to save money. I may be fourteen, but it sounds like a dumb reason to me. Especially since Jared and I are going to have to share a room. I've always had my own room. Nothing about this is right.

I read those *Diary of a Wimpy Kid* books to help prepare myself for middle school. They're really funny and I thought they showed how bad middle school can be. The truth is, it was a lot worse. At least Greg Heffley didn't have to deal with his mother pleading guilty to child abuse and having it reported on the front page of the paper. Other kids make fun of you when you have a bad hair day. They sure got a lot of mileage out of my mother being a child abuser.

Greg also didn't have to deal with his parents getting divorced during his eighth grade year. The weird thing is that my parents used to fight— lots of yelling and arguing. That stopped when my mom got arrested. I figured things were better. Then one day, my dad just moved out. The next thing I knew, they were telling us they were getting divorced.

My mom is still living in our old house, but they're trying to sell it. It really bothers me that they're selling my house. My room is there. My basketball hoop is in the driveway. My tree fort is in the backyard. I'm in the ninth grade now, so I never use it anymore. Still, it's not right. But I'm a kid, so I have to live with it.

CHAPTER 54

Sarah Bennett
Saturday, October 25, 2014

I went for a run the other day. On my way back, I saw Karen Driscoll walking toward me on the other side of the road. I started to hyperventilate, so I had to stop running and bend over. Crouched on the side of the road, I saw her feet crossing the street toward me.

"Are you okay?" she said. I had no choice but to raise my head, and when I did, I realized it wasn't her. The woman who had stopped was much older, much taller, much heavier.

"It's just a stitch," I said. "I'm fine, thanks." I walked the rest of the way, wondering how I could have seen a resemblance that wasn't there.

I'm still here in Middleton Falls. I'd rather be some place else, but my kids are here, so here I'll stay. At least until they go off to college. Every time I see a police car, my heart races. I count to five at every stop sign. I drive well under the speed limit at all times. I don't want to give them any reason to come after me again. It's all part of the PTSD. Unfortunately, knowing that doesn't make it go away.

James' leaving was a real wakeup call, partly because there was no fight that preceded it. One morning after the kids had left for school, he announced calmly that he needed a break. Of course he needed a break. We all did. He'd been shouldering a lot of responsibilities for a long time, and the atmosphere in our house was certainly depressing. I didn't want him to leave, but I understood why he wanted to. Besides, I figured it was temporary.

I started taking antidepressants. I had no choice. With the pills, I felt enough better that I could function, so I asked Meredith's counselor whether she should take them as well. After a referral to a psychiatrist, Meredith got a prescription.

A month later, I went to see James at his office. We hadn't seen each other since he left. All the arrangements for the kids had taken place on the phone. It felt like he was avoiding me. He didn't get up from his chair when I walked in, just gestured toward one of the visitor chairs.

"You look better," he said.

"I feel better. Your leaving gave me a jolt."

"Then it was the right thing to do. I wasn't sure. I want you to know it was a hard decision."

"When are you coming home?"

"I'm not."

I twisted my wedding ring while I tried to decide how to respond. Finally I said, "Look, I know I haven't been a lot of fun lately, but I still think it would be better for our family to be together. What we need is a fresh start, not an end. Before we give up on sixteen years of marriage, we should go someplace new and start over."

"I spent too much time building my practice here. I don't want to leave it."

"I get that. I just think a fresh start would be good for all of us, and I thought you agreed with me."

"I do, sort of. The problem is I don't want a fresh start with you. There's too much baggage there. We could move across the country and there'd be no guarantee you're going to get over this. I need normal. The kids need normal. I just want to be happy. This past year has been hell. I want to forget it, but I don't think you're going to be able to."

"What are you saying?"

"I'm seeing someone."

I felt like I'd been hit by an airbag. "Were you having an affair?"

"No. Nothing like that. It's all new."

"And you're going to give up on a sixteen-year marriage to be with someone you just met?"

"I've known her for a while. It's just the dating part that's new."

It never occurred to me that James would be with another woman.

"Who?" I said.

"Kristy."

"Jared's mom?"

"Yes."

"And it's serious?"

"Yes."

There was nothing else to do. I knew James well enough to know that my marriage was over. I solved my depression with pills. He solved his by falling in love. The problem is that, when the newness wears off, he'll go back to taking out his frustration by swearing and throwing things. And I won't be there to protect my children.

I was at a severe disadvantage in the divorce. Neither one of us had any money, but James had his partner, Phil, representing him, and James himself knows a bit about divorce law. My parents loaned me some money to hire a lawyer. It would have been good if I could have hired Barry, but I couldn't afford him. Instead, Betsy got me some names of people to consider. I finally chose Kim Duquette, mostly because she only wanted a $2,500 retainer. And I like her. She used to be a social worker before she got divorced in her forties and went back to law school. I told her the whole story about the court case. I even told her about James' history.

"Did you ever tell anyone else about James' violence?" she said.

"No."

"Nobody at all? Not even your therapist?"

"No."

"Was he ever violent with the children?"

I told her about what happened with Nick.

"But you didn't tell anyone about that either?"

"No."

"Why not?"

"Lots of reasons. Because I was ashamed. Because I wanted to make my marriage work. Because I was afraid James would quit counseling if he thought Jasmine was biased against him. And I never expected he would hurt one of the children. Then, when the charges were pending against me, I was afraid that if the violence came out, the children might be put in state custody. It may sound crazy, but I knew Jasmine was a mandatory reporter, and given how out of proportion everything was at the time, I couldn't risk it."

"Do you think he's a batterer?"

"No."

"Then what is it?"

"He's a normal human being who doesn't always do well managing his stress."

James wanted full custody of the children. So did I, but I knew I couldn't survive a divorce trial. I couldn't even handle walking into a courtroom. Just walking into the building for monthly appointments with Pam had taken all of my resolve.

James probably didn't want a trial either. We obviously both have issues we'd rather not have aired. I'm sure my depression would not have impressed the judge. James must have been afraid I would raise the issue of his violence. I told Kim she could mention the violence in her negotiations, but that I didn't want it part of the public record. James doesn't deserve to be labeled. Besides, if there is one thing I've learned these past two years, it's that everything is a compromise.

There weren't any assets left to fight about, but like many things it still came down to money. I couldn't afford to take care of the kids without a lot of help from James. We agreed to share physical custody, alternating weeks and holidays. James got full legal custody. In exchange, I got a small amount of alimony for five years as well as a little child support.

When the divorce was final, I lost my healthcare coverage. I had to stop seeing Jasmine. My medication will run out soon. Fortunately, Meredith is still covered by James' insurance.

I haven't been able to find a job with benefits. The problem is that this town is too small. I'll never get another job in my field because of my criminal record, and there's little left here for me to do. Right now I have two part-time jobs. In the mornings, I'm a caregiver for an elderly shut-in. He's a sweet old man who likes my tuna casserole and delights in the chocolate chip cookies I bring from home. He seems to be blessed with an ability to remember only the good things that have happened to him.

I also work part-time delivering prescriptions for the Rite Aid Pharmacy. The hours are flexible, which means I'm available to the kids when I have them. I make enough to get by, but not enough to pay the mortgages on the house. As soon as the house sells, I'll move into something smaller. Hopefully, I can make the kids a new home.

The weeks away from the kids are hard. But after the eight months without them, I've had lots of practice. My mom calls me every night that the kids are not here. And Samson keeps me company. It's lucky that Kristy is allergic to dogs.

My sister and I talk regularly these days. Amelia's coming for Christmas this year for the first time. I'm looking forward to it.

I'm waiting on the front steps when James pulls into the driveway. The girls tumble out of the back seat. Nick's head in the front is the same height as his father. He'll be driving soon. James goes around back to open the hatch and get the kids' backpacks. He waves to me and, as he shuts the hatch, his wedding ring glints in the sun.

As soon as she has her backpack, Meredith runs to me, her blond hair streaming behind her, and her dimples as deep as they can go. Her smile reminds me there was never really a choice.

I'll never forgive the system for what it did to my family. Because forgiveness implies acceptance, and our society shouldn't tolerate a system that wreaks havoc with such impunity. I might be able to forgive the individuals involved if they ever asked, but I know they won't. For my own mental health, I just let it go. Most of the time.

It took me a while to realize it, but my life isn't over. I'm just beginning a new chapter. I'm no longer a wife, but I'll always be a mother. My own mother has proven it's a lifetime job. I'll probably still make mistakes. Who doesn't? I'm not looking forward to ten more years of Kristy, but for the sake of the kids, I'll pretend I like her. These next ten years are about the kids. After that, I may do something for me. If they no longer need me here.

AUTHOR'S NOTE

For four years, I worked as a prosecutor in my town. I was proud of my job because I saw myself as one of the "white hat" guys. I jokingly referred to my colleagues who shifted to defense work as going to the "dark side." And, on some level, I believed it. The only way you can work in a job requiring you to judge other people with such dire consequences is to believe you are on the right side of things. You have to convince yourself the people you are prosecuting are guilty. The only problem is they're not all guilty. Not by a long shot.

I didn't realize how skewed the criminal justice system is until I was falsely accused of a crime. At the time I was taking a sabbatical, but planning to eventually return to work as a prosecutor. The actual event that triggered the charges in my case was an interaction with my daughter similar to the one in the story. In my case, the charges were ultimately dismissed, but not until my family had suffered under the weight of a criminal justice system run amok for six months. Fortunately, my case did not involve a felony or a no-contact order. Even so, my family was severely and irreparably damaged.

When I was charged and read the affidavit of probable cause, I couldn't understand how there could have been a witness who signed sworn statements accusing me of things that did not happen. I couldn't understand how my daughter could have corroborated such a wild account. I couldn't believe the police officer reported that I admitted guilt. I was emotionally destroyed. My lawyer made repeated requests to the prosecution for copies of the interview recordings. It took two months to get copies of the interviews and another month to get drawings that were allegedly done by my daughter and the witness. Those months were hell.

After watching the recordings, I realized how the charges came about. The witness got so many of the facts wrong because he was guessing. He saw a few snippets of what happened in his sideview mirror while he was driving away and filled in the blanks. The manner in which the police questioned him encouraged him fill in those blanks with facts that would make the situation incriminating. The helpful officer who interviewed the witness even drew him a diagram to aid his memory. In addition, unlike Meredith, my daughter had not actually corroborated that version of the events in her interview even though the interviewing officer apparently believed she had. This second helpful officer also drew visual aids to help my daughter remember what had happened, then mistakenly reported that my daughter had drawn them. Fortunately, that error was recorded. Apparently, it also never occurred to the officer that an eight-year-old would be intimidated by being interviewed in a stark interview room by an armed and uniformed officer. Interestingly, that same officer still maintains I made the admission she mistakenly attributed to me. Of course, it's not recorded.

In all fairness, I think the witness was well intentioned. He probably thought my daughter was an at-risk child and that, by using the words suggested by the police, he was somehow helping to protect her from a historically abusive parent. Unfortunately, he played into the hands of the police officers trying to make a case.

I felt better after watching the recordings because I assumed that, as soon as my lawyer brought these mistakes to the attention of the prosecutor and the court, the charges would be dismissed. That hopefulness was short lived. What I learned was nobody wanted to hear it.

Our criminal justice system was founded on the premise that you are innocent until proven guilty, but nothing could be further from the truth. From the moment you are accused of a crime, you are fighting an uphill battle. That's because it is a system of people, not justice. Whenever people are involved, there is necessarily a psychological component. Police officers are supposed to be fact finders, but that's not how they see themselves and it's not how they behave. Prosecutors are supposed to be both neutral evaluators and zealous advocates—two roles inherently at odds. Judges are supposed to be neutral evaluators as well, but an underfunded court system encourages expediency over justice.

By the time I was able to prove that the witness' testimony had been tainted by the police, it was too late. The case was in the system and had taken on a life of its own. I wanted to go after the police for their misconduct, but my experienced defense attorney thought it would backfire. With more than thirty years of experience and a degree in psychology, Robert Keiner knew something I didn't know at the time—

many people who work in the system are psychologically incapable of admitting their mistakes. Cognitive dissonance is a real problem. In summary, the accused is the bad guy. They are the good guys because they protect the world from bad guys. If they made a mistake, they would actually be the bad guys. They can't be both good guys and bad guys, so they can't have made a mistake.

Unfortunately, the things that would have helped my family emotionally at the time were ill advised from a legal standpoint. I wanted to proclaim my innocence publicly and attack the police. My attorney feared that would put the system on the defensive and necessitate a trial. Instead, he badgered and cajoled the prosecutors until they agreed to drop the case. Even then, they wouldn't or couldn't admit they had made a mistake.

This story was born as a way for me to heal. I realized that a few changes in circumstances could have destroyed my family. I also realized that, as a prosecutor, I had frequently requested no-contact orders in domestic violence cases without fully considering the consequences. I suspect that what happened to the fictitious Bennett family is not unique.

I am now acutely aware of the more than a thousand people who have been wrongly convicted and subsequently exonerated, many of them irrefutably by DNA evidence. A significant number of those people were not exonerated until after they had spent decades in prison. Most exoneration cases have one thing in common: police conduct that biased an investigation.

I could have sued the police department that wrongly accused me and I might have won, but I thought it was more important to get them to change their ways. I brought my case to the attention of the police chief. Tom Hanley understood that the system is biased and has expressed a willingness to update the department's policies and protocols in an effort to reduce that bias. It is a step in the right direction.

Dr. Lapitas is a fictional character, but everything he says is backed by scientific research. The misinformation effect is real. The human memory is elastic. Thus, as long as police officers think they know the answers and are allowed to ask questions in a leading manner, people will continue to be wrongly accused and convicted. Also, many police agencies in this country have a practice of drafting statements for witnesses to sign. Harried witnesses sign those statements without paying much attention to the wording. Months or years later, when the matter goes to trial, they review those statements and what is in them becomes their memory. The practice may be more expedient than requiring witnesses to write their own statements, but it also creates witnesses who are more sure after the fact than they were when they witnessed an event. Such is the nature of memory.

The proposed investigation protocol I drafted for Chief Hanley is based on recommendations by the Department of Justice and the Innocence Project and has been updated to account for recent research on memory. It includes child-interviewing procedures that are designed to minimize trauma to the child as well as reduce bias. In order to encourage compliance and ongoing education, there is also a peer-review component. The proposed protocol is available at my website: www.teriames.com.

Clearly, the police are not the only ones in the system who need to change their approach. District or state's attorneys are almost always elected, which makes them acutely aware of political consequences. Further, their underlings, the type who are willing to sacrifice their personal lives for the opportunity to get trial experience, are inherently competitive. They don't like to lose. After they have invested time and energy into a case, dismissing it feels like quitting, a form of losing. Prosecutors would also be well advised to adopt a peer-review approach to their cases. Sometimes, only someone without prior exposure to a case or a political agenda can accurately assess its merit.

Obviously, appointed judges are more likely to make unbiased decisions than elected ones; however, they are still human beings and therefore prone to human bias. Like all human beings, they will go to great lengths to avoid admitting to themselves and others that they were wrong. At this point, awareness and education are my only suggestions.

ACKNOWLEDGEMENTS

It took a village to write this book. I appreciate that so many people were generous with their time and expertise. Special thanks to Antonia Losano and Amy Rast for editing help, constructive criticism, and encouragement. Thanks also to Barbara Kolysko, Jennifer Murdoch, Tamara Chase, Esq., Sarah Kearns and Sarah Star, Esq. for reading drafts.

I am grateful to my editor, Barbara Bamberger Scott. She turned plot weaknesses into strengths.

Unlike Sarah Bennett, I was not alone during my time of crisis. Thanks to Betsy Cartland, Kathy Foley, John Quinn, Deb James, Tamara Chase, Amy Rast and Kerri Duquette-Hoffman for providing the support that made the ordeal survivable.

Last, but not least, thanks to my father, Allan Ames, for a lifetime of moral support.

READING GROUP QUESTIONS

1. Who or what is the true antagonist in this story?
2. How does Sarah mature as a mother during the story? How does she mature as a person?
3. There are references to the judge being a "baby splitter" or a judge who splits thing down the middle rather than make difficult decisions. It is also a reference to the Bible story of King Solomon who was applauded for determining the real mother of a baby by threatening to split him in half and awarding the baby to the woman willing to give him up. How do the judge's decisions compare to that of King Solomon?
4. Is Owen's assessment that Tamara is coldhearted and closed minded fair?
5. Is Karen's case against Sarah really a vendetta? Should Karen have recused herself from the investigation?
6. Is James a batterer? Should he be prosecuted for assaulting Nick?
7. Who or what is most to blame for destroying the Bennett family? Until what point could it have been avoided?
8. The title is based on a quote from Tamara justifying her decision to subpoena Meredith. Which other characters engage in moral balancing?

CPSIA information can be obtained at www.ICGtesting.com
Printed in the USA
LVOW08s2358270616

494335LV00004B/139/P